PRAIRIE TOWN

OTHER FIVE STAR WESTERN TITLES BY LAURAN PAINE:

Tears of the Heart (1995); *Lockwood* (1996); *The White Bird* (1997); *The Grand Ones of San Ildefonso* (1997); *Cache Cañon* (1998); *The Killer Gun* (1998); *The Mustangers* (1999); *The Running Iron* (2000); *The Dark Trail* (2001); *Guns in the Desert* (2002); *Gathering Storm* (2003); *Night of the Comancheros* (2003); *Rain Valley* (2004); *Guns in Oregon* (2004); *Holding the Ace Card* (2005); *Gunman* (2006); *The Plains of Laramie* (2006); *Halfmoon Ranch* (2007); *Man from Durango* (2007); *The Quiet Gun* (2008); *Patterson* (2008); *Hurd's Crossing* (2008); *Rangers of El Paso* (2009); *Sheriff of Hangtown* (2009); *Gunman's Moon* (2009); *Promise of Revenge* (2010); *Kansas Kid* (2010); *Guns of Thunder* (2010); *Iron Marshal* (2011)

PRAIRIE TOWN

A WESTERN DUO

LAURAN PAINE

FIVE STAR
A part of Gale, Cengage Learning

GALE
CENGAGE Learning

Detroit • New York • San Francisco • New Haven, Conn • Waterville, Maine • London

Set in 11 pt. Plantin.

LIBRARY OF CONGRESS CATALOGING-IN-PUBLICATION DATA

Paine, Lauran.
    Prairie town: a western duo / by Lauran Paine. — 1st ed.
      p. cm.
    ISBN-13: 978-1-59414-942-9 (hardcover)
    ISBN-10: 1-59414-942-9 (hardcover)
    I. Paine, Lauran. Marshal redleaf. II. Title.
    PS3566.A34P718 2011
    813'.54—dc22   2011007371

First Edition. First Printing: June 2011.
Published in 2011 in conjunction with Golden West Literary Agency.

CONTENTS

★ ★ ★ ★ ★

MARSHAL REDLEAF

★ ★ ★ ★ ★

I

Chet Redleaf held the cards against his chest, leaned across the table, and spoke in a low voice. The room was hazy with smoke, there were four other tables, all occupied by card players, some having poker sessions, at least one set of four gamblers engrossed in blackjack, and toward the rear of the card room where lamplight barely reached three swarthy muleteers, who spoke rarely, were playing pedro.

Redleaf said: "There was no leather behind the hub."

His companion glanced up briefly, then returned to the study of his cards. "There usually ain't when that happens."

Redleaf eased back, eyeing his friend. "Lester, when they wear out and you pull a wheel, there is something left. A torn piece of leather, a little ball of it mixed in the grease."

His adversary folded his cards, placed them face down before speaking, and studied the even features across from him—the very dark hair and eyes, the softly bronzed skin—and faintly, sardonically smiled.

"What are you trying to do? Chet, being town marshal don't make you a Pinkerton man." Lester, who was powerfully built, was about the same age as Town Marshal Redleaf, but with Irish blue eyes, carroty-colored hair, and a slightly tipped nose. He sat, gazing across the table. "Nothing happened. The stage burned out a hub and warped an axle. It got here on a wobble. Chet, if there ever was a grease retainer, it just purely got chewed up and spit out along with the grease." Lester Riley reached for his cards. He'd had his say and he thought the topic closed.

The marshal fanned his cards, glanced at them, then looked up to say: "They told me over at the corral yard a leather was put into each wheel two weeks back."

"All right. So one leather was maybe neck or belly leather. Did you have 'em take off the other three wheels?"

"Yes, all the other leathers were in place and showed almost no wear. Lester, there wasn't any leather put into that fourth wheel."

Riley looked up, annoyed. "All right. Somebody over there forgot and didn't want to admit it and get fired, so he lied. What the hell difference does it make?" Lester shrugged powerful shoulders. "The stage company'll have to buy a new axle, maybe a new wheel or hub. Are we going to play cards or not?"

Marshal Redleaf said nothing. They dealt about six or eight hands with the pots going one way, then the other way. Those swarthy muleteers left and about a half hour later one of the poker sessions also broke up. Its players had all been local cowmen. They nodded to the town marshal on their way toward the heavy red drapery that separated the card room from the saloon.

Lester Riley raked in a pot worth 60¢ and smiled across the table. "That old man who runs the livery barn's going to be waiting up for me."

"Why? Didn't you put your horses in the public corrals?"

"Yeah. But I bought hay and grain from him, and I know him from years back. He can't sleep if someone owes him money."

Redleaf critically examined his cards as he said: "He must use a lot of coal oil then, Les."

"I'll guess. You got four aces?"

"No."

"Four kings. Four of something?"

Redleaf placed a mongrel hand face up for his friend to see, waited until the last players from the nearest table had departed, then said: "I'll tell you why I keep coming back to that missing grease retainer."

Riley was gazing at the worthless hand, three horizontal wrinkles across his broad, low forehead. "You didn't have anything," he eventually said, and leaned back still looking puzzled.

Redleaf ignored his friend's expression. "There is something I didn't tell you."

Riley's voice was flat with annoyance as he said: "What?"

"The stage was six miles north of town when the wheel began smoking and wobbling."

Riley threw up his hands and leaned to rise. He looked thoroughly disgusted.

The town marshal acted as though he had seen none of this. "There were no passengers, just the whip and a young buck the company's training to drive."

"Chet, damn it, everyone knows that."

"Sure. I'll tell you something they don't know. While the whip and his helper were hoisting the near side to take the wheel off to examine the damage, the box of light freight inside the coach on the floor disappeared."

Les Riley gazed steadily at his companion. "Disappeared? A crate of light freight? Where was it to be delivered?"

"To Manion's General Store here in Mandan."

"What d'you mean . . . disappeared? How could anything disappear out of a stagecoach when there were two men pulling a wheel?"

Chet leaned back, too. The card room was empty. Even the fragrant tobacco smoke was dissipating. "It was there when they stopped. When they were putting up their tools, it was gone. Someone was in the rocks or trees on the offside and, when they were straining to lift the wheel to block it up, sneaked down from the offside, opened the door over there, and took the box."

Riley did not seem entirely convinced anything like that had happened, but he did not dispute it. He instead asked a pointed question: "Why should someone want to steal a box coming here to Manion's? Maybe they'd make off with some corsets, a lady's button shoes, or maybe a box full of that dry oatmeal folks mix with milk and feed to babies."

Redleaf said: "They made off with four thousand dollars in greenbacks."

Riley started in his chair. His eyes sprang wide open. For half a minute he sat, staring. Realization, at least a theory, settled in his mind as he loosened in the chair again. "Rodney Manion was trying to sneak four thousand dollars down to Mandan mislabeled as fry pans or something?"

Chet barely inclined his head, and Riley reddened. "That old skinflint. Too cheap to hire an armed guard or outriders." Riley was not fond of the General Store's proprietor. Not very many people were in the Mandan Valley country.

Marshal Redleaf carefully fashioned a rice-paper cigarette and lighted it while waiting for his friend to recover from both shock and indignation. He trickled smoke while eyeing Riley's high color and smoldering gaze. When Riley was about to launch into additional denunciations, the lawman held up his hand with the quirly in it.

"All right. He tried to save money and be clever at the same time and it didn't work. He's going to regret it for the rest of his life. But that's his end of it. My end of it is that there's no other lawman in the area. Also, where the box disappeared was beyond the town limits but well within my operating range."

"Whoa," Riley said softly. "Your authority doesn't extend beyond Mandan's town limits."

Redleaf did not dispute this, he simply stated what had been a recognized fact of life west of the Missouri River since before either he or Lester Riley had been born. When town marshals were the only duly elected and authorized lawmen in a countryside, if people knew of the limitations they were not supposed to exceed, they neither mentioned it, nor neglected to run for a town marshal any time a law had been broken, and usually in areas miles beyond the legal limits of a town marshal.

Redleaf said: "How long have we known each other?"

Riley's eyes narrowed. "Since I first hauled freight into Mandan. Wait a minute, Chet, I know what you're thinking. I've got some freight to haul out of Mandan for the blacksmith. I've been loafing in Mandan for two weeks but that's about over. I'll be hauling out in a day or two, so I can't help you."

Redleaf began counting the loose silver in front of him on the table. Riley watched this in silence until Redleaf had pocketed his winnings and leaned to rise as he said: "How much did you rake in?"

Riley moved coins before answering. "Lost two dollars and thirty cents. You?"

"Two dollars and thirst cents to the good. Come on, winner stands a round."

When they got out to the bar, most of the patrons had departed earlier. What remained were a sprinkling of range men, a few strangers, probably passing through and stranded in Mandan until the morning stage left town tomorrow, and some townsmen, probably unmarried men.

The barman was a large, massive, beetle-browed individual named Jack Hudson whose normal amiability concealed a temper local saloon patrons knew better than to incite. He winked at Riley and Redleaf, set up a bottle with two jolt glasses, and leaned to watch the lawman pour as he said: "Maybe one of those epidemics is settling in." At the quizzical looks he got for leaving that statement hanging in mid-air, Hudson leaned lower and spoke so softly his words did not carry ten feet. "Joe Manion was taken down sick and had to go home to bed. His clerk said he was red as a beet, didn't hear when someone spoke to him, and wiped tears from his eyes with shaky hands. I looked up them symptoms in my *Doctor Sunday*'s medical book. Seemed to me they fit the signs of cholera, or maybe tick fever, or possibly the bloody flux or lung fever."

Redleaf pushed the bottle away and leaned comfortably while holding his little glass. "I don't think it's catching," he told Jack Hudson, tilted his head, dropped the whiskey straight down, and remained rigid, eyes fixed unblinkingly dead ahead until the almost overpowering urge to shudder from head to heels had passed, then he let go with a long, silent breath of inflammable air and leaned against the bar.

Jack Hudson smiled. "One-third Indian ain't real Indian, is it? A full-blood or even a half-breed would have had tears down his face, he would have been suckin' air like a whale out of water, an' he'd have been grippin' the bar with all his strength."

It was exactly for this reason Chet Redleaf went through his act of iron self-control every time he drank straight whiskey.

Lester Riley had no inhibitions. After downing his jolt, he panted, swore, brushed water from his eyes with the back of a hairy hand, and glared at Jack Hudson. "Where did you get that whiskey?" he asked.

Hudson straightened back, groped beneath the bar, brought up a brown bottle, turned it so lamplight fell across the label, and read aloud: " 'Green River Whiskey. Distilled at Green River, Wyoming by the Green River Fermentation and Bottling Works.' "

Hudson put the bottle in his hand beside the bottle Redleaf and Riley had poured from, and pointed out that they were identical. He also said: "That there is Mormon whiskey."

Riley glared. "Mormons don't make whiskey. They don't

drink it, neither. Well, they're not supposed to drink it."

Hudson showed big strong, even white teeth in a bleak grin. "Mister Riley, they make it. This here is genuine Mormon whiskey. The feller who passes through a couple times a year delivering it is a Mormon. Maybe a jack Mormon, but still a Mormon."

They paid for the whiskey, went out into the softly warm springtime night, and stood breathing deeply of air as clear as glass while looking up and down Mandan's main thoroughfare.

Les Riley was still slightly breathless. "Maybe the Mormons're trying to kill us non-Mormons, Chet."

Marshal Redleaf laughed. "You won't have to worry. You'll be hauling out of the territory in a few days. Good night, Les."

"Good night, Chet. I'll look you up when I pass through next time, maybe win back some of what you taken off me tonight."

Marshal Redleaf stood watching Riley cross the wide, dusty roadway on a diagonal, southerly course in the direction of the solitary lighted lantern at the lower end of town where the livery barn and public corrals were located.

He remained out front of the saloon long enough to roll and light a smoke, take the pulse of his town, finish his quirly, and walk across the road and northward to the rooming house where he had quarters, and just before bedding down reminded himself very firmly to talk to the town blacksmith first thing in the morning.

II

Enos Orcutt was at the café counter having an early breakfast when Marshal Redleaf walked in, nodded at other diners, and sat down beside the town blacksmith. They exchanged greetings before Redleaf ordered breakfast and turned to say: "Enos, I heard you were shipping out some freight."

The bull-built man, about ten years older than Marshal

Redleaf, turned as he nodded his head. "Yeah. Made up ten pair of tires for the stage company on an order from somewhere up in Montana. Why?"

"Is Les Riley going to haul them?"

"Part way. Over as far as rail's end and the steam train will take them north." The blacksmith's gaze hardened a little. "What's your interest?"

"When are you figuring on sending them on their way?"

Orcutt reached for his cup, half drained it, put it slowly aside, and straightened back off the counter. "Once more, Chet . . . why? What business is it of yours?"

"I need Riley for a few days. That coach that wobbled into town yesterday. . . ."

Orcutt nodded. "The one with the warped axle and burned-out hub?"

"Yeah. It was robbed up there where the driver and his helper were removing the wheel. Four thousand dollars in greenbacks coming down here to Rodney Manion's store."

The blacksmith sat like stone for several seconds. "I heard about the wheel. In fact, I even went up there to see if anything could be done to salvage the axle. No one told me about a robbery."

Marshal Redleaf went back to his earlier topic. "I need Les as a deputy, Enos. Do you have to ship those tires right away?"

Orcutt leaned on the counter again, eyeing his half-finished meal. "No, not right away. We had some slack time so we made up the whole order. It isn't due to be sent north for another ten days." The blacksmith turned his head. "Four thousand dollars? Without no gun guard?"

Redleaf sighed. "Yes."

"What d'you need Riley for?"

"I'm going up where they raided the coach, try to find tracks, and go from there. Les is a good man to have along. He's rid-

16

den with me before a couple of times."

Enos wagged his shaggy head of graying hair. "Four thousand dollars?"

Redleaf smiled. "Can you tell him you'll be another week putting the tires together for shipping?"

"Yeah. I told him it'd be a few more days. Maybe by today. Yeah, I can tell him that. How did they get the money?"

Redleaf patiently explained, then leaned forward to eat breakfast while the blacksmith sat down again, had another cup of black java, and finally arose, cuffed Redleaf roughly on the shoulder, and departed.

When Enos Orcutt got down to his shop, the big, brawny younger man who was learning the trade from him finished tying his mule-hide shoeing apron and jutted his jaw toward the roadway. "Riley was just here. He went over yonder but he'll be back. He's sort of anxious to load up and haul out."

Orcutt stepped back to scan the roadway but it was empty in the direction of the barn and corrals. He watched his apprentice finish with the apron, then said: "Walt, we've got to go over those tires again." At the look he got from the big, younger man, Orcutt offered what he hoped would be a convincing explanation. "There were some soft spots. I didn't notice them until yesterday. Overheated iron. We've got to make damned sure that's fixed or we'll never get paid. It shouldn't take more'n another couple, three days. We'll sandwich it in between our other work."

Walt leaned down to plug horseshoe nails in the slits on the outer edge of his apron below the knees. "Sandwich it in when?" he asked grumpily. "We've got work lyin' around here that should've been finished last week."

The bear-like older man strolled to the front opening of his sooty shop and gazed northward, in the direction of the jailhouse. His attention was pulled away by someone calling his name from the middle of the road. Orcutt fidgeted as he watched Lester Riley's approach.

The freighter smiled as he came up and said: "I've been going over harness and running gear."

Orcutt reddened, told his lie, saw the disappointment settle across the freighter's countenance, and that made him feel more ashamed of himself than he'd felt in years.

Riley finally said: "Another week?"

Orcutt nodded. "Sorry, Les, but soft steel in wagon tires won't last one day's run. Walt and I'll go over them as quick as we can. I'll hunt you up when everything is ready."

Riley nodded, turned northward, passed several small business establishments including the café, passed Manion's General Store, and turned in at the pool hall just south of the saloon. Orcutt stood a long time gazing at the front of the General Store. $4,000? What in hell would Rod Manion want with $4,000, which was more money than Enos made all year?

Walt called, Orcutt went back down inside the shop, and plucked his apron off a wall peg, ready for the day's work.

On the opposite side of the road, Marshal Redleaf was finishing his first coffee and smoke for the day when he saw Les Riley shuffle into the pool hall. He killed his smoke, dumped the empty cup into a bucket of greasy water behind the wood stove, picked up his hat, and went across the road.

Les was not shooting pool because, excluding the old man who owned the place and who did not shoot pool, there were no other customers.

When the town marshal walked in, the old man nodded at him. Like most older people in the territory whose experiences with Indians had left them anything but well disposed even toward part-blood Indians, the old man did not smile. He never smiled at Marshal Redleaf.

Les Riley was crafting a brown-paper cigarette. He glanced

briefly upward, went back to finish his handiwork, light up, and say: "Good morning, Chet."

Redleaf smiled as he returned the greeting. The old man had been waiting for someone to dig out two bits for the use of a table. It did not appear the one-third Indian lawman and the freighter were going to do this soon, so he dug out a ragged newspaper and sat down to read it.

Chet asked about the load his friend was to haul out, and Riley told him the story of poor steel and more delay. Redleaf was sympathetic, and said: "I can pay a dollar a day, which ought to help defray the feed bill down yonder."

Les inhaled, exhaled, studied the lawman for a long moment, then said: "The last time I rode with you an idiot shot a horse out from under me."

Redleaf continued to smile amiably. "Those horses will eat a lot of hay between now and next week, Les. All I want to do is go up there and see what I can find. Whoever rode off with Manion's money sure as hell isn't sitting up there waiting to be caught. A dollar a day?"

Riley blew smoke, shook his head, and wordlessly followed the town marshal across the road and southward in the direction of the livery barn.

The liveryman was a balding individual with a droopy big nose that resembled an oversize strawberry and was nearly as red. As he saddled two horses, he addressed the town marshal. "Heard somethin' it's hard to believe. That crippled stage that limped into town yestiddy was raided of a box full of money comin' here for Rod Manion. Ten thousand dollars I was told."

For the first time today Les Riley smiled as they led the horses out of the runway before mounting. On the way up through town he dryly said: "Sure would be nice if a man could increase his money the way it's done in rumors, wouldn't it . . . or were you lying to me?"

"Four thousand is what Manion told me."

"He could be lying."

"Why?"

"I don't know. I'm about out of the makings. You got any?"

Redleaf passed over his Durham sack and papers. They rode a full mile warming out the horses before easing over into a lope. It was a splendid late springtime day with air so clear they could see mammoth firs atop a jagged mountain ridge thirty miles distant.

There had been traffic since the day before. There were saddle horse imprints, wheel marks, now and then cloven tracks where deer or perhaps wapiti had crossed the road.

Riley had a question as they were approaching rugged, forested land where low foothills began. "How did they happen to rob that particular stage?"

Chet was squinting ahead as he replied. "I told you . . . there was no retainer in that fore wheel."

Riley pondered that until the quirly was warming his fingers. He smashed it out on the saddle horn. "Are you telling me someone deliberately left that leather out so's the coach would have to stop up ahead?"

"Nope. Not exactly. What I think is that the leather was deliberately left out so's the hub and axle would burn, like they did, and whoever left out that leather had a friend, maybe two or three friends, trailing the coach until it stopped, then they sneaked down, got the box, and that was that."

Riley scowled at his companion's profile. "Getting this out of you is like pulling teeth. How did they know Manion's money was in that box?"

Redleaf did not know. "It only happened yesterday."

Riley was not satisfied with that so he said: "Someone had to know Manion was going to have his money on that particular stage. And someone at the corral yard had to know which coach to leave a grease retainer out of . . . Chet?"

"What?"

"Manion or his clerk knew the money was coming. Someone across the road knew how to cripple exactly the right stage. What the hell are we doing up here in the trees and rocks? There's at least one man at the corral yard who can answer those questions."

Redleaf was reining toward the east-side burn and did not speak again until he had dismounted to tie his animal. When the freighter had done the same, Redleaf pointed to scuffed dust where there were no pine or fir needles, and his companion started backtracking the sign. As he was doing this, he asked a question: "Did you talk to that cranky old goat who manages the stage company in Mandan?"

Redleaf was on the far side of the tracks, also watching them, as he replied: "Nope. Didn't go near him."

Riley stopped in his tracks. "Why not?"

"Because I don't think it could have been one of his yard-men, Les. That coach was not going north from Mandan, it was coming from up north down to Mandan."

Riley was silent for a while, then began tracking again because Redleaf was already moving northeastward into the timber. The second time they halted was where horse droppings indicated at least three horses had been tethered among the big trees for perhaps several hours, and that made Les Riley roll his eyes because it meant that whoever had been trailing the coach until it stopped had not only taken off the money box, but had not fled in haste. They had lingered in this place for several hours.

"No reason to run," Redleaf said. "A crippled stagecoach couldn't cover ten or eleven miles in short of a couple of hours."

They found the smashed box hidden in a little ravine with pine limbs piled atop it. They found it by following the tracks of men who had walked back and forth many times to drag the pine limbs.

The address painted in black was Manion's store in Mandan. There was one more word on the smashed box in black paint. *Drygoods.*

They flung off the pine limbs, saw bruises in the wood where a steel instrument had been used to pry boards loose, to break some of them, and to knock one side of the box awry. Here, the tracks were harder to define because of needles. They finished examining the box and backtracked to the area where there were fewer needles, more rocks and dust. Here it was possible to trace outlines without difficulty.

Redleaf was experienced at reading sign. So was his friend. But the ideas that ultimately firmed up in Les Riley's mind baffled him less than they troubled him. From the beginning of the raiders' trail one thing had been obvious. The thieves had not been wearing boots; they had been wearing moccasins.

Riley hunkered across from the town marshal saying nothing. He had seen all he had to see so he eased his shoulders against a rough-barked pine tree and waited.

Redleaf quartered through the area, returned eventually where his companion was resting, sank to one knee, and said: "It doesn't make sense."

Riley cocked a quizzical eye. "What doesn't?"

"Moccasins not boots."

Riley spoke flatly. "I've heard of hold-outs ever since I got into the freighting business. I've met folks who've seen 'em slipping around in the timber or watching roadway traffic. The Army didn't corral them all." Riley pointed to the ground. "There's your proof, Chet."

Redleaf got comfortable, tipped back his hat, and squinted southward where a midday heat haze was firming up to make the world in the direction of Mandan undulate like an ocean of grass.

"Les," he eventually said, "it doesn't make sense. In the first place, if it was hold-outs, how in hell could they have known about Manion's money?"

"They didn't know, Chet. They just trailed a stagecoach until it was off by itself and crippled, then they snuck ahead and. . . ."

"Naw. Les, hold-outs don't shoe their horses. You saw the shod-horse marks back where the horses were tied. Hold-outs that I've heard about steal a lot of things . . . guns, horses, cattle, dresses and pants off clotheslines . . . but not money. Where they live in hidden places deep in the mountains, they've got less use for paper money than they have for anything." Marshal Redleaf stood up to dust off. "When you was in school do you remember reading about the Boston Tea Party?"

Riley remembered. "Yeah. A bunch of men dumped some tea off an English ship into the water."

Redleaf nodded. "Yeah. Indians! You remember that? They were settlers dressed to look like Indians." He stopped beside the tracks and pointed. "Everything we saw up here was different from anything Indians do, Les. Except for those moccasin marks." Redleaf started toward their tethered horses, still speaking. "Those settlers who dumped the English tea wanted the Indians to get blamed. So do these sons-of-bitches."

III

On the ride back the marshal sifted through ideas that didn't fit as well as a few that did. He knew what folks would say in town the minute they heard about moccasin tracks. Instead of brooding over that he had roof tops in sight by the time he rationalized that into something that could be helpful.

If enough people became angry over Indians raiding the stagecoach, it should—at least he hoped it would—distract them from what really happened back there. If there was enough denunciation about Indian raiders, whoever in Mandan knew what had happened up there, how, and why it had happened, would probably feel safe.

He did not say anything about this. Not even after dusk when he and Les Riley had handed back the livery horses and went over to the café for supper, and later strolled to the jailhouse for some coffee and relaxation.

It was Riley who finally put things into perspective; he did not mention the moccasin tracks. He said: "All right. That grease leather was taken off up north, maybe at Berksville, the place where most local stages lie over, then head back, but that don't explain how someone knew the money was in that box."

Redleaf handed his friend a cup of hot coffee, returned to his chair, and sank down. "You said they trailed the coach and raided it when it was forced to stop. You said they didn't know there was any money. They just got lucky."

Riley shifted in his chair, eyed the steaming coffee that was too hot to drink, and muttered his reply: "Yeah. Well, that's how it seemed up there."

"But not down here?"

"No. I don't believe that much in coincidences." Riley leaned to put the cup aside, then settled back, legs pushed out. "It's got to be someone right here in Mandan, Chet. Manion's clerk. Maybe that cranky old man who manages the stage company. Maybe Manion himself shot off his mouth."

Redleaf was almost smiling as he regarded his troubled friend. "You're pretty good at backtracking," he said. "Let's backtrack right now. Let's go talk to Manion. Why did he need that money? Did he owe someone four thousand dollars? Maybe he was going to invest it in something. Someone he was doing business with one way or another knew he'd need four thousand dollars. If Manion will tell us that, we can hunt him down."

Les Riley shot up out of his chair. "That's what I been trying to figure out."

As the lawman rose, he smiled in the direction of the roadside door as he said: "You get good ideas, Les."

The Manion residence was on the south side of a dusty side road on the east side of town. It was one of the few painted residences in Mandan. Even from a distance it had a look of prosperity. The little picket fence out front was painted; the gate did not sag. Beyond, there was a wooden walkway to the elevated porch. The house had two stories and there was a light in the parlor as well as in one second-floor room as Riley and Redleaf approached the front door.

Light temporarily blinded both men when a graying, tall, and statuesque woman opened the door. She did not know Les Riley, so she bobbed her head in his direction, but she knew Marshal Redleaf and greeted him with a smile as she moved aside for them to enter.

The interior of the house smelled wonderfully of recent cooking. There was a log fire at one end of the overly furnished parlor where the men felt heat. Redleaf introduced Riley to Rod Manion's wife. She acknowledged his presence with another quick, brusque little nod.

Redleaf asked about her husband. She told him she had sent for the doctor from up at Berksville and that he should arrive tomorrow. When the lawman asked if they could talk to her husband, the tall woman hung fire, eyeing them both, before curtly nodding and turning to lead the way.

Rodney Manion's upstairs bedroom smelled of some variety of dried and crushed flowers that had been simmered in hot water.

The storekeeper recognized his callers. He was propped up in the bed, pale, drawn, and unable to remain still; he either tapped the counterpane with his fingers, or jumped his eyes around the

room, across the ceiling, down to the faces of his visitors, or at
his wife, who stood primly by, hands firmly clasped over her
stomach.

Riley unobtrusively sat on a chair that was near the farthest
reach of an overhead lamp. Marshal Redleaf stood at bedside,
smiling downward. "You're looking pretty good," he told the
man in bed, and got a waspish retort.

"You aren't going to find those thieves in my bedroom, Chet."

Redleaf grinned as though it had been a joke. "Rod, we found
the box, some tracks, but nothing else. What we'd like from you
is some information."

The storekeeper's brows dropped a notch. "What information? Chet, they're putting miles between Mandan and them
right this minute."

Again Marshal Redleaf ignored the waspishness. "Why did
you need that four thousand dollars, Rod?"

Manion's pale blue eyes stopped moving and remained fixed
on Redleaf's face. "For business," he explained. "For increasing
the inventory. For having money on hand to cash voucher
checks for stockmen."

Redleaf watched the older man closely. "Right away, this
week? Couldn't you have waited until the stage company could
put a gun guard on the coach?"

Manion's gaze sprang from Redleaf to Les Riley and back. "I
was running low on cash," he answered, deliberately not meeting his wife's stare from half in shadows. "In business a man
has to keep a supply of cash on hand. If I'd waited until the
stage company put a guard on, I might have had to wait until
next year."

"You could have hired one, Rod."

Manion snorted. "It's not up to me to provide protection for
the stage company."

Redleaf guided the conversation back where he'd wanted it

earlier. "You didn't have any other reason for withdrawing that money from your Denver account and having it sent down here disguised as drygoods?"

Manion steadied his gaze with an effort. "Just for business purposes. If you operated a general store, you'd know what I mean."

Redleaf twisted to trade glances with the freighter. Both the storekeeper and his wife noticed this. The tall woman spoke sharply to Marshal Redleaf. "Do you doubt his word, Chet?"

Redleaf smiled at her, and evaded a direct reply. "What I'm trying to figure out is who knew he had sent for that money. Someone besides your husband knew it was coming." Redleaf turned back to face the man in the bed. "I'll do my damnedest to get it back for you, Rod, but I can't do it alone. Who knew you had sent for the money?"

Manion stared at the far wall a few inches over Marshal Redleaf's left shoulder. It became so quiet in the room it was possible to hear a large old clock ticking down in the parlor.

"Howard knew," the storekeeper finally said. "My wife knew."

"No one else?"

The ticking clock reached the ears of everyone in the upstairs bedroom before Manion spoke again. "A man staying down at the rooming house named Henry Nye. He knew."

Redleaf s dark brows shot up. He knew everyone in Mandan and its environs. He had never heard that name before. "Who is he, Rod? How did he happen to know the money was on its way down here?"

Manion glanced at his wife as though for support. She remained flintily erect and expressionless. Manion brought his attention back to Marshal Redleaf. "He's a mining engineer. Chet, I can't tell you more than that."

Riley arose, hat in hand. He'd felt the intensity of the looks Manion had shot at him. He said—"I'll wait downstairs."—and left the room. Behind him the storekeeper's wife also departed. She caught Riley on the ground floor to ask if he had accompanied Marshal Redleaf north to the site of the theft, and, when Riley told her that he had, she looked intently at him as she asked what they had found up there.

Riley regarded the statuesque woman thoughtfully, and decided now would be a good time to start circulating the moccasin story. He had no way of knowing what the tall woman's reaction would be, but he found out right after he said: "Yes'm. We found the box where they'd tried to hide it. We found where their horses stood and we found moccasin tracks. Plenty of them."

The tall woman straightened to her full height, clasped both hands across the front of her apron, and fixed Riley with a fiercely triumphant look. "I knew it! I told Rodney he was losing his mind if he did business with that man!"

She spun around and went stamping back up the stairs and passed Chet Redleaf midway without even looking at him. He paused to watch her disappear beyond the door of her husband's room, shrugged, and continued down until Les Riley said: "For what it's worth, she asked me what we found up yonder, and, when I said we'd found moccasin tracks, she looked like she was going to explode and went charging back upstairs."

They left the house, turned west beyond the neat little picket fence, continued until they were on Mandan's main thoroughfare, then turned south again toward the rooming house near the lower end of town.

Not a word passed between them until they were approaching the darkened porch of the rooming house, then Les Riley brushed the marshal's arm and spoke in a lowered tone of voice.

"You believe in hunches? I've got one now. We're going to be halfway home when we walk in on this Nye feller."

The rooming house had a set of rules nailed to the roadway

door. Chet knew them by heart. He had lived here for five years. The front door was locked tight sharply at 10:00 P.M. and would not be unlocked until 5:00 the following morning. Roomers were to remove boots before going to bed. Tobacco chewers would find a spittoon in each room. If they missed it, they would be charged extra for cleaning up.

As they pushed inside, a crippled old man turned to scowl from his elevated position on a chair. He had been jockeying a clean glass chimney on the hall lamp. When he recognized Redleaf, the scowl did not leave. He was gingerly getting down from the chair as he said: "You know rule number seven. No overnight guests unless paid for in advance."

The marshal ignored this to ask where a man named Henry Nye was staying. The old man jerked his head. "Room Six. Opposite your room." The old man's scowl changed slightly. "No trouble in the house, Chet. What's he wanted for? Any bounty on him?"

They brushed past. Redleaf rattled the door with a knotty fist. They had to wait a couple of minutes after a deep, growling voice told them to be patient.

When the door finally opened, Henry Nye had lighted a lamp, which was behind him. Redleaf and Riley stood like statues. Henry Nye was not only an Indian; he was one of the biggest Indians either of them had ever seen. He was easily six feet and four or five inches tall and he was built appropriately for that height. Riley guessed he had to be at least two hundred and fifty pounds.

He returned their stares, motioned them into the room with an arm like an oak, stuffed shirt tails into his britches, and eyed Chet's badge. He said: "I hope it's important, Marshal. Being awakened from a sound sleep never helped my disposition much." He pointed to a pair of chairs. "Sit down." He went to a coat hanging from a peg, produced two thick cigars, and offered them to his callers. They both declined, so the big man lighted one stogie and tossed the other atop a dresser, dropped down on his bed, and scratched his head.

His hair was coarse, straight, and very black. He wore it short. His features were neither thick nor fine, but somewhere between. He was, in fact, a handsome man, and certainly impressive. His hair was graying at the temples. He glanced briefly at Riley, put his attention upon Chet Redleaf, and removed his cigar to speak.

"What can I do for you, Marshal?"

Chet cleared his throat. Henry Nye would have been a shock in broad daylight. In the smoky lamp glow he looked big enough to wear a saddle. Chet explained about the stolen money, how it had been stolen, and ended up by saying he and Les had just come from a visit with Rodney Manion and that Manion had mentioned Nye as one of four people who had known the $4,000 was coming to Mandan.

The big man chewed his cigar for a moment, black eyes fixed on Marshal Redleaf. One thing was becoming clear about Henry Nye; he was not a man who could be hurried. He removed the cigar again and spoke while examining the length of its ash.

"Marshal, I'm a mining engineer with a diploma and a degree from a Massachusetts University. I'm not a stage robber. I knew the money was coming because Mister Manion is investing in a location I discovered while vacationing in the mountains northeast of Mandan two years ago." Nye plugged the big cigar back between large white teeth and continued to stare at Marshal Redleaf. "I heard about the theft from Mister Manion yesterday. That's about all I can tell you."

Chet had a question. "Who did you tell that you and Rod Manion were going into the mining business together?"

"No one. Not a soul." The black eyes were fixed unblinkingly on Redleaf's face.

Les Riley sighed noisily and looked at his friend. "So much for your idea, Chet."

But the lawman was not finished. "When did you arrive in town, Mister Nye?"

"Four days ago. I came up on the northbound coach from Daggett. I've been on the road for five weeks. I had to go back East to arrange for mining machinery. It should arrive within the next ten days . . . Marshal?"

"Yes."

"Did you go over the place where the box disappeared?"

"Yes, and we found the box, among other things."

"Then why aren't you out with a posse? The longer you wait, the farther off they'll be."

Chet arose, hooked both thumbs in his shell belt, and said: "Because chasing them would most likely take us all over hell, and there's someone here in Mandan who can give me some answers, if I can find him."

The big man spread hands the size of hams. "I'm not your man."

IV

It was late when Chet brewed coffee atop his office stove. Mandan was quiet, at least until some night-prowling varmint stirred up the town dogs. Les slouched in a chair squinting in the direction of the roadside door as Marshal Redleaf went to his chair, saying: "What was that you said . . . if we found Nye, we'd be halfway home?"

Riley yawned behind a thick hand before answering. "It's a start, ain't it? Moccasin marks up yonder and one hell of a big Indian who talks like a schoolteacher. All we got to do is connect the moccasin sign with the big Indian."

Marshal Redleaf inhaled deeply of the coffee's aroma. "We started out to find out why Rod needed all that money. Well, we found out, and you know what? We're just as far from sorting things out as before. Maybe more so. Now we've got Henry Nye to add to our list."

When the coffee boiled, Redleaf drew off two cups, passed one to his friend, and returned to the table with the other cup. "It's late," he stated, and tested the coffee, which was too hot.

Riley agreed. "Must be after ten o'clock."

"You want to go with me while I roust Manion's clerk out of his blankets?"

Riley's raised cup stopped in mid-air. "Right now? What's wrong with waiting until morning?"

Redleaf smiled bleakly. "Nothing. I just feel like doing it now. I never liked Howard Ballew."

Riley sipped coffee in silence. When the cup was empty, he rose tiredly, hitched at his britches, re-set his hat, and ran a palm along the slant of his jaw to make a raspy sound.

They left the jailhouse lamp lighted, emerged into an empty, dark roadway between outbursts of barking by local dogs, and turned north as far as an empty site between two buildings, crossed the Westside alley, and angled among other empty places to reach a small house where old logs had been sheathed over in front with planed boards.

Manion's clerk lived alone. When he had first arrived in town three or four years earlier, there had been the usual speculation. By now people accepted him, so most of the gossip had died out. But Ballew had never contributed to it earlier, and still did not. He was a close-mouthed, lean six-footer with a lipless wide mouth, curly brown hair, a prominent Adam's apple, who looked to be in his middle thirties and, while he was co-operative at the store, kept to himself when not working there.

Chet Redleaf's reason for disliking the tall man was difficult to define. He had tried to analyze it a couple of times and gave it up. One thing he knew was that Howard Ballew did not like

Indians. Not even Indians who were mostly white. But that recognizable subtlety had not actually annoyed Chet. He'd been encountering it since late childhood, and had shrugged it off because it was not really a common thing among people he had known.

As he raised his fist to rattle the door, Les Riley brushed his arm and jerked his head. Mystified, Chet followed his friend down off the porch and around behind the house where there was a pole corral and a three-sided shed. Inside the shed was a tall bay horse eating calmly from a raised manger. He turned a curious stare at the two men climbing into the corral but went right on chewing.

Les chummed his way up close, put a hand on the bay's neck, and motioned for the lawman to do the same. The bay horse was sweaty. He had been ridden not very long ago.

They groped in darkness for the saddle and blanket. The blanket was also sweaty on the hair side. The saddle, draped high by one stirrup, still felt warm on the sheep-pelted skirts.

Les dryly said: "He's not going to be asleep after all."

They returned to the front of the house. As they were approaching the door, Chet lowered his head softly to ask a question: "How did you know from here that horse had been ridden?"

Riley held up a hand for absolute silence. The sound of the animal masticating reached them through the utterly silent dark stillness.

Chet raised his hand to rattle the door, and this time there was no interruption.

First, a lamp guttered to brightness, then the sound of someone stamping into their boots was audible; after that there was a quiet interval before a tall, lean, and sinewy man opened the door with a six-gun in his fist. When he recognized Redleaf, he lowered the gun, stepped aside for his visitors to enter, and without a word or a smile closed the door while gesturing them toward chairs.

The parlor was not much larger than an ordinary bedroom and it was chilly. As Chet moved toward a chair, he managed to brush the iron wood stove. It was cold.

The tall man turned up his parlor lamp to spread light, and, as he was doing this, the marshal asked if he had any ideas about Manion's money and what had happened to it. The tall man finished fiddling with the lamp before shaking his head as he sat down. "The only thing I know is what Mister Manion told me when he came back from the stage company's office where they'd told him his box had been stole off the rig while it was stopped."

"He was pretty upset, Howard?"

The store clerk almost smiled. "Upset? Yeah. He was about to have a screamin' fit. He broke into a sweat, mumbled, and flung his arms around. Finally he went home. I heard he was flat out in bed with the doctor comin' from up at Berksville."

The clerk leaned back as though he was deriving some satisfaction from all this. "You know Mister Manion as well as I do, Marshal. There's nothin' on this earth that'll set him off like losin' money. Nothing at all. All he thinks about is makin' money."

Ballew paused to gaze at his visitors. He had a lantern-jawed, long face. He looked from Chet to Les Riley and back. "You got something on your mind?" he asked.

Redleaf smiled. "Howard, why did Mister Manion tell you he was sending out for that money?"

It was a trap, and for once one of Chet's traps was properly sprung. The lanky man answered without hesitation. "He said we was running short on operating capital to cash vouchers with and such like."

"Who did you tell he was sending for the money?"

Ballew's long face acquired a rock-hard cast; he glared at the lawman. "No one. Is that what you're doin' out here tonight, tryin' to involve me with his money gettin' stolen?"

Marshal Redleaf's reply was calm. "What we're trying to do is find anything at all that'll help us figure out what happened. Did Mister Manion mention any business propositions or investments, anything like that?"

Ballew's mood was no longer co-operative. "He wouldn't discuss things like that with me. I just clerk in his store. We aren't partners or anything like that."

The visit ended shortly after this, and, as Riley and Redleaf were carefully picking their way across refuse-littered back lots in the direction of the lighted jailhouse, Les said: "Well, he knew the money had been sent for. You got that much out of him, and so far he's the only one outside of Manion, his wife, and that big Indian who admitted knowing that."

Redleaf opened the jailhouse door for his companion to precede him as he replied. "That's just about everybody we've talked to. Are you getting tired, Les?"

Riley reddened as he entered the warm, lighted office, dropped down in the chair he'd vacated an hour earlier, and scowled at Redleaf. "Yeah, I'm tired, and I'm going down to my wagon to bed down right after you tell me why you didn't ask Ballew how come his horse was sweaty so late at night."

Chet draped his hat from a wall rack of antlers before seating himself. "Because he's the only suspect we got so far that's been out of town late at night."

Riley looked perplexed. He seemed about to speak when the marshal beat him to it.

"We wouldn't be likely to pick up his tracks from all the other tracks around town, so I guess we've got to keep watch over him. Not while he's at the store, but afterward. In case he makes another ride late at night. And he rode that horse fairly hard. I'd say a man who rides hard late at night heading away from home, then returns the same way, isn't pleasure riding."

Les Riley eyed the coffee pot atop the wood stove, but, when he rose, he walked past to the roadside door and spoke with one hand on the latch. "How about that big Indian?"

Chet leaned back, hands behind his head. "If we had a telegraph in town, I'd send out some enquiries about him. Since we don't, I guess we'll have to keep an eye on him, too." The marshal rose to approach his friend with a smile. "You sleep in tomorrow. I'm going to have another talk with Rod Manion. I think I know why he didn't want to talk about his four thousand dollars."

Riley nodded. "Yeah. Because of his wife. She went up those stairs like the devil after a crippled saint when I mentioned moccasins. Good night."

Redleaf closed the door after the freighter, returned to his table, rolled and lit a quirly, and sat in thought for a half hour before locking up from outside and heading for his quarters at the rooming house.

The roadway door was locked. He knew better than to rattle it because the old man either slept like the dead or pretended to. He went along the west side of the old building, hoisted his window, and climbed inside. For precisely this reason the window was never locked.

He had the lamp lighted and was coiling his shell belt and holstered Colt when someone rapped lightly on his door. He draped his hat from a nail in the wall, crossed over, and opened the door.

Henry Nye filled the opening, fully clothed and smelling strongly of cigar smoke. Redleaf jerked his head, closed the door, and pointed to the only chair in his room. Nye eyed it warily, decided not to put it to the test, and went over to lean against the window sill as he said: "You've been busy tonight,

Marshal. I looked all over town for you. I knew you'd be back directly because the lamp was lighted in your office and the stove hadn't been dampered down."

Chet sank down on the edge of his bed. "Yeah, we've been busy. What can I do for you?"

The big man's very dark eyes shone in the lamplight. "Tell me about those moccasin tracks you found up where the coach stopped."

Redleaf thoughtfully considered the large man. "Not much to tell, Mister Nye. They were all over the place, but mostly in dusty places where a little kid could have seen them."

"Hold-outs, Marshal?"

Chet gently shook his head. "I'd guess they weren't Indians at all but white men wearing moccasins to make it look like the robbery was done by Indians."

"But you do have hold-outs in those northward mountains, Marshal. I'm not much of a redskin. I was born and raised in a religious compound in upstate New York. But there's always something in the remembering blood, I think. When I was prospecting up there a couple of years ago, I got the feeling that I was being watched, so I began sneaking around to do some watching of my own."

"And you saw Indians?"

"Yes. Several times. They never approached very close. My guess was that I was in an area they hunted over, or maybe camped in. I pretended I didn't see them. Marshal, maybe you're right. Maybe it was whites wearing moccasins, but I know for a fact you have hold-outs back in the mountains who wear moccasins."

Chet began rolling a smoke. The large man watched him in silence. When he had lighted up, he smiled at the big man. "I could use some help, Mister Nye. It might be in your interest to lend me a hand. I'd like to get Mister Manion's money back.

But mostly, I'd like to know who stole it."

Nye eyed Redleaf warily. "Well, I'd like to see you recover the money, Marshal, but I'm a stranger to this country, and I'm not a manhunter, so I don't know what I can do."

Chet kept his smile up. "I'll arrange for a saddle animal for you and some supplies. If you'd ride back up where you have that mining claim and sort of settle in like you're going to stay for a while and, when those Indians scout you up again, see if you can maybe catch one, or let them catch you."

Nye's black brows climbed. "Why?"

"Because, Mister Nye, I've got a feeling that if those hold-outs scouted you up, they scout up other folks who either pass through their mountains or camp up there."

Henry Nye's face cleared. He was thoughtful for a moment before saying: "Marshal, what kind of Indians are up there?"

Chet laughed. "Darned if I know. Wild ones I guess."

Nye missed the humor. "I can speak a little Mohawk. Darned little. And they sure as hell aren't woodlands people, are they?"

Chet leaned to stub out his smoke in a smashed-flat tin can that served as an ashtray. "They could be Crows, or Southern Utes, or maybe a mixed band." He straightened back. "As sure as I'm sitting here, there'll be some who speak English."

Nye seemed to accept that, but he mentioned something else. "Tell me, Marshal, are there stories of them killing travelers or hunters up there?"

Chet shook his head. "Not that I've heard. My guess is that they'd do just about anything to avoid something like that, because, if they did it, their mountains would be crawling with soldiers and posse men." Chet could not resist so he also said: "Of course, there's always got to be a first time. Do you own a six-gun?"

Henry Nye continued to lean on the sill for a long silent moment before pushing upright as he answered: "Yes, a six-gun and a Derringer, but I'm not a very good shot . . . maybe if I took something up to give them. . . ."

That was an excellent idea. "Three things they'll be short of, Mister Nye, are salt, sugar, and coffee. You'll do it?"

Nye smiled. It was the first time Redleaf had seen him look other than solemn or annoyed. "Yes, but suppose we keep this between the two of us. If there are men down here in Mandan involved with that robbery, I'd just as soon they didn't know I was going into the mountains to find Indians who might have seen them, might be able to identify them as the thieves."

Chet agreed to meet Nye down at the livery barn an hour before sunrise to see him on his way. After the large man closed the door and crossed the hall to his own quarters, Chet sat slumped on the edge of his bed, wagging his head because now he dared not sleep, or, as tired as he was, he'd never awaken in time to help the big man get organized for his trip to the mountains.

V

Riley killed almost a full hour at breakfast. He also sat out front of the jailhouse in morning chill for a long time, and finally went stamping down to the rooming house.

Chet was returning from the wash house, an old gray towel draped over his shoulder when the freighter entered from out front. Les said: "Have you seen Manion yet?"

Redleaf hadn't. He had not gone to bed until shortly before sunrise, which was shortly after he'd seen Henry Nye heading north in the darkness.

They entered Redleaf's room where Les leaned indolently, waiting for the lawman to finish dressing, buckle his weapon belt into place, and reach for his hat.

Out front Les said: "If you're going to see Manion, I'll make coffee at the jailhouse."

As Redleaf passed the café's steamy window, he was tempted to turn in. Instead, he walked the full distance to the storekeeper's residence and was admitted by Manion's wife, who greeted him but did not smile as she did so.

Upstairs she remained primly erect while Redleaf approached the bed. Rod Manion needed a shave. He had been fed; the tray was still on a small table at the bedside. He looked enquiringly at the town marshal.

It had been Redleaf's hope that Mrs. Manion would not remain in the room. She was clearly not going to leave, so Chet placed his old hat carefully aside, drew a chair close to the bed, and said: "Rod, tell me about the mine."

Manion's tall wife unexpectedly emitted a loud snort of derision and stamped out of the room, slamming the door after herself.

Redleaf listened to angry footfalls going down the stairs before speaking again. "I talked to Henry Nye."

Manion seemed to loosen beneath his blankets. To emphasize his relief at being alone with Chet, he also heaved a great sigh before beginning to speak.

"Henry came to the store a while back for supplies. We got to talking. He offered me a half interest for five thousand dollars. He drew up papers and I gave him one thousand out of my office safe." Manion pointed toward a small table with a marble top. "In the top drawer, Chet."

Redleaf went to the table, picked up a small but fairly heavy little doeskin pouch, and returned to the bedside with it. Manion said: "Open it."

The pouch contained four gold nuggets. The smallest one was slightly larger than a bean. The largest nugget was about the size of Chet's thumbnail. Manion handed him a glass half full of water. Chet dropped them into the water one at a time. They sank like lead. He leaned back on the chair. "They're gold

all right," he said. "The next question is . . . how do you know
Nye is as genuine as his nuggets?"

Manion smiled slightly. "I've been gambling on my ability to
judge folks for a lot of years. In my business, where you got to
extend credit, you learn to make judgments about people.
Henry's genuine."

Chet gazed at the water glass, thinking that if Nye wasn't
genuine, if Manion had misjudged this time, Chet had presented
the big Indian with the means to leave the country. He said: "I
hope you're right, Rod. Now I've got one more question. Does
your clerk have friends out in the country somewhere . . . maybe
a girl he's sparking?"

Manion slowly wagged his head on the pillow. "He don't
spark girls. At least I've never known him to in the three or so
years he's worked for me."

"How about friends?"

Manion's pale eyes were fixed on the lawman. "You know
Howard. He puts in long days at the store, maybe has a drink at
the saloon. Otherwise he don't mix much."

Chet was leaning to arise when Manion stopped him.
"Howard . . . ? You think Howard . . . ?"

"He knew the money was coming, Rod."

"So did Henry Nye. So did my wife. Maybe others knew,
too."

Chet smiled and stood up without mentioning Ballew's night
ride. "Yeah, and that's my problem. Rod, I'll find your money, if
it can be done. Get back on your feet." He gave the older man a
rough slap on the shoulder, and departed.

Manion's tall wife was waiting for him in the parlor. As he
came down the stairs, she said: "I told him from the beginning
he was losing his mind, that Henry Nye was another educated
redskin who'd learned white ways and like all of 'em was out to
use what he knew about white folks to get even with them."

Chet's temper was stirring, but, as he put on his hat, he smiled at her while going to the door. "I sure hope you're wrong," he said, and let himself out.

By the time he reached the jailhouse, his anger had died. Les had hot coffee. Chet told him what Manion had said. When he told him about the nuggets, Les's brows climbed like twin caterpillars. "If something like that got out, there'd be folks up there with picks and shovels scouring every hillside and meadow."

Chet rolled a smoke. He was hungry but this would dampen the feeling for a while. After lighting up, he told Les about his pact with Henry Nye, and the freighter stared back without saying a word for a long while. Not until Marshal Redleaf had drawn himself a second cup of coffee to take back to the table with him.

"And suppose that big Indian just keeps on riding? Suppose he's in cahoots with the men who robbed the coach?"

"We'll be skunked," replied Marshal Redleaf. "But I'll bet my wages for a year he'll do what neither you nor I could do. He looks like an Indian. I don't. Not enough like one to go up there and try chumming with them."

Les slumped in his chair, sipping coffee. Into the silence that settled between them the blacksmith's big, muscular apprentice appeared from out front to tell Riley the blacksmith wanted him to know the wagon tires would be ready to ship north by the middle of the following week.

After the younger man had departed, Les gazed dispassionately at Marshal Redleaf. "Whatever gets done had better get done before next week."

Chet nodded. He was thinking ahead. "I'll watch Howard Ballew tonight. You can do it tomorrow night."

Riley looked doubtful. "Not if you were up all last night. All we need is for you to fall asleep tonight, if Ballew rides out again. That'd set us back another few days and I'm freighting north next week come hell or high water. You bed down and I'll spy on Ballew."

Chet left Riley out front, walking southward, while he headed for the café, ravenous as a bitch wolf. Jack Hudson, the burly barman, was at the counter when Redleaf sat down. Hudson looked around, nodded, and went back to his meal until after the café man had come and gone, then he put down his tools and said: "The whip who brought in the morning stage from Berksville came in for an early jolt this morning before he had to take another coach southward. I guess they're short of drivers. He told me there was some kind of ruckus up in Berksville a few days back. Something about a corral yard drunk gettin' troublesome. The marshal up there flung him in one of his cells and by God the hostler had one thousand dollars on him, which is pretty good for someone who don't make more'n, at the very most, thirty dollars a month."

Hudson continued to look steadily at Marshal Redleaf after he had finished speaking. The café man brought Chet's platter and departed. Hudson nudged the lawman. "You don't suppose that yardman got part of Rod Manion's money, do you?"

Redleaf picked up his knife and fork as he answered. "If he did, Jack, he sure as hell got an awful big share of it."

Hudson left the café. Chet finished eating and walked out into the sunshine, looking southward. There was no one in front of the livery barn. He struck out in that direction with an idea firming up in his mind that had occurred to him at the café counter.

Riley was out back with his wagon. When Chet came up behind him, he was already stating his reason for being there. He told Les what Hudson had told him, and added a little more. "If you'll take the stage north and find out all you can from that yardman in the Berksville jailhouse, I'll spy on Ballew tonight."

Les tipped down his hat to keep sun glare from his eyes and gazed at the town marshal. "On one condition," he eventually said. "That you go down to your room right now and get some sleep. Ballew will close the store about six o'clock. If you sleep between now and then, I'll go north, and, if that's the yardman who removed the grease retainer from the coach that got robbed, I'll get it out of him one way or another."

Chet nodded. "See you in the morning." He left Riley gazing after him, went directly to his quarters, shed his boots, gun belt, and hat, dropped onto the bed, and within five minutes was asleep.

When he awakened, early evening was settling. In the roadway two arguing men were using language most of Mandan's residents, particularly the female segment, did not approve of. Chet rolled up into a sitting position, yanked on his boots, stood up to buckle his gun belt into place, grabbed his hat, and went down the dingy hallway to the roadway where he paused to clear his pipes, rub his eyes, and stare at a small crowd of onlookers who were watching two head-to-head big freight wagons whose angry drivers were demanding that each other back clear and make way.

The road was blocked. There was buggy and light wagon traffic behind both wagons. Horsemen could go around the big rigs, as could people on foot, but nothing else could pass.

Redleaf walked out into the roadway, down the near side of the closest wagon, which had entered town from the north, stepped to the hub from the ground, used improvised hand holds to climb higher. The onlookers were motionless. The opposite teamster was no longer shouting. The man whose wagon the lawman was climbing on, baffled at the abrupt silence, leaned to look down his near side.

44

Redleaf's face came even with the teamster's face. The teamster was a swarthy, beard-stubbled man with too-long hair and soiled clothing. He saw the badge.

Chet reached, got a handful of shirting, and heaved backward with all his weight. The freighter squawked, let go of his lines, and reached frantically for something that would break his fall. When he hit the ground on his back, some rough men among the onlookers laughed. Chet came back down to the hub, jumped to the ground, leaned over the stunned teamster to disarm him, flung his six-gun toward the crowd on the sidewalk, and started toward the other huge wagon.

This time the freighter could not be taken by surprise. He saw the town marshal coming for him and slammed off his binders, leaned back on the lines, and yelled for his eight large mules to move backward. They obeyed. It was to the teamster's credit that he could back his hitch without crimping the front wheels. His wagon was half empty, which made it easier to be backed.

Redleaf stopped to watch, turned slowly toward the other teamster who was struggling to catch his breath, hoisted the man to his feet, and said: "You get up there and do the same. And don't you ever come down Main Street again with that big wagon. You use one of the back alleys. If you don't, the next time I catch you out here, I'll impound your outfit, auction off the mules, and raffle off your wagon. Now get up there."

It required fifteen minutes for the big wagons to squeeze as closely as they could to one sidewalk or the other, and inch past one another. The drivers did not even look at each other as they did this.

Marshal Redleaf stood on the plank walk in front of the saloon, watching. When the road was clear, he went down to the café for an early supper. The counter was empty when the café man came along, drying both hands on a soiled towel and smil-

ing. He was a taciturn man but he had observed the interlude in the road. He said: "That was a good lick, Marshal."

Chet acted as though he had not heard. "Steak, spuds, coffee, and pie if you've got it. What time is it?"

"Half hour before six."

A pair of townsmen entered the café, both bachelors. One was the blacksmith's helper, the other a yardman from the stage company's corral yard. They exchanged nods with the marshal and went farther down the counter.

When Redleaf had finished and stood up to pay, he asked the yardman if the late-day stage going north had left town. It had.

Outside, the fading day had a faintly smoky cast to it as though it might rain, but as nearly as Redleaf could tell there were no clouds.

He crossed to the jailhouse, pulled a chair to one of the little, barred front windows, and got comfortable. Across the road he could see customers inside the General Store being waited on.

He had one interruption and took advantage of it. The elfin, small, bowlegged man who owned the livery barn poked his head in to say he'd seen the tussle in the roadway and to compliment Redleaf on the way he'd handled it. Chet asked the liveryman to saddle a good horse and leave it in a stall. At the quizzical stare he got about this, the marshal simply said: "I might want to use him, and I might not. But if I've got to, I'd like to have him rigged out and ready."

The bowlegged older man winked conspiratorially, closed the door, and went hiking briskly southward.

Chet drew off a cup of java, rolled a smoke to go with it, and got comfortable at the window again. Failing daylight had sheathed Mandan in soft tan. It had not appeared to get any darker for the last hour or so, nor would it. At this time of year the days were longer, and, even when dusk eventually arrived, it settled with infinite slowness.

Chet had finished his coffee, put out his quirly, and was sitting in near darkness behind the thick walls of his jailhouse by the time he saw Manion's lanky clerk bolt the front door of the General Store from the inside, blow down the mantles of the three lamps that lighted the store, and shed his apron and sleeve protectors while standing at the roadway window, looking up and down the roadway.

Chet sighed, got to his feet, went through the rear storeroom behind his office, and out into the alleyway. It was lighter out there than it had been in the jailhouse.

He walked to the north intersection of the alley with a side road and waited for Ballew to enter the saloon for his usual nightcap.

He did not enter the saloon when he emerged from a dogtrot but stopped on the plank walk in front of the General Store to glance around before striking out in the direction of his little house on the west side of town.

VI

The lingering dusk was more of an obstacle than an ally. Redleaf could not follow the store clerk across the open area between the alley and his residence without being seen. He watched Ballew stride toward his residence while using the alley and its flanking buildings to conceal himself, but Ballew looked neither right nor left. Chet got the impression that the lanky man had something on his mind. He hoped it might be supper and that Ballew would take his time about rustling it up and eating it. It was time for the lawman to make a decision, but he waited to make it until he saw Ballew climb through corral stringers behind his house to fork a bait of hay to the big brown horse.

Horses were usually fed twice a day, once in the morning, once in the evening. It was also customary to feed a horse that was to be ridden an hour or two before he was saddled and

bridled. Chet had to gamble this was Ballew's reason for feeding the bay before feeding himself. He turned back down the alley in the direction of the livery barn in a swift walk. There was no one around as he went up the runway, looking for a saddled horse in a stall. What he found was a large, powerfully built dark mare with a blazed face and a couple of white socks.

He led her out, snugged up the cinch, checked the bridle, and, because he did not know her, he led her out back and turned her twice before cheeking her to get astride. She acted thoroughly tractable. He walked her up the alley. She was one of those strong animals with lots of bottom that telegraphed all this to the man on her back through the seat of his britches. He swung off a few yards shy of the northward intersection, trailed the reins, and moved ahead until he had a clear view in the gradually increasing evening of Ballew's distant house.

There was a light burning. Chet's tension slackened off a little. He rolled and lit a smoke, growled at the big mare when she tried to reach over someone's old wooden fence to bite heads off some flowers, and decided that, rather than run the risk of being discovered, he would remain in the alley until Ballew rode away. Otherwise, he could have scouted around through the increasing darkness to be closer. The main risks of doing this included the fact that his mare might nicker at the smell of the bay horse, or the bay horse might alert Ballew that a rider was out there somewhere, by nickering first. The light abruptly flickered out.

Redleaf still stood in front of the big mare. He was not certain but he thought he saw a silhouette move from the rear of the house toward the corral. Finally he left the alley with the mare close on his heels, and continued to walk until he could vaguely make out the house, the corral, and the horse shed. He saw nothing but he heard the sounds of a man rigging out an animal, turned to swing across leather, and hold the mare on short reins

in case she decided to nicker. She didn't, but she clearly knew the bay horse was ahead in the warm night; she stood like a statue, head raised, ears forward.

Redleaf hoped she wasn't horsing, otherwise she would certainly fidget and eventually trumpet to the gelding she could scent but not see. If she had done those things, Redleaf would have had something hair-raising to say to the liveryman when he got back to town. *If* he got back to town.

The big mare was strongly curious about the scents up ahead but she neither offered to nicker nor to fidget. Chet sighed. He was not a man who rode mares. He wouldn't have been astride this one if he'd had a choice. The sound of a ridden horse heading northward eventually told the town marshal all he had to know. He waited until the sounds were almost indistinguishable, then allowed the big mare to follow.

After about a mile of trailing the bay, the big mare seemed to understand what her rider was doing. It may have been coincidence, but, when Ballew suddenly halted up ahead, the mare stopped dead still. When Ballew rode on, the mare moved out. She kept the distance without pressure from the reins. Chet leaned to pat her neck. She would not change his opinion of mares but she encouraged his admiration of her as an individual mare.

Full darkness made it possible for the marshal to worry less about being seen, but he still had to be alert in case the store clerk did as he had done earlier, stop to listen. They were about three miles north of town when Ballew eased over into a lope. Because a loping horse made more noise than a walking horse, Chet could keep track of his prey without trying to keep up with him. He knew the country they were passing through. It was flat to rolling. The closer they got to the uplands, the more uneven it became. He knew the territory up ahead, too, but that

did not help any in trying to guess where the store clerk was going.

When Ballew hauled back down to a walk, Chet eased ahead a little so as not to lose the sound of the big bay horse. He was speculating about Ballew's destination, not about why he was out here, when the big mare missed a lead as her head came up and swung slightly to her left. Chet could see nothing out there, but the mare had either heard or smelled something, so he eased her back a little.

Ballew turned west in front of a solitary old twisted pine tree, which was evidently a landmark he had been seeking in the darkness. Chet halted, listened, and also moved westerly when Ballew's sound was very faint. He thought he had hung back too far and squeezed the big mare to close up the distance a little. She obeyed but there was no horse sound up ahead. There was no sound at all.

Chet acknowledged a shrill little silent alarm in his head, stopped, and swung to the ground with one hand raised to the mare's cheek piece in case she nickered. If Ballew was still moving, he was crossing sand, or perhaps something as sound absorbent like deep dust, because Chet could not hear a thing.

The moon was coming. Farther out high rims were bathed in an eerie glow. Chet started walking with the big mare. There was concealment up there, but northward where some uneven low hills appeared, not out where he was leading the mare. He had lost Howard Ballew.

He tried to recall ever having seen ancient lava dust up here, something anyway that absorbed sound, and could not for the life of him remember anything but hard ground, tall grass, rolling countryside, and very few trees. The mare plodded until something brought her head up very abruptly as she leaned back slightly on the reins. Chet halted, but whatever had caught her attention was invisible to him, and soundless.

He waited a long while before moving out again, and he was now beginning to feel uneasy. Ballew had not been swallowed up by the night, nor had Chet encountered anything like sand or deep dust, but it only belatedly occurred to him that the store clerk was no longer riding. It was the big mare that brought this realization home when she finally sucked down a deep breath and raised her head.

Chet's fingers closed down like a vice before she could whinny. She tried to toss the hand off, failed, and, when he finally eased up enough for her to breathe, she was too occupied doing that to try to nicker. Ballew was up ahead. Someone was, anyway, and whoever it might be was being silent and perhaps wary. Chet turned back to find something to tie the mare to and had gone no more than a hundred yards when a silhouette seemed to rise up out of the earth directly in his path. It had to be a fairly solid silhouette because it cocked a Winchester.

Chet yanked the mare to a halt, hoped the silhouette could not see him do it, and eased his right hand slowly toward his hip holster to tug free the tie-down thong.

A sharp voice said: "Both hands over your head!"

Chet obeyed. The silhouette did not move for a full minute, then it slowly approached, carbine held belt buckle high in both the man's hands. When they were close enough to see each other's features, the armed man said: "Well, well, well. He was right. It was you that got the saddled mare from the livery barn. Marshal, use your left hand to lift out the six-gun and drop it. But if you think you can beat a trigger pull, you just go right ahead and try it."

Chet, left-handed, lifted out his weapon and let it fall. He was trying very hard to place the coarse-featured face of the man fifteen feet away. His effort was interrupted by a voice he had heard often speak from behind: "Who is he, Cuff?"

"The marshal from Mandan. You cover him, and I'll see if he's got any hide-outs."

The rearward man was silent as he took several forward steps and halted to await the results of his companion's search. Chet gave up on the man who had caught him. If he'd seen him before, he could not remember it. But the man behind him was Howard Ballew. As the stranger stepped back, eased down the hammer of his Winchester, and grounded it, Howard Ballew walked around where he could see Redleaf's face. He was holding an uncocked Colt in his right fist. He gave his head a little wag before speaking. "Too bad, Marshal. Turn west and walk ahead of me. Stay on the left side of the big mare. I'll tell you when to halt."

Chet had said nothing to this point and did not say anything now as he turned and started walking. He was angry with himself for having been captured so easily. Without question the man who had captured him had already been out there, watching Ballew's back trail. That being the case, Chet had no one to blame for being caught but himself. He should have suspected Ballew was riding to a rendezvous. If he hadn't been concentrating so hard on keeping track of the store clerk in the darkness, he probably would have realized both he and Ballew were inevitably going to meet someone out here.

"Halt," Ballew said, and raised his voice a little. "Fred, it's the town marshal."

Another man Chet did not remember having seen before came up the gentle slope of a swale, carbine slung carelessly over his shoulder. He was thick, weathered, and bearded. He eyed Redleaf in silence until Ballew ordered the marshal to proceed down the slope, then the bearded man fell in beside him, studied Redleaf's profile as they walked, and finally said: " 'Breed Indian. You're the lawman down at Mandan?"

Chet nodded, eyeing the scattered horse equipment down

where there was a camp.

The bearded man smiled. "I thought it was supposed to work the other way . . . white skins gettin' caught by redskins."

Chet turned, scanned the bearded man's face, then replied: "Naw. If that was true, there wouldn't be any white skins. It worked the other way. White skins always slipping up on red-skins."

The bearded man nudged Redleaf toward some upended saddles and told him to sit down with his hands in his lap. He did not seem very fierce or hostile, maybe because he did not have to seem that way. But the other stranger and Howard Ballew were different. They sank down on the ground, eyeing their prisoner, clearly troubled by this unexpected situation.

The bearded man who had been called Fred ignored Redleaf as he rummaged for a plug of chewing tobacco and bit off a cud of it. He addressed the store clerk. "Well, Howard . . . ?"

Ballew did not look at the bearded man when he spoke. "I stopped and listened. He didn't make a sound an' it was too dark to skyline him while he was moving."

Fred turned to expectorate, turned back, and addressed the other man Redleaf did not know. "Cuff . . . ?

"I was fixin' to come to camp behind Howard. I thought I heard somethin' so I got flat down an' here he come, leading that big mare. He wasn't no more surprised than I was."

Fred sprayed amber again. "The point is . . . what do we do with him?"

Ballew sounded vindictive when he replied to that. He prob-ably was embarrassed about not having known he was being trailed. "Nothing we do but shoot him. We can't take any chances. An' we don't have all night. It's a long ride back to town to get the money out of the store safe an' go over and burn old Manion's feet until he tells us where he's got his sav-ings hid."

Chet stared at the clerk. "What money?" he blurted out. "Why would he have four thousand dollars sent down here if he already had money?"

Ballew raised sulphurous eyes to the marshal. "Because he wouldn't touch his savings to save his damned soul. I happen to know he's got a lot of money cached somewhere in town. And there's the money I've taken in at the store since he's been sick at home. It's not a whole lot but it hadn't ought to be left behind."

Chet stared at Ballew. "Then why didn't you bring it with you tonight?"

Fred chuckled. "Howard, he ain't dumb."

Ballew ignored that to snarl his reply to Redleaf: "Because Miz Manion comes in an' counts the receipts. Not every day but I could never tell when she might do it. If that damned money and I was gone, she'd tell her husband, and sure as hell we'd never find his savings."

The man who had caught Chet fidgeted. He was holding his carbine across his lap. "You don't have to explain nothin' to this son-of-a-bitch, Howard, and we're wastin' time. It's gettin' late. We got a lot of ridin' to do before we get this done with. Howard, you want to shoot him or do you want me to do it?"

Fred spoke up: "Maybe we'd ought to take him along, sort of like life insurance."

The man called Cuff snorted about that. "Fred, for Christ's sake, we're goin' to have enough to do without watching him, too."

Fred caved in. "Have it your way, Cuff. Howard . . . ?"

Ballew leaned to push up off the ground. When he was upright, he said: "On your feet, Redleaf. We're goin' for a walk."

VII

As Cuff and Fred watched Ballew herd the town marshal up the easterly slope, a very distant, faint pewter light appeared. Evidently the moon had arisen sometime before and had been obscured by clouds. Now, where the ghostly paleness appeared, visibility was not helped much but the heavens took on an unusual luminosity. Redleaf did not notice. Neither did the man walking behind him a couple of yards. When Ballew thought they had walked far enough, he halted and started to give an order when somewhere behind him in the direction of the camp a horse loudly trumpeted.

Instinct flashed a warning to both the prisoner and his executioner. Horses whinnied like that at the scent of other horses, riders, something that aroused their curiosity without frightening them. Howard Ballew twisted to look back. Redleaf was too far ahead to rush him. He cocked his head to listen as he said: "Riders. They're coming from the north."

Ballew faced forward. "Get flat down an', if you make a noise, I'll blow your head off. There's only supposed to be one."

Redleaf moved a little closer to the store clerk before lying down. To keep up the tension he said: "They're angling toward your camp. You hear them?"

Ballew hissed at him: "How can I with you spouting off every couple of minutes? Shut up!"

Chet held his upper body off the ground with his elbows, peering northward. He whispered—"Sounds like maybe four or five of them."—closing both hands around piles of loose soil, dust, and tiny rocks.

Ballew also raised up. "I don't hear anything." He turned with a deep scowl and Redleaf raised up, hurled the fistfuls of dirt, and sprang ahead. Ballew instinctively raised both hands as his eyes filled with dirt. He made a sound in his throat as instinct told him to get back, get clear. It was too late. Redleaf hit Ballew with his shoulder, bowling him over. The store clerk would have had his hands full even without being blinded and in pain from his eyes. Redleaf hit him twice, the first time as Ballew was rolling his head. That blow grazed upward through Ballew's hair at the temple. The second strike landed squarely against Ballew's jaw below the ear. He arched suddenly, and just as suddenly went limp.

Chet took the six-gun, dropped it into his own holster, stood up, listening, and was reassured by the lack of sounds from the direction of the camp, and sank down to check on the unconscious store clerk.

He straddled Howard Ballew, gazing westward. In a soft voice he said—"I owe you, old mare."—stood up, flexed his knuckles, and eyed the pewter sky. Enough time had elapsed so he tipped Ballew's six-gun upward and fired one shot. Echoes chased one another in all directions.

He shucked the empty casing, plugged in a fresh load, and walked northward until he felt safe, then turned westerly, and finally halted on the gentle slope of the same shallow arroyo where Ballew's friends were waiting. The odds were not in Redleaf's favor except for one factor. Fred and Cuff had heard one gunshot out where Ballew had marched his captive to be shot. They would expect Ballew to return to camp soon. Chet started southward on the lip of the arroyo until he could hear a man's intermittent grumbling. He went back a few yards from the edge of the arroyo, still moving parallel to it. When the grumbling became distinct, desultory conversation between Fred and Cuff, Redleaf turned westward in a silent stalk.

The burly, bearded man called Fred spoke in a manner that was evidently characteristic of him: "You're like Howard, you're forever expectin' the sky to fall on you. We still got plenty of time. Here, have a drink."

The less resonant, faster-paced voice of Cuff replied: "An'

suppose someone finds his body out here?"

"Have a drink, damn it. Nobody's goin' to find . . . Cuff, who would have a reason to be out here? Just us an' Paul, an', if he hasn't come by now, he ain't coming. Hey! Don't drink it all!"

Redleaf belly-crawled to the lip of the shallow place, put his hat aside, raised his head, and had better visibility than he'd had before the moon had located that thin place in the overcast. He could see Fred facing him and Cuff with his back to the slope.

Without a sound he eased Howard Ballew's six-gun ahead, rested the butt on the palm of his left hand, and waited for that desultory talk to resume before cocking the weapon. It was not a very long wait. Cuff finally pushed up off the saddle he'd been leaning on. "What the hell is taking him so long? Fred, if we waste another damned hour, we might as well forget goin' down there tonight. It'll be daylight before we even reach Mandan."

Fred remained unperturbed. "All right. Then we'll ride down there tomorrow night. One damned day ain't going to make much difference. Cuff, you been worryin' ever since we left Berksville."

"Yeah, I been worrying. I told you six months ago Jim Brooks was a damned drunk. Now they got him in jail up there, and, believe me, Fred, he'll tell 'em everything. He's got jelly for backbone."

Fred remained unruffled. "If he tells them, what can they do about it? We're out here in the middle of nowhere, it's too dark for 'em to track us, even if they knew it was us that left the tracks."

Cuff shook his head. "They don't have to track us. All they got to do is send word down to Mandan about Brooks takin' out that grease leather, an' sure as hell he'll tell them he done it, if they throw him up against the wall a few times. You know what'll happen then? The law an' most likely half the town'll be waitin' down there for us."

Fred made a scornful snort. "You're puttin' the horse behind the cart. In the first place the law of Mandan is out yonder with a slug in him. In the second place, even if Brooks tells them everything an' they send the word down to Mandan that him and us, Howard, and the blond feller who works for that Mandan blacksmith, got Manion's money, all they will know is that we left town. That's all. We left town in the night an' could be riding in any direction."

Redleaf spoke into the silence that followed Fred's argument. His voice carried perfectly. He neither raised it nor sounded very menacing, but, as he was speaking, he watched the pale men in the swale very closely: "Put your hands straight out in front of you."

Cuff, already tightly wound, started up off the ground. Fred's surprise was just as complete but his temperament was different. He sat perfectly still, gazing up the slope in the direction of Redleaf's voice. He was not sure whose voice it was from up there, but he knew it was not the voice of Howard Ballew.

Fred put both hands in front, arms rigid from the shoulders. Cuff, half bent around toward the slope, had a twisted face with bared teeth showing.

Redleaf spoke again. "You better do it or you'll never leave this place standing up. Face forward, you bastard. Put your arms out in front like your friend is doing!"

Fred muttered something indistinguishable without taking his eyes off the top-out where Chet was prone. Cuff gradually eased down, faced ahead, and raised his arms.

"The guns," Chet said. "One-handed and toss them backward."

They disarmed themselves as he had ordered. As Fred did this, he asked a question. "Where's Howard?"

"Back yonder with a bad headache and a sore jaw. Stand up. Both of you. Now walk toward the sound of my voice."

Cuff was angrily silent but Fred spoke as the pair started eastward up the gentle slope. "Marshal, a man workin' for wages just keeps on pluggin' and hopin' and one day he's old and ailin' and he's still workin' for wages."

Chet rolled to his feet as the men came closer, gestured with Ballew's handgun for them to walk out where he had left their companion, and told Fred to keep quiet, but Fred was a wily individual and kept up his harmless ramblings until it dawned on Redleaf that what Fred was doing was letting Howard Ballew know they were coming.

He approached the burly, bearded man from behind, swung the pistol barrel in a short, fierce arc, stepped back so as not to be struck by the falling body, and looked straight at Cuff, whose mouth was hanging slack. "Get down there and tie him," Chet said. "Use his belts and cinch them up tight."

Cuff knelt, touched the unconscious man, and raised a hand. "You cracked his skull . . . he's bleeding."

"Tie him and keep your mouth closed."

It did not take long. Cuff pushed up to his feet with most of that earlier defiance gone. When Chet gestured for him to start walking again, he obeyed without a word or any hesitation.

Ballew was still lying where he'd been knocked unconscious, but his body was beginning to make small, spasmodic jerks as consciousness slowly returned. Chet told Cuff to sit down with his hands in front. He rolled the store clerk onto his back, hoisted him, and propped him against a knee. Ballew groaned, raised a feeble hand to explore his jaw, which was turning purple and was also swelling. He looked into the marshal's face from a distance of about twelve inches, let his head tip forward slightly as he turned toward Cuff.

Redleaf stepped away from them a few feet and sank to one

knee with Ballew's six-gun hanging loosely. Ballew finally said: "Where's Fred?"

Cuff told him, and glared. "How in the hell did you make a mess out of somethin' as simple as shootin' an unarmed man, Howard?"

Ballew did not respond. Chet answered for him: "He heard riders out yonder when that mare whinnied."

Cuff's brows dropped. "Howard . . . what's wrong with you? You spent all your life in stores? That damned mare is comin' into heat. She'd whinny at her own shadow."

Ballew still would not raise his head. Chet went over them both for hide-outs, did not find any, and got comfortable in the cooling night. He would have worried about other riders coming to this place if he hadn't heard Cuff and Fred discussing the other men involved in stealing Manion's money, and who had met out here with the store clerk to be led back to town to get even more of the store owner's wealth. Only two of them were not out here. Jim Brooks, the corral yard hostler up at Berksville, and big Walt Prentice, the town blacksmith's helper. And maybe a third man, someone named Paul.

He did not worry about Brooks, who was probably still in the Berksville jail, trying to explain that thousand dollars he'd been carrying when he'd been locked up. He did not particularly worry about Enos Orcutt's helper down in Mandan. If Prentice had not arrived at the rendezvous by now, it was highly unlikely that he would. Redleaf's surprise at learning there were two men in his town who were involved in stealing Rod Manion's $4,000 did not last long.

Ballew asked if anyone had brought the bottle of whiskey from the camp. Cuff would not even look at him, so Chet answered: "No. When we saddle up to head for Mandan, maybe we can find it for you."

Ballew slumped. Cuff cast a sidelong glance at Redleaf and

asked if he could get a chew from his shirt pocket. Redleaf nodded, cocked Ballew's six-gun, aimed it at Cuff's middle, and did not lower the hammer or let the gun hang slackly until Cuff had his cud in place behind his left cheek. He looked across at Redleaf, spat, and said: "How long we goin' to sit here?"

"Until there's enough daylight for me to keep an eye on all of you. Then we'll saddle up and leave."

"It's gettin' cold."

Chet nodded agreement about that. "Sure is. What do you want me to do, build a fire?"

Cuff turned aside to spray tobacco juice again, faced forward looking menacingly at Marshal Redleaf without speaking.

The chill increased as dawn hung just beyond the farthest curve of the world. Someone behind them in the direction of the empty camp called out gruffly: "Where the hell is everybody?"

Chet smiled a little. Even with an oversize headache that Fred could not avoid having right at this moment, he was still garrulous.

Chet jutted his jaw at Cuff. "Tell him."

One more spray of tobacco juice, then Cuff called out: "We're settin' over here like sage chickens waitin' for dawn."

"Who is? Was that you, Cuff?"

"Yeah, it was me. I'm over here. So is Howard, an' the town marshal is settin' here with us, holdin' a gun."

"What the hell's he waitin' for?"

"Dawn. Some daylight to see by. I just told you that. Are them belts still tight, Fred?"

"They're tight. Too tight, an' my head feels like there's a kickin' mule inside it tryin' to bust out."

Cuff looked at Redleaf, expecting him to react some way to Fred's dilemma. Chet sat there without moving or making a sound. Occasionally he would glance eastward where the sun would appear before too long. He was cold and hungry and had been wondering about Les up in Berksville, and big Henry Nye in the mountains looking for hold-outs. If he could get his prisoners back to Mandan and locked in the cells down there, maybe he could send word to Berksville for Riley to return, but there was no way he could reach Henry Nye. He hadn't even been sure where Nye would be in the mountains. Trying to find him would be impossible.

Ballew suddenly swung his arms to keep warm. There was a streak of sickly gray spreading along the eastern world, the cold was as bad as it would be for the rest of the day. Fred called profanely that his legs and arms were stiff and sore.

Chet finally rose, gestured for his prisoners to walk westward, and paced along behind them until they reached the burly, bearded man whose old hat had been punched down over his ears by the force of the blow that had knocked him senseless. Cuff knelt to free his friend without looking at Chet for instructions, nor looking at him afterward as he helped Fred stand up, and steadied him. Fred lifted his hat with both hands. He had a thick mane of iron-gray hair. Even so, there was a slight matting of blood-encrusted hair where the gun barrel had come down. His eyes were bloodshot.

None of them looked presentable as they trudged back down the gentle slope where their horses were already moving along, cropping grass.

VIII

If the big mare was horsing, she did not do it as hard as most mares did. Even so Chet kept her away from the other horses as the little group started riding southeastward in the cold early morning. By daylight they all looked dirty, haggard, unshaved, and sunken-eyed. Two of them, Ballew and the man called Fred, had not been helped much by the whiskey Chet had found at the camp. Ballew was morose, but Fred, possibly with a thicker skull to go with his garrulous, rather practical disposition, slouched along like a man who was resigned to his fate. Once he said: "Marshal, you don't get paid enough for the hours you got to put in."

Redleaf responded tartly: "I suppose you do."

Fred did not look back where Redleaf was bringing up the rear as he replied: "Yeah, I think so. We miss a little sleep now 'n' then an' once in a while got to postpone a meal, but we make as much in two months as you make all year. I know because I was a town marshal once."

Chet's interest was piqued. "Where?"

"Over in Idaho. North end of the Snake River. . . . Marshal, suppose you could pick up as much from us as you'll get as a lawman for the next year?"

Chet looped his reins and went to work over a cigarette. "I wouldn't take it," he said matter-of-factly. "I don't like missing meals and losing sleep. Fred, tell me about the blacksmith's helper down in Mandan."

The bearded, burly outlaw raised his hat gingerly to explore his injury before replying: "Nothin' to tell."

"He was the one who saw me leave town. How did he get word to you and Cuff?"

"Heliograph mirror from upstairs at the rooming house. Marshal, you're lettin' a real fine opportunity get away from you."

Redleaf smiled. "Is that a fact? You boys got four thousand dollars from that crippled stage an' there are five of you. That's not a hell of a lot of money per man for all the ridin' and worryin' you had to go through."

Cuff spoke for the first time since they'd been astride. "Amen. That's the gospel truth."

But Fred ignored that to say: "That was for openers, Marshal.

We was to get maybe as much again, maybe more, from the storekeeper's cache down at his house. And on the way out of the territory we'd pick up a little more from stages and what not."

Howard Ballew put a venomous look upon Fred. "You always did have a tongue hinged in the middle that flapped at both ends. Shut up!"

Fred was not particularly intimidated. He eyed Ballew briefly before addressing him. "If I was in your boots, I don't think I'd criticize other folks. You led him right to our camp, and fell for a schoolboy trick when you walked out a ways with him."

Ballew ignored the other man. In fact, he did not speak again, even after they could see roof tops in the distance, but Cuff did. He'd been evaluating his situation. "I got a question for you, Marshal. What would it take for you to look the other way for fifteen minutes before we reach town?"

Redleaf gazed dispassionately at the speaker. "Whatever it is, you don't have it."

Fred, who had already asked a similar question, eyed Cuff sardonically. But he did not speak.

Chet led his prisoners down the west side alley with late-day shadows beginning to emerge, left the horses with a big-eyed hostler, and marched his prisoners to the jailhouse. On the way people stared, some gathered out front of the saloon and General Store to speculate aloud. Down in front of the blacksmith's shop no one emerged to stare, but, as Redleaf followed his prisoners into the jailhouse, he knew that his arrival back in town with prisoners would reach the shop before very long, as it would spread elsewhere through town.

He had the prisoners empty their pockets atop his table, took them into the cell room, and locked them into cells. He was returning to the office when Fred called after him. "How are you goin' to prove anything?"

Chet did not answer. He slammed and barred the cell-room door, left the office with a thrusting stride, heading toward the lower end of town. People watched but prudently made no attempt to accost him.

Enos Orcutt and his helper were out back under a sooty overhang struggling profanely to pry a large rear wheel off the axle of a jacked-up dump wagon. Neither man looked up as the marshal came out and stood under the ancient overhang, watching.

That livery barn day man who had cared for the horses came rushing into the shop, eyes wide. He got halfway through before he saw Marshal Redleaf, standing there. Evidently his purpose in arriving had been to give Orcutt the latest news—that Redleaf had returned to town with some prisoners—but, when he saw the marshal, he did an abrupt about-face and walked as swiftly back out of the shop as he had walked into it.

Orcutt and his big, powerful apprentice finally got the wheel jarred loose. They braced on both sides of it to work it free. As it began moving, Enos looked over the shoulder of his helper and said: "Damned cowmen never put grease on nothing until it's too late, then they complain that wagon makers don't make 'em like they used to."

Walt Prentice looked around, saw Redleaf in the shade, nodded, and braced for the final rocking to get the wheel off. When it came, its weight nearly caused both the men holding it to fall.

Prentice rolled it to an upright, and carefully leaned it there, while his employer walked over to Marshal Redleaf, wiping both hands on a dirty old rag. He said: "You been out of town. Folks have been speculating. Did you find anything?"

Redleaf did not take his eyes off the big apprentice who was shaking his head as he examined a rusted, badly pitted wagon axle. "Yeah, I found something, Enos."

Walt Prentice looked around, showing interest. Redleaf jutted his chin. "Him."

Neither the blacksmith nor his helper moved. They stared until Chet rested his right hand upon the handle of his six-gun, then Enos Orcutt turned with a bewildered expression to stare at his helper. Prentice ignored Orcutt. He began drying both palms down the outside-seam of his trousers.

Chet said: "Take off the apron, Walt. I want to see what you got beneath it."

The big muscular man stared at Redleaf. "What are you talkin' about?" he demanded.

Redleaf repeated it. "Take off the apron!"

Prentice pulled down a big breath and used both hands to untie his shoeing apron as he let his breath out.

Chet's intuition was right. He raised his left arm to push the blacksmith away, gripped his gun with the other hand, and, as the shoeing apron fell to the ground, Prentice pushed out both hands, palms up. He was not wearing a gun belt beneath the apron.

Chet gave another order. "Pull up your pants' legs."

Prentice obeyed until the tops of his boots showed. There was no hide-out weapon. As he was straightening up, he smiled. "What else you got in mind, Marshal? We got a lot of work to do around here."

Redleaf jerked his head, still gripping the gun handle. "Walk up the middle of the shop to the roadway. Cross over out there and walk up to the jailhouse."

Enos Orcutt's bewilderment had not diminished but his patience had. "What the hell are you doing?" he demanded of the lawman. "He's been right here with me all day. Yestiddy, too."

Chet replied without taking his eyes off Walt Prentice. "He didn't have to be anywhere else, Enos. There were five men involved in stealing Manion's box off that crippled stage. Your

66

helper here was in it up to his hocks."

Orcutt's bewilderment deepened. He looked from one of them to the other, then made a fluttery gesture with his hands. "Chet, are you sure you know what you're doing?"

"Dead sure, Enos. Prentice, like I said, walk up through to the roadway."

As the powerfully built large man started moving, Chet lifted out his six-gun. Prentice passed within ten feet of him. He kept on walking. Inside, where daylight rarely reached, the shop was black with layers of soot. There were anvils bolted to massive old oak rounds. There was a forge where the metal canopy was warped from heat and greasy black from many fires. There were tools along the south wall held in place by loops in a long leather hanger. There were other tools where someone had left them.

As Chet started up through behind Orcutt's apprentice, the big man passed close to an anvil where tools had been left. Chet was watching closely, but the big man knew this would be the case. As he started past the anvil, he did not look around or downward, but he listed a little, and before Orcutt or Redleaf saw a change, Prentice had picked up a pair of tongs used for pulling metal from the forge, turned on the balls of his feet, and hurled the tongs as hard as he could.

Redleaf instinctively ducked. Orcutt, who was behind him, was slower. The tongs were wide open when they hit him in the chest.

Prentice hurled a pipe-handled shoeing hammer and fol- lowed this with a horseshoe nail-hole pick. The pick struck Chet in the shoulder as he was tipping his gun muzzle. There was little pain but the momentum moved his body to the right as Walt Prentice broke away in a lunging run, and emerged from the shop into the roadway as Chet fired.

The bullet punched a hole in Enos Orcutt's most cherished copper bucket. Where it exited it left a jagged place large enough for a man's fist to fit through. Neither Orcutt, who was recovering from being struck by tongs or Marshal Redleaf who was swinging his gun for one more shot before Prentice disappeared across the road into the livery barn, were concerned with the bucket. Chet went rapidly toward the roadway. Enos started after him, but stopped up near the anvil where Prentice had counter-attacked and prudently remained there. He did not have a gun.

Redleaf was in the shop doorway when a waspish explosion across the road was followed by a board on the front of the shop a foot away, bursting apart under the impact of a bullet. Deeper in the barn's runway a man's startled squawk suggested where the big apprentice blacksmith had gone. Chet looked left and right, then started over there, but kept to the right of the doorless barn opening in case someone shot at him again from inside the old building.

No one did. He got across without incident. Northward people were tumbling from buildings on both sides of the roadway to gape southward. Redleaf did not hesitate in front of the barn. He knew Prentice would be trying to get a horse to flee on. He did not believe Prentice would be foolish enough to break clear of the barn out front, so he slipped down among the old cribbed pole corrals toward the rear alley. There was noise inside the barn. Redleaf was almost to the alley when he heard a frantic voice say: "Get the hell away. I don't need no saddle."

Chet widened his steps and was at the juncture of the barn with the alley when he heard a horse rise up and come down in a hard lunge. Prentice was astride bareback. Chet settled against the north side of the barn, raised his weapon, and, when the big blacksmith's helper came charging out of the barn, Chet was ready. But Prentice did not turn right up the alley, he turned left, which was southward. Chet jumped to the center of the alley and yelled. Prentice twisted and fired twice. Chet fired once.

Prentice was firing from the back of a terrified, running horse. Chet was stationary with a large target dead ahead. The big man slumped, dropped the six-gun he'd got at the barn to grip the running horse's mane with both hands, while Chet lowered his Colt and remained, wide-legged, in the middle of the alley, watching.

Several noisy townsmen came running down through the barn from up the roadway. Chet ignored them even when they burst out into the alley yelling questions at him. Prentice was down low over the horse. As distance made it difficult to see him clearly, Chet yelled up the barn runway for someone to saddle him a horse, then resumed his position, expecting Prentice to fall any moment. He did not fall.

He was getting small in the afternoon sunlight by the time Chet was handed a pair of reins, mounted without even looking at the animal beneath him, and started southward from town in a slow lope. He was half a mile along before he thought there was something familiar and looked down. He was riding the same big mare he'd ridden before. He swore. She had already been put through a hard ordeal. If Walt Prentice didn't fall to the ground up ahead, that fresher animal he was straddling would very probably draw away from the big mare as the horse race went on.

Redleaf did not push his animal. He did not particularly want to overtake Prentice; he wanted to keep him in sight until he collapsed with his mount running out from under him. But the big mare viewed things differently. She thought this was supposed to be a horse race and steadily widened her stride, eyes fixed on the other horse, the one she thought she was supposed to catch.

Chet laughed, eased back on the reins until she was down to a lope, patted her roughly on the neck, and said: "You are some critter, Mamie, or whatever your name is. When we get back,

I'm going to buy you if I can. Not to ride, mind you, but just to turn you out, and, when I find a two-legged female that can match you for brains, marry her."

Far back several townsmen were coming in a flinging run, coattails flapping, hats being pulled down. Chet watched them, faced forward, and saw Walt Prentice aiming for a bosk of white oaks. He corrected the big mare, aiming in the same direction. He did not hurry. In fact, he rode steadily slower until he was down to a walk. If a man was like a wounded deer, sometimes the best thing to do was to sit patiently and just wait.

IX

Walt Prentice was off the horse among the trees. Chet could make out a fidgeting animal in speckled shadows, but he could not locate its rider. He thought that, providing the big man's gunshot wound was serious, he would be flat on the ground among the trees. He knew Prentice had dropped the six-gun he'd acquired back at the livery barn, and a reasonable assumption would be that he was now unarmed. Most of the cemeteries west of the Missouri River had occupants who had bet their lives that someone had been unarmed when they hadn't been.

He waited, and, when those flinging riders from town came sliding to a halt nearby, sprang to the ground, and rushed forward, Chet stood beside his mount with a hand raised. He knew the townsmen. One of them gestured in the direction of the bosk of trees and called loudly that they had seen the fugitive ride in there.

There were five of the excited townsmen, all armed, all agitated. Chet told them to stay back out of the way. Not to use their weapons no matter what they thought they saw up ahead. He stood with the mare's reins draped from an arm and rolled a smoke under the scowling looks of the townsmen. After lighting up, he ignored them to kneel, facing the trees. The horse was no longer excitedly moving and there was no sighting of Enos Orcutt's apprentice. Chet smoked, eyed the sun, glanced around at the muttering townsmen, and faced forward again.

A townsman said: "What'n hell's the sense of doin' nothing? There's enough of us to surround them trees."

Chet replied without taking his eyes off the distant bosk. "He's wounded. We're not going to do anything. It's up to him."

"You hit him?"

"Yes."

"Then he's likely dead in there an' evening's coming."

Chet stubbed out his smoke, glanced at the patiently standing big mare, and ignored the townsmen. Waning daylight cast thickening shadows angling in the direction of the trees. The waiting men were not so distant from town they could not detect the fragrance of smoke from supper fires.

A man called from in among the trees. "Redleaf, you can set there all night, I'm not coming out!"

Chet's reply was dryly spoken: "That's all right with me, Walt. In the morning we'll come in and wrap you in a blanket and haul you back stiff as a ramrod."

The townsmen were impatient. One of them departed in the direction of town, too disgusted to remain. Chet allowed the big mare to crop feed to the length of her seven-foot reins, and continued to wait.

Dusk was sifting in like faint soot when the same voice called from the trees: "Redleaf! Why me?"

"Because I've got all your friends except Brooks in my cells, and the one called Fred told me you signaled from the rooming house with a mirror when I left town. He also told me all the rest of it. Walt, I can set out here for as long as it takes. You're not going anywhere, not even after dark. We'll get completely around your trees after dark and, if you try slipping away, you're going to get yourself killed. Walt, for you this is the end of it.

71

The others'll get supper and a bed up off the ground tonight. You'll get yourself shot to death. It's not worth it."

There was no more conversation until dusk was fully down, then Prentice called again: "You got a canteen, Marshal?"

Chet did not but one of the townsmen had and called to Prentice: "Yeah, there's water! There's also some whiskey."

The blacksmith sounded tired when he finally caved in. "All right, Marshal? I'm not armed!"

"All right. Walk out with your hands even with your shoulders. No one'll shoot."

"Just one arm, Marshal, the other one's busted an' I can't raise it."

"Walk out. Leave the horse."

Every man out there watched the darkening gloom of the trees. No one moved or made a sound. It seemed to be an interminable wait, but it was actually only about ten minutes before Prentice appeared as a pale silhouette backgrounded by tree gloom. He was leaning heavily on a crooked length of deadfall wood and halted just clear of the trees until Chet re-assured him, then he continued to walk.

The townsmen muttered as Chet rose from his stooping posi-tion. He growled at them to stay where they were and not to touch their weapons. He was walking toward Prentice when he said that.

The big man had blood on his shirt and trousers. Even in poor light he looked like someone who had been butchering beef. His color was ashen, which Chet could not make out, and he was listing heavily to the side of the tree limb he was using as a support. Redleaf stopped fifteen feet distant. They eyed one another for a moment before Walt Prentice fainted. One mo-ment he was standing there; the next moment he was lying on his face.

Chet called for the townsmen to fetch the big mare and come

up where he was standing. As they were obeying, he knelt to roll the large man on to his back.

Prentice had a shattered right arm with glistening white bone ends protruding through flesh and shirt cloth. It was not just a broken arm, it was a lifelong, crippling injury, and he had tied off the flesh above the wound with a torn piece of cloth, but there had been a considerable loss of blood. Even in poor light, the townsmen lined up as solemn as pallbearers.

Chet gave orders as he examined the tourniquet, eased the lifeless-appearing lower arm inside Prentice's shirt front, and wiped blood off his hands in the grass.

"One of you fetch the horse in the trees. We'll boost him across a saddle and ride on both sides to keep him from falling off. One of you gents can ride the bareback horse."

A townsman leaned to stare as he said: "How much blood's left in him? He's soaked with it."

Chet ignored that: "Bring up a horse!"

They had to grunt because even though there were five of them, including Marshal Redleaf, Prentice was not just heavy he was also inert.

They started back with dusk darkening toward full darkness. There was no moon but the night was warm and would probably remain that way for another couple of hours. Their progress was very slow, but, by the time they had lighted windows in sight, they had worked out a fairly efficient method of keeping the unconscious man atop a horse.

In the alley behind the livery barn they eased Prentice to the ground, and, while the townsmen were handing reins to the night hawk, Chet went searching for a blanket.

They placed Prentice on the blanket and went awkwardly up the back alley to the rear door of the jailhouse, carried him inside where Redleaf lighted a lamp, and laid him out flat on the floor. The townsmen left, presumably making a beeline for the saloon, leaving the marshal to care for the unconscious large man whose shattered arm was becoming very swollen above the tourniquet and corpse-colored below it.

He got water, some clean rags, and washed away most of the dried blood. Enos Orcutt arrived, looked shocked at what he saw, and spoke in sepulchral tones when he said: "I'll send someone up to Berksville for the doctor. Marshal? Are you sure he's alive?"

Chet nodded as he rose, drying his hands. "He's alive. He'll lose that arm sure as hell. When he comes around, he may not want to face that, Enos. And I've got a feeling we can't wait for the Berksville doctor."

Orcutt looked horrified. "What are you talkin' about?"

"See for yourself. The lower arm's shattered with bone splinters all through it. The slug must have hit him squarely in the back of the arm. Look at it. He looks like a half-butchered sheep."

Orcutt felt for a chair and sank down, staring from the man on the floor to the town marshal. "Chet, for Christ's sake. . . ."

Redleaf hurled the bloody rag at the floor and turned on the blacksmith. "All right, Enos. You're his boss. It's up to you, but it looks to me if someone doesn't amputate that arm below the shredded part he'll never make it. Go ahead, loosen that tourniquet. See what happens. If he's got to lie here until tomorrow afternoon when a stage can get down here from Berksville, I wouldn't bet you a plugged *centavo* he'll live long."

"Marshal, cuttin' that arm off isn't going to. . . ."

"Kneel down here while I hold the lamp. Now then . . . do you see that dirt in the meat? He'll have an infection in his body by morning that'll kill him no matter what a doctor tries to do."

Redleaf hung the lamp back on its ceiling hook and leaned from the hips against his table, gazing at Orcutt's helper.

Other townsmen arrived. Chet growled at them the moment they opened the door. As they retreated after a good look at the bloody man on the floor, there were no more interruptions until those men had returned to the saloon and or to their homes around town to tell what they had seen. Then both Enos and Marshal Redleaf got a surprise.

Big Jack Hudson walked in out of the darkness without his little bar apron, but still wearing his pink sleeve garters above the elbow and his elegant brocaded vest with three cigars in each upper pocket. He closed the door, ignored Redleaf and Orcutt to stand a moment staring at the ashen man on the floor, then he crossed closer, sank to one knee, growled for someone to lower the lamp. When Redleaf complied, the big barman rolled up both sleeves and made a careful, thorough examination.

It was quiet enough inside the office to have heard a coin drop. Hudson stood up, fished forth a large handkerchief, wiped his hands with it while continuing to stare at the unconscious man, and said: "That arm's got to come off."

Enos was staring. "Jack? You know anythin' about this sort of thing?"

Hudson replied, still gazing at Walt Prentice: "A little, Enos. I was hurt in the back durin' the war and ended up helpin' surgeons. Almost two years of it." Hudson pocketed his handkerchief before resuming. "I've helped take off enough arms and legs to make a damned big pile." He paused again, this time to gaze at the other two men before passing his final judgment. "But I'll tell you right now, I've seen 'em like this hundreds of times. He's lost too much blood. The shock will likely kill him."

Enos remained in his chair near the roadway door, but he eased slowly back in it, looking at his helper. It was Redleaf who spoke next. "Could you take the ruined part off, Jack?"

Hudson nodded. "Yes. I've got a satchel of surgical tools in the storeroom across the road." He looked at Orcutt. "Who are his next of kin, Enos?"

Orcutt had no idea. "He never said. In fact, he never hardly ever talked about himself."

"Well, now, Enos, I'm not goin' to take it on myself to amputate that arm. You are his friend. He worked for you. Unless you can come up with a name of someone else around town who was closer to him, it looks to me like you're the one who's got to say yes or no."

Orcutt did not move or speak. He sat, staring at the man who had been his helper, evidently unable even to think about this kind of a responsibility. Hudson looked at Redleaf, and Chet raised and dropped his shoulders. He'd told Enos practically the same thing and had got no more response than Jack Hudson had.

Hudson was not a procrastinator. By nature he was forceful and decisive, and in this situation he was also dispassionate. Not because Prentice had turned out to be an outlaw, but because he privately did not believe Prentice was going to survive with or without the amputation. He had, in Hudson's view, waited far too long before surrendering.

Enos finally asked if Chet had any whiskey. He had a bottle behind his desk and set it up where the blacksmith could take a couple of long pulls from it. He offered it to Hudson, who declined with a curt head shake as he said: "If we're goin' to do this thing, I'll go hunt up my tools. If we're not, I've got a saloon to run."

Orcutt leaned with both arms on his legs, looking steadily at his helper. The whiskey did not contribute much, if anything, to the decision he finally made. "He'll most likely hate me . . . all of us . . . when he wakes up and finds we taken off one of his arms." Hudson solemnly nodded his head in silence. "But at least he'll be alive," the blacksmith stated. "All right, Jack. Let's take it off."

Hudson turned without a word, slammed the jailhouse door after himself, and walked briskly through the night in the direction of the saloon. Enos had another couple of pulls from the lawman's whiskey bottle, after which Redleaf put it back in the dusty box where he kept it. He did not know whether Hudson would require him and Enos to help in the amputation or not, but if Hudson did require it, the last thing Redleaf wanted was a drunken blacksmith.

Hudson returned fifteen minutes later with a black leather satchel, half an armload of clean towels, some laudanum, and a bottle of whiskey that he placed on Redleaf's table. He rolled up his sleeves past the elbows, washed his hands at the office basin, dried them while gazing at the inert man, and slowly began to scowl as he finished drying his hands.

He approached Prentice, knelt for a long time looking and listening, then straightened back very slowly, looking up. "He's dead."

X

Redleaf rolled Prentice into an old canvas and left him on the storeroom floor, had a pull from his whiskey bottle, skipped supper, and went down to the rooming house tired enough to sleep the clock around. The last two things he'd done at the jailhouse was sluice the office floor with a bucket of water, and bring food from the café to his prisoners. He did not tell them about Walt Prentice.

The old man who operated the rooming house was friendly for a change as the town marshal came along. He had some questions to ask concerning several things he'd heard, and got no answers as Redleaf closed his door. The whiskey that had seemed to have no effect on Enos a while back had an effect on the town marshal. He slept like a log, did not hear someone rattling his door after midnight, and did not open his eyes until the sun was rising.

He did not anticipate a pleasant new day. For one thing he had to find the local carpenter, have him measure Prentice for a pine box, then muster diggers for the grave hole, and haul the body out there to be put down. For another thing, he was worried about the big Indian who had volunteered to search the mountains for hold-outs who might have witnessed the robbery of that crippled stagecoach. He was also worried about Les Riley whose excursion up to Berksville could have ended up with Les being in trouble up there.

On this last score he need not have worried. The heavy fist that had rattled his door at the rooming house in the wee hours had been Riley. He'd arrived back in Mandan about midnight.

They met at the café but said very little until they were across the road in the privacy of the jailhouse, then Les told Redleaf a lot of things that the lawman already knew, and which Les had coaxed out of the prisoner up in Berksville. Redleaf then told his friend about Walt Prentice, about his prisoners, and, when he had finished, Les made a gesture of resignation. "I'd have done better to stay home," he asserted. Redleaf took him over to the saloon where they drank beer and ate corned beef sandwiches, and that revived Riley's mood a little.

Then Chet told Les about the big Indian, Henry Nye, and Les cocked his head quizzically. "And you want me to go into those damned mountains and find him."

Chet smiled. "No. I doubt that you could. All we can do is wait."

"Hell, you don't need any Indians to identify your prisoners, Chet."

Redleaf nodded. "Yeah. But there's no way I can get that information to Henry Nye."

Riley hunted up the town carpenter and took him to the jail-house to measure the corpse while Marshal Redleaf went to see Rod Manion. When he had finished his recitation, the store-keeper, who looked much better than he had looked at their last meeting, stared in wide-eyed astonishment. "Walt Prentice was one of them? I can't believe it. I've waited on Walt at the store dozens of times. He was a nice feller, good-natured and all. And Howard? My God, I'd have trusted him with my life."

As Chet arose to leave, he dryly said: "Maybe Judas Iscariot was a nice feller, too, Rod. I've yet to meet an outlaw who would tell you he wasn't a nice feller. Anyway, they're locked up . . . the live ones . . . and you're lucky they didn't get back down here to roast your toes until you told 'em where your cache is."

"And Henry's in the mountains by himself?"

"Yes."

Manion wagged his head, was still wagging it as Redleaf went downstairs and was waylaid by Manion's tall wife who wanted to know if the rumors going around town were true. He listened to her before agreeing that for the most part, at least as far as the basics were concerned, they were indeed true. He did not tell her about Henry Nye. She already knew about Howard Ballew.

When he got back to the jailhouse, Les and a grizzled, tall, pale-eyed older man were sharing cups of coffee while they waited. When Chet arrived, his friend inclined his head in the stranger's direction and said: "This here is the U.S. marshal from Albuquerque, Paul Scott."

Chet acknowledged the introduction, eyed the lean, hard-eyed older man, and went after a cup of coffee for himself as he asked what he could do for the stranger, and got back a brusque reply as the hard-eyed older man tossed three folded papers on the table, then sat back, watching Marshal Redleaf unfold them, spread them flat, and read them.

Les Riley, who'd made idle conversation with the stranger until Redleaf returned to the jailhouse, sat straighter in his chair, showing interest, so he clearly had had no previous knowledge concerning the stranger's purpose in being in Mandan. Chet flattened the papers carefully and re-read them before raising his eyes to the older man's weathered countenance. The federal officer looked straight back as he said: "They're in order, Marshal. That's the superior court judge's signature on the bottom."

Chet continued to gaze at the hard-eyed man. "I only got them locked up yesterday and you're from Albuquerque. How did you know I had them. Albuquerque is a hell of a distance from Mandan."

The older man made a death's-head smile. "I didn't know until I arrived in town last night and heard the talk at the saloon. I was on my way up north, looking for Ballew, Cuff Waters, and Fred Holden. We got word a couple months back down in Albuquerque that they was somewhere up around Berksville."

"I see. And you were on your way up there?"

"Yep. Looks like you saved me a lot of time, Marshal Redleaf."

Les Riley looked puzzled. "Are those federal warrants, Chet?"

Redleaf looked at the papers under his hands as he nodded. "Yeah. Warrants for Howard Ballew, a man named Holden, a man named Waters. Charges are mail robbery among other things. Federal offences."

Les turned slowly toward the hard-eyed older man and sighed. "Hell of a note. We do all the work and the federal government comes along and takes the prisoners."

The older man laughed. "Except for luck I wouldn't have been able to do it. I was expecting to have to hire a horse up in Berksville country and start hunting for them." He rose and unconsciously adjusted his gun belt. "I've got to eat, then I'll find out when the next southbound stage leaves, and by then, Marshal, you can have 'em ready."

Chet nodded. He and Les watched the older man cross to the door and close it after himself. Les made a little fluttery gesture. "Just like that," he said, sounding annoyed.

Redleaf studied the warrants briefly, leaned back, scratched his head, and put a quizzical gaze upon his friend. "Why just Howard, Cuff, and Fred? That feller you talked to up at Berksville was in with them. So was Walt Prentice."

"Maybe only those three robbed the mail," stated Riley.

Chet got to his feet, crossed to the cell-room door, and disappeared down the corridor, leaving Les still in his chair where he heard Redleaf ask Fred and Cuff if Brooks and Prentice had been their associates for long. The garrulous outlaw answered.

"Three, four years. They still got Brooks in jail up in Berksville?"

Chet ignored the question. "How about mail robberies, Fred?"

Cuff growled before his companion could reply. "We told you all we're goin' to say. Go ask Walt."

Chet's reply to that shocked his prisoners. "Walt is dead. After I locked you boys in, I went after him. He made a run for it, got shot, and died last night in my office."

Chet did not wait for the shock to pass. He fixed Fred with an unblinking stare as he said: "Who is Paul Scott?"

Only Ballew's eyes widened. Cuff and Fred looked blank.

He had another question: "Did you rob mail stages using the same system you used to rob the coach with Manion's money on it?"

Fred pushed out a hand to grip one of the steel bars. "We used downed trees across the road or rolled boulders out there. Anything that would force a stage to stop."

Chet studied them from beyond the steel bars. They looked

dirtier and more beard-stubbled than they had looked the day before. "Did Brooks and Prentice help at robbing mail stages?"

Fred and Cuff exchanged a look. Cuff shrugged and Fred answered. "Yeah. Prentice did the planning."

Chet hesitated before asking his final question. "Who helped Walt plan the raids?"

The prisoners were silent. Fred returned to the edge of his bunk, sat down, looking at the stone floor. Eventually he said: "All of us worked out the plans."

Chet waited for more, and, when Fred did not add anything, Chet said: "Just you, Cuff, Howard, Walt, and Brooks . . . no one else?"

Not one of the prisoners looked at Redleaf as Fred replied: "No one else."

Cuff nodded his head in verification so Marshal Redleaf returned to the office, closed the cell-room door, and met the faint frown of Les Riley as he crossed to his chair at the table. Les said: "Naw, not the U.S. marshal. Where'd you get such a crazy idea?"

Redleaf patted the legal documents. "Three warrants, Les."

"They're official, aren't they?"

"Yes. Official blanks that are filled out as they are needed. Les, you heard 'em just now. Prentice, Brooks, and Ballew were with Cuff and Fred when they raided mail stages, but this here U.S. marshal shows up with warrants for the only prisoners I've got. And it was just luck that he happened to arrive in town the day I locked them up. Why didn't he have warrants for Brooks and Prentice? They stole federal mail, too."

A raw-boned man with carroty hair and freckled skin poked his head in from out front to announce that the coffin was ready.

Les went down to the livery barn for a light dray wagon that he parked in the alley behind the jailhouse. He and Marshal Redleaf carried Prentice out there, then drove across town to the carpenter's shop where the three men fitted Enos Orcutt's defunct helper into the box. The carpenter nailed the lid down.

Les drove back the way they had come, halted behind the saloon, and waited until Marshal Redleaf returned after hiring a pair of local loafers to get their tools and drive out to the Mandan cemetery with Riley and Redleaf and dig a grave.

It was pleasant out there, mostly because the cemetery was shaded by huge old trees. While the diggers worked, Chet and Les leaned in wagon shade, watching. Eventually Les spoke while crushing a tick between his thumbnails. "There were five of them?"

Chet side-stepped a direct reply. "What I know, Les, is that the federal marshals I've had to deal with over the years don't go after a gang of outlaws without all the warrants they'll need. And . . . if they've been keeping track of mail robberies, they know how many highwaymen stopped and robbed stages. This one only talked about the three men I got in my cells."

Les finished squashing the tick and flicked it away. Fifty feet ahead the noise of men digging in soft earth continued. "All right. Now then . . . just who is this man?"

Chet watched the diggers for a while before answering. "I trapped three by following one 'way to hell and gone out where there was to be a rendezvous."

Riley looked around swiftly. "And the other one was already in the *juzgado* up at Berksville. That makes five. Are you saying they were waiting out there for another man?"

"I'm saying, when I crept up on to them they were setting in their camp, talking. Twice they said something about someone named Paul, like he was supposed to show up at the rendezvous, too."

Riley stared. "Paul?"

"Yeah."

Les faced forward to watch the diggers for a while before

speaking again. "Naw. No one's that big a damn' fool. If he's one of them, he sure as hell wouldn't use his right name."

Redleaf nodded agreement because the same thought had been troubling him. But there were other discrepancies. He turned to glance back in the direction of town. There was a slight heat haze back there. He could see men in the stage company's corral yard, harnessing a hitch for the southbound stagecoach. He faced forward to watch the diggers briefly, then said: "Let down the tailgate and help me get the coffin out. They can lower Prentice when the hole's deep enough and cover him."

Riley did not say a word until they had the box on the ground and one of the diggers, who had been watching, called to say the hole wasn't deep enough yet. Les called back: "When it is, put the box down in it, cover it, and come back to town!"

The diggers leaned on their shovels, watching Marshal Redleaf and his companion kick off the brakes and turn in the direction of Mandan. One of them tossed aside his shovel, clambered out of the grave, and rummaged in an old coat he'd dropped when the heat and digging had made him sweat. He held up a half-full bottle. The other gravedigger laughed and climbed out to perch on the edge of the grave.

They sat up there in tree shade, passing the bottle back and forth. One of them jerked a thumb in the direction of the pine coffin. "Did you know him?" he asked.

The other man drew a soiled sleeve across his lips before replying. "Yeah. Worked for Enos Orcutt. Seemed like a nice feller, Alfred, except that I got to tell you I always had a feelin' about him."

Alfred turned watering eyes toward his companion. "You never did no such a thing. Every blessed time we come out here and get to talkin' about whoever's in the box, you got to say something like that . . . what're you holdin' your hand out for?"

"Because I'm thirsty, you old screw."

"Here. Now don't hog it, Alfred. You know what your wife used to say."

Alfred handed back the bottle and raised a sleeve to his watering eyes. "What did she use to say?"

"Well, that was before she run off with that drummer with the curly brim derby hat and them spats over his shoes."

"I know who she run off with, for Christ's sake. What did she use to say?"

". . . Who?"

"My wife, for . . . you emptied the bottle, Homer. I got half a notion never to come here an' dig another grave with you. . . . What are you lyin' down for?"

"I'm sleepy."

"Get your scrawny butt up off the grass an' let's finish this hole or we'll miss supper. Get up, Homer."

XI

The U.S. marshal was smoking a long, thin cigar when Redleaf reached the office after leaving Riley to return the hitch and rig to the lower end of town. They exchanged a nod and the federal officer removed his stogie as he said: "There'll be a southbound coach leaving Mandan in half an hour. They told me it was late, but then I've rode darned few stages that was on time."

Chet went to his table, sat down, and put his hat aside. "We just buried Walt Prentice," he said.

Marshal Scott showed no concern. "It happens. Maybe we'd better get them other ones up here in the office and go over them."

Chet did not move. "They don't have any hide-outs."

"Well, I'd like to talk to one of them for a few minutes before we walk up yonder to the corral yard." Marshal Scott smiled through a rising trickle of fragrant blue smoke. "It's my custom,

Mister Redleaf, to explain exactly what I expect from them, and what'll happen if they don't do it."

Chet leaned back. "Marshal, do you know how many outlaws were in that band?"

Scott's hard gaze went to Redleaf's face and remained there. "Yeah. You got three of them, one is dead, and I heard in the saloon last night that another one is in jail up at Berksville."

Chet nodded. "Five," he said, and Marshal Scott nodded his head without taking his eyes off Redleaf. "That's the number I come up with," he said.

"You handed me warrants for only three of them."

Scott took a long pull off his cigar before replying. "I knew Prentice was dead and that Brooks was in jail up yonder. That's all they talked about at the saloon last night. Some of those gents were out there when Prentice surrendered to you." For a moment Marshal Scott gazed steadily at Redleaf before slowly removing his cigar to examine the length of ash. As he spoke his voice was different: "You got something bothering you, Mister Redleaf?"

Chet had no opportunity to answer, the door burst open, and Les Riley sprang into the room, looking wild-eyed and breathless as though he had run all the way from the lower end of town. He started to speak, saw the federal officer sitting there, relaxed and comfortable, and checked himself, forced a poor excuse for a smile, and crossed to the stove with his back to the other men to draw off a cup of coffee.

Chet was round-eyed. The federal officer trickled smoke, showed no expression at all, but kept his eyes on Riley's back until Les turned slowly, cup in hand, ignored the federal lawman, and looked directly at Redleaf as he said: "Have you fed your prisoners?"

Chet hadn't. It was slightly past high noon. He hadn't been thinking of that during his conversation with Paul Scott.

"No. In a few minutes. Why?"

Les jerked his head. "Go down there and look," he said.

Redleaf's stomach knotted. He stared steadily at his friend for a moment or two, then rose, took down his copper ring of keys, and hauled back the oaken cell-room door and disappeared in the dinginess as Les Riley put his gaze upon the hard-eyed man across the room from him whose legs were thrust out full length and crossed at the ankles. Paul Scott gazed directly back, smoke lazily rising. He did not remove the stogie but spoke around it. "What's this all about?"

Riley did not reply. Redleaf bellowed from the cell room and came charging back to the office. He said: "They're gone!"

Marshal Scott stopped puffing but otherwise showed nothing and did not move in his chair.

Riley, who had caught his breath and whose agitation had been sustained as long as it could be, nodded at his agitated friend. "Yeah, they're gone. And they had a gun when they ran down the alley to the livery barn. Howard had the weapon. He shoved it into the liveryman's gut. That's how they got three horses." Riley considered his coffee and put the cup aside without having tasted its contents. "They went west from town and headed straight north."

Les faced toward the stove, and turned back with his Colt aimed directly at the federal lawman. Scott's eyes widened slightly, went from the gun to Riley's face, then back to the gun as Riley cocked it. No smoke rose from his cigar. He removed it carefully and shook his head in Redleaf's direction. "You've got an excitable friend. Right now he's out of his mind."

Les's teeth showed in a cold smile. "While we were out yonder planting Walt Prentice, you were in and out of this office three times. Folks saw you come in and go out. The last time was about fifteen minutes before Howard Ballew shoved a gun in the liveryman's belly." Riley did not take his eyes off the federal marshal. "Chet, let me guess. Those cell doors was unlocked. Maybe it's about time for you to quit hanging your keys on that nail behind your desk."

Paul Scott slowly drew his legs back and began to lean slightly in his chair.

Riley spoke quietly to him. "You come up out of that chair and I'll blow you through the wall."

Scott remained expressionless but his gaze sharpened. "Mister Redleaf," he said, "you better control this idiot before someone gets hurt."

Chet's mind had been working very fast since the discovery that someone had unlocked the cell doors of his prisoners from the outside. For some time now he had been prepared to believe the worst about Paul Scott. But right now he addressed Riley, not Scott, as he began moving around behind Riley and the wood stove in the direction of the cell-room door. He did not draw his weapon until he had the door pulled back, then he wigwagged with the six-gun while simultaneously addressing Scott.

"Reach across with your left hand and drop the gun. Keep both hands in sight."

Finally Scott came up off the chair, looking from one of them to the other. He did not have the chance of a snowball in hell and knew it. Two weapons were aimed at him from a distance of less than thirty feet, and even though only one gun was cocked there was not a gunman living who could draw, aim, cock his weapon, and fire before those other two guns could blow him apart.

He dropped his weapon and shook his head in Redleaf's direction. "You're crazy," he growled.

Chet did not speak; he gestured with his gun barrel and followed Scott down to one of the empty cells, slammed the door on him, jammed the padlock closed, put up his weapon, and said—"You'll have time to think."—and hastened back to the office.

Riley was not there but the roadway door was wide open. Across the road three men burst forth from the saloon with Les Riley out front. One of them had a carbine, the others had only their belt guns. As Riley led his recruits past the pool hall, he bellowed in the doorway. Two pool players dropped their cues and ran outside.

Redleaf went back across his office, pulled the chain through the trigger guards of his racked weapons, took three carbines, and left in a lope heading toward the livery barn. When he got down there, the noise and confusion had attracted other townsmen, but of these onlookers none rushed forth to volunteer, which was probably just as well because by the time Marshal Redleaf had kept one carbine for himself and handed the other two around, men were swinging up across leather.

He led them out into the alley and northward. The badly upset liveryman had pointed with a rigid arm in that direction, yelling even after the posse riders were flinging up the alley. There was more excitement in town as information of the escape got around. It was a good thing Chet Redleaf was not there to hear some of what was being said.

Jack Hudson from the saloon, along with Enos Orcutt and the pool-hall proprietor, went down to the jailhouse, entered the office, saw the cell-room door ajar, and trooped down there to gaze with some surprise at the solitary prisoner.

Scott glowered. He told them what he wanted them to believe, said Redleaf was crazy, and demanded to be released. Not a word was said as the three townsmen turned on their heels, marched back to the office, carefully barred the cell-room door from the office side, and walked up to the saloon for a drink.

Hudson had served Scott over his bar. The pool-hall

proprietor was one of those people who had seen Scott enter the jailhouse several times during Redleaf's absence and Enos Orcutt, the Mandan blacksmith, had been sufficiently benumbed by recent events, including the death of his helper, not to have a whole lot of faith in anyone, particularly if he did not know them, and that disagreeable-acting man locked in one of Redleaf's cells was a perfect stranger to Enos. He was thinking of something else: "How did they unlock their cell door? Chet keeps his key ring on that nail behind his desk. Hell! Do you expect that's why he locked that feller up? He got the key ring and freed those sons-of-bitches?"

The pool-hall proprietor turned a jaundiced gaze on the blacksmith. "Did you see that feller enter an' leave the jailhouse three or four times while Chet and Les Riley was out at the cemetery? Well, I did. An' I say keep that feller locked up in there until Chet returns an' I don't give a damn whether he's a federal marshal or the President of the United States."

Big, burly Jack Hudson solemnly re-filled three glasses and stoppered the bottle before placing it under his bar top. "They're not goin' to get far," he prophesied. "Chet's got seven men with him an' it don't seem to me those outlaws had that big a head start."

An old gaffer, slumping in a chair beside the unlighted big old cast-iron wood stove, peered from sunken eyes at the other men as he said: "You don't know them mountains or you wouldn't make no such a statement, Jack. All them outlaws need is fast horses an' no more'n a half hour's head start. If they can clear the foothills and get up in there, take my word for it, the devil hisself couldn't find them, tracks or no tracks. I know. I scouted up Indians for Gen'l Miles through them damned mountains for three years."

The old man's statement dampened the grim enthusiasm of his listeners. They had their drinks and left the saloon in silence, all but Jack Hudson, who leaned on his bar top, gazing around his empty place of business, finally settling his eyes upon the ragged old scarecrow slumped in a chair beside the stove. Jack straightened up, filled a shot glass, took it over to the old man, and jerked his head in the direction of the platters of corned beef, coarse bread, and pickles at the free-lunch end of the bar. "Fat up," he growled. "Leave the whiskey here until you've the pleats out of your belly."

The old man raised tired eyes. "I got no money, Jack."

"I wouldn't take it if you did have," the big, burly man growled. "Quit settin' here, feelin' sorry for yourself. Go over there and fill up."

"Jack."

"What?"

". . . If you got a broom, I'll sweep out for m' food and the whiskey."

Hudson stood a moment, gazing downward. "Did you really scout for General Miles?"

"Yes, for a damned fact. And for a friend of his who didn't have the brains God give a goose. Feller named George Armstrong Custer."

Hudson's eyes widened. "Him, too?"

The old man's eyes crinkled. "Ten years of it. From up along the Canadian line south to New Mexico."

"The Army retired you?"

The old man's mouth pulled wide in a bitter smile. "The Army don't retire nobody under twenty years, an', if it's an enlisted man, he don't get enough to buy a knothole to pee through. For civilian scouts . . . they give you a medal with a pretty ribbon on it and turn you out to grass."

Hudson returned behind his bar when three strangers walked in, beating off dust after a six-hour stage ride. He served them, listened to their grumbling, and, when they departed southward in the direction of the rooming house because there would not be another eastbound stage leaving Mandan until morning, Hudson watched the gaunt old man methodically eating at the free-lunch end of his bar.

He called up to him: "What's your name?"

The answer was barely distinguishable because the old man did not swallow before offering it. "Bud Leslie. I've been in here before. Mostly when it's cold outside."

Hudson nodded. He remembered the old man but until today had not distinguished him from several other old men without families who huddled around his stove in wintertime, sometimes buying a 5¢ beer, more rarely buying a 10¢ jolt of whiskey. "Bud, I got a proposition for you."

The old man turned his gaunt face with the sunken eyes, chewed, and said nothing.

"There's an iron cot in my storeroom out back. All you can eat. I'll get you some decent pants and shirts down at Manion's store. You wash glasses, keep the place swept out, haul in stove wood in winter. Six dollars a month cash."

The old man chewed, swallowed, pulled a filthy sleeve across his mouth, and turned back to the mammoth sandwich he'd made as he said: "I'll do it, but there's got to be more work'n that, Jack, because I don't take no charity."

Hudson continued to lean and watch the old man. "All right. Keep the backbar dusted an', before you bed down every night, go across the alley and put a shovelful of lye down the holes in the outhouse. I'll think of other things."

Bud Leslie took his sandwich back to the chair by the stove, sat down, and grinned as he reached for the little glass of whiskey. "I bet you will," he said, and dropped the whiskey straight down.

Hudson laughed, swabbed his bar top almost without thought, and, as townsmen began drifting in, he said: "Start first thing in the morning. When you get through there, go settle in at the storeroom."

XII

Redleaf's riders reached the foothills on sweaty horses. They had fresh tracks that far, so they'd been able to make good time, but there was nothing to see—no movement, not even any dust, which meant the escaping outlaws had not spared their stolen animals to get far enough ahead to be into the timber by the time the townsmen reached the foothills. They took time out to dismount, loosen cinches, roll smokes, and gaze up ahead where tiers of trees, most of which were at least a hundred feet tall, made a place of perpetual gloom as the country sloped steadily upward, in some places almost precipitously upward.

A squinty-eyed thin man with skin like parchment and a prominent Adam's apple that bobbled when he talked raked bent fingers through graying hair and said: "I been pot-huntin' them hills for some years, an' I'm here to tell you that's bad country up there. A man can get lost up there who ain't ever been lost nowhere else."

Les Riley eyed the speaker coolly. "How far back in there have you been?"

The thin man gestured toward the nearest high ridge. "About that far. Maybe six, eight miles." He lowered his arm. "I can guide you that far. But if them renegades went in a different direction. . . ." The thin man spat, shrugged, and remained silent.

When they were astride again, still following gouged tracks left by shod horses digging in with each jump, Redleaf began to suspect that the escaping outlaws had indeed gone in a different direction. They were pushing in among forest giants when the tracks turned eastward paralleling the highest ridge above them.

For a long while nothing was said. Chet read sign in the lead and the others followed him. Once, a posse man, sounding uncomfortable, mentioned the possibility of an ambush that could put them all face down in the dirt. No one replied; it was highly unlikely outlaws, fleeing for their lives, would risk losing the time an ambush would take.

They were crossing a soggy meadow where mosquitoes arose in the thousands to plague the horses when Chet swung off, retrieved something from the grass, and rode onward while examining it. When he was finished, he passed the object over to Riley and concentrated on reading sign. It was a cracked short length of leather, ragged at both ends where it had torn loose, with a Conway buckle in the middle. It could have come from a cheek piece or perhaps from the length of leather beneath a horse wearing a double-rigged saddle, but one thing was certain—it had not been lying in that damp place very long, otherwise it would have showed rust and the leather would have been soggy, not dry.

Someone made a wry comment. "It come from the livery-man's equipment all right. He never soaped nor oiled a piece of leather in his life."

Redleaf paused on the near side of a gravelly top-out that had been wind-swept down to bedrock in places, handed Les his reins, and crept up to lie flat on the rim. He had an excellent view of the countryside to the east, west, and north. The trouble was that all that magnificent view had varying degrees of timber denseness. It was not possible to see down through to the ground. But what Redleaf was looking for was not on the ground. It originated there but did not stay there—dust.

He saw it higher upcountry northward, but eastward as though the fleeing riders were trying to gain height while at the same time hastening eastward. He lay for a long time watching, trying to guess the route of the escaping outlaws, and, when he was satisfied, he returned to the others, who had been squatting in tree shade while their animals rummaged for whatever was edible up here, of which there was precious little because grass did not grow where resin-impregnated pine and fir needles formed carpets six to ten inches deep.

When they were moving again, Chet twisted toward Les Riley directly behind him and said: "What we should have done was go straight up the stage road northward."

"Is that where they're going?"

"Yeah, but my guess is that they'll cross it and keep going eastward. Maybe they know the country over there. If we'd gone up the road, we could have cut them off."

Riley dryly said: "Sure we could have, and, if we had a crystal ball, we could know when it's going to rain."

Shadows began inching around from behind the big trees, frail at first but strengthening as time passed. Redleaf pushed the horses as much as he dared. He did not want to have to call a halt for the night because he did not believe the outlaws would do that.

It was that thin, homely man with the squinted eyes who thought this would not be so. He told the others that no one in their right mind, including outlaws, rode through the night in a damned forest where anything could happen to a man and damned well might happen—even if he wasn't straddling ridden-down saddle stock. Whether this observation was true or false, it put a little heart into the others as Chet finally had to dismount and walk ahead of his animal to make out the tracks because dusk arrived much earlier in stands of big timber than it did where there was no timber.

They reached the stage road, slid their animals down a crumbly embankment to reach the center of it, and halted to listen. The only thing they heard was an invisible animal who had been routed out of its bed by their arrival, and grunted irritably as it fled through the underbrush.

Redleaf rolled and lit a smoke. They were about three hundred yards south of the place where the crippled stagecoach had been forced to halt—and had been robbed. Riley and another man got down to bend close to the ground for tracks. They found them, followed them across to the opposite clay-bank, straightened up, and gazed at deep gouges where horses had been forced to climb up a very steep bank of soft soil. They told Redleaf where the outlaws had gone and pointed eastward. He nodded absently, picked up his reins, and turned northward up the middle of the stage road. Riley and the man who had scouted with him exchanged a look but said nothing. No one said anything in fact, but they watched Redleaf as men would have done who felt like challenging his decision.

Dusk darkened both sides of the roadbed. Out there, however, there was better light. There were weak stars for a while, until eventually they brightened and coldly blinked, by which time the posse men were riding blind. Redleaf did not lope, did not even lift his horse over into a trot, but he kept riding, so the men behind him did the same. It was a warm night, which was a blessing since most of the riders had flung out of town in such haste they'd had no time to go after coats and jackets.

By the time moonlight added a little to visibility, though, the warmth was fading. Redleaf headed directly toward a gunsight notch in the skyline where the road passed through, halted slightly below it, and swung off to rest the horses. He and Riley walked up to the pass and stood in silence, looking downhill where a fifty-mile swale in the mountain chain ended in the moonlighted dim distance where the country rose up again gradually toward another gunsight notch. Between one pass and the other there was primitive country. That thin man with the Adam's apple came up behind them and said: "Ain't no different as far as a man can see, but as long as a man stays on the road he'll come out somewhere. If he gets to foragin' around in the trees on either side of the road, he'll get lost sure as hell."

Les turned. "I've freighted this road for a lot of years, friend, and you're right. But Berksville's up there."

"Anythin' in between?"

"Nope. Some grassy meadows you can see through the trees now and then but no settlements of any kind that I ever saw."

The thin man made a laconic observation. "Well, boys, they're up there maybe, an', if they are, they won't be too far ahead. Folks can't abuse saddle stock like they been doin' an' not end up on foot if they don't rest 'em. Nothing's harder on horses than mountainous country. They been pushing those animals like they thought they was made of iron . . . they're up there, gents. From here on it'd pay to ride off the road where the needles will deaden our sound."

It was sound advice, but Redleaf had already decided on a course that was consistent with his idea about the men they were pursuing, and it went back to that earlier robbery of the stagecoach. That time, the outlaws had skulked downcountry parallel to the road on the east side until they found the coach where it had halted. He mounted and turned off the roadway into the easterly timber where it was as dark as the inside of a boot except in rare instances where little grassy glades caught moonlight.

It was Redleaf's opinion that those stage robbers must have had a camp up here somewhere. For that reason, when they came upon one of those grassy places, he would scout around and across it. It was slow going, and, although from time to time they dismounted, looking for shod-horse tracks, they had no success, so they fanned out on foot, leading their animals to form a wide-ranging sweep northward. Redleaf believed as that shrewd, squinty-eyed man believed that the outlaws were somewhere up ahead and probably not too distant. Twice he called a halt, took Les Riley, and scouted ahead on foot.

They found nothing. On the hike after the second scout Chet said they would wear themselves and the horses down doing this. When they got back to the others, he suggested off-saddling, making a dry camp, and getting some sleep. The squinty-eyed man shook his head but said nothing. The others were willing to rest. They would have liked a warming fire but no one suggested it.

The moon soared, stars flickered, occasionally a nocturnal forager rustled fir needles or undergrowth, and the chill deepened. Riley went out to look at the horses and returned to say the squinty-eyed man was gone. There was a little muttering about this, but since the horse he had been riding was still with the other animals the unanimous opinion was that he had gone on a scout.

He had. In fact, when he eventually returned to camp and a drowsy posse man was roused by his presence and challenged him, the lanky man said: "Just settle down, friend. I went for a walk. Back home in Virginia I was raised up walking in the mountains."

His voice roused the other men. They wanted to know if he'd found anything. He answered while moving over where Marshal Redleaf was sitting with his back to a giant red fir tree. "Yes, sir. I found some horses. I didn't go up close. Didn't want them smellin' me and gettin' scairt. Hard to tell from a distance but there was at least three of them in a little park about a mile an' a half ahead down the far side of this here top-out."

Everyone was wide-awake. Les asked about the riders of those horses but the Virginian's reply was disappointing. "Didn't see hide nor hair of 'em. Didn't find their camp, neither, even though I slunk around lookin' for it. But they got to be over there, boys. That's why I hurried on the way back. We got about two hours more of darkness, then dawn'll come and it'll be too late for us all to sneak back there and set up an ambush. Wherever those gents are hid out among the trees, they sure as hell don't figure to go nowhere without their horses. All's we got to do is get in place and be stonestill when those fellers come out for their animals." The Virginian tapped Redleaf's shoulder lightly. "You're the chief."

Chet rose, popped the stiffness from his legs by flexing his knees, picked up a carbine, and jerked his head. Without a word the others also rose.

The Virginian took the lead. They never lost sight of him, but occasionally his zigzagging route left the others temporarily in doubt.

Les nudged Chet. "Who is he?"

Redleaf did not know the man. "Haven't any idea. I don't recall seeing him around town."

The Virginian stopped beside a huge sugar pine with reddish bark. The others walked right up on to him and might have passed by if he hadn't stepped out in front with an arm raised for silence. He turned and pointed toward a palely lighted clearing of no more than ten acres. There was stirrup-high grass out there and it was still green. At this elevation grass did not turn brown and go to seed until much later than it did at lower elevations.

The posse men crept close to the final fringe of trees that surrounded the grassy place and halted. Riley thought there were five animals over on the far side of the glade. Someone else said it was no more than three horses. That was the number they had expected to find so it was easy to believe there were no more than three animals over yonder. Any more would have made problems for them; the outlaws had escaped from town on three stolen horses. The issue was seemingly resolved when Chet told them to spread out among the trees, some of the men to start circling to the left, the others to start around the meadow on the right. When they were in place, they were to hide and wait for dawn. As soon as the riders of those horses appeared, they were to throw down on them.

The Virginian was smiling broadly; this had been his suggestion. He led off on the left-side surround. Riley led off in the opposite direction, and Marshal Redleaf leaned his carbine against the handsome big sugar pine and hunkered down to wait.

Everything appeared to be progressing satisfactorily until a cougar screamed somewhere southward. The cat could have been close or he could have been farther than he seemed to be, but his scream carried perfectly to those dozing horses. They came awake in a moment and ran in panic toward the center of the glade. Where they halted, milling, unwilling to run in among the trees, Chet Redleaf counted nine horses.

XIII

The horses remained poised to panic, but as moments passed without another scream, they gradually came down from their high and cropped grass, occasionally testing the air for a scent. As time passed even that kind of uneasiness waned.

Redleaf felt like swearing. There was no way the outlaws could have acquired that many horses; he had been on their trail from town and they had not come upon any ranches or any free-grazing ranch animals. He scowled toward where the horses were beginning to spread out as they ate. There was only one explanation—he and his companions had set up an ambush for men who'd had nothing to do with the jail break. He shoved up to his feet, twisted to brush himself off, and saw the stonestill silhouette of a man not thirty feet distant among the trees.

They regarded each other for a moment before the shadowy silhouette raised a carbine, holding it low in both hands with its barrel aimed squarely at the lawman. It was not a posse man.

Even before the weapon came to bear Redleaf sensed something different. After the gun was aimed, he said: "Are those your horses?"

The shadow did not respond. Neither did he look away from Redleaf. To the right where more huge old overly ripe trees hindered visibility a second silhouette appeared and spoke. "You must have a good reason for prowling these mountains in the dark, Marshal."

Henry Nye came soundlessly forward. He had no carbine, just a holstered Colt around his middle. He looked even larger in the gloom.

Chet eased his breath out slowly, looked once again at the first silhouette, then faced the big Indian. "Yeah. We had a jail break. Three of the men who took Manion's box off the stagecoach got set free by another member of the gang, and came up here, riding hell for leather."

Nye thought about that for a while before asking a question. "You got 'em dead to rights?"

"Yes. If I'd known how to contact you, I'd have done it. We won't need any Indians to identify them."

Henry Nye glanced in the direction of the statue-like silhouette. "Come on over here, Owl."

The silhouette was a lean young Indian whose attire was about equal parts white man's clothing and tanned deerskin. He grounded his Winchester while looking straight at Redleaf, and neither spoke nor nodded as he was introduced to the lawman.

Henry Nye rubbed the tip of his nose while gazing at the young buck. He told him about the fleeing outlaws and the Indian grinned, showing perfect white teeth in the chilly predawn. Chet asked Henry Nye if the Indian thought it was amusing that he and his posse men had ridden themselves to a frazzle in pursuit of outlaws.

Nye shook his head, looking bemused. "No. But in the middle of the night someone in the camp heard horses whinnying and roused the others. They scattered through the timber on foot. Some of them saw three riders going past at a dead walk on very tired horses."

The Indian said: "White men."

Nye nodded. "White men."

Chet was interested. "In which direction?"

"North," stated the big Indian, and shifted position a little. "Where are your friends, Marshal?"

Redleaf gestured. "Around the clearing waiting to catch someone coming out after those horses."

"It might be a good idea to leave them out there for the time being." Henry Nye jutted his chin in the Indian's direction. "These folks would just as soon as few people as possible knew they are up here." Nye switched his attention to the Indian. "Do you suppose you could take a few men, find where those outlaws are camped, and steal their horses?"

Again the buck broadly smiled. "Yes. Will you keep these men away from the camp?"

Nye nodded his head, and the Indian faded out among the trees.

Nye got comfortable on the ground, gazing out where those nine horses were eating. "You're wondering how I found these people. Well, I didn't find them, they found me. I was bumbling around north of here a few miles. It was getting dark, so I made camp near a little creek, slept like a dead man, and in the morning, when I opened my eyes, there they were. Six of them, sitting there like a row of rocks with blankets around them." Nye grinned. "I invited them to breakfast. Of the six three could not speak English. They were the older men. The younger men, like Owl who was one of them, all spoke English."

Chet had a question. "If they're so shy about folks knowing

they are up in here, why didn't they just let you ride on?"

"Curiosity. By the light of dawn they could see my hide was about the same color as their hide. If I'd been a white man, they would have let me ride past." Nye paused to look at Redleaf. "They need friends, Marshal. They have a main camp about seven miles northwest of here beneath a big granite over crop. It's in a beautiful big meadow, a regular picture-postcard setting. They need many things. Medicine, for example, woolen blankets, warm clothing that is better than split-hide shirts and britches. They need iron cooking pots, gunpowder, and lead. It tugs at a man's heart to see how they live, as wary as coyotes, always fearful someone will see them and tell the Army where they are." Henry Nye squinted eastward where a feeble paleness was beginning to appear. "I'm not going to say I saw any hold-outs up here." He turned questioning dark eyes on Redleaf.

Chet was agreeable. "Nor am I."

Nye accepted that. "Then all we got to worry about is your posse men." He brushed himself off as he stood up. Chet also got to his feet. Nye gestured in the direction of the fish-belly sky. "If you'll round them up, Marshal, and take them back the way you came to that boggy meadow down there, I'll deliver their horses to you and with any luck the outlaws, too." Nye looked long at Marshal Redleaf. "It's got to be done without the outlaws seeing the Indians."

Chet turned to watch the horses briefly. "How do you do that, Mister Nye? Those outlaws know someone is behind them. I think they only have one gun among them, but, if I'm wrong, someone could get killed."

Nye looked thoughtful. "I wouldn't pretend to know how these people stalk wild game and kill it with rocks, but I know for a fact they do it. I'd say your outlaws wouldn't be too much trouble for them." Henry Nye shoved big hands deep into trouser pockets and changed the subject. "How is Rod Man-ion?"

"Much better. Did you know the feller who clerked for him at the store?"

"Yes. Ballew, wasn't it?"

"He was one of the band who robbed the coach. He's one of the outlaws your Indians will be after. Another one was the town blacksmith's helper. He's dead. There was another one we didn't know about until he showed up pretending to be a federal lawman, and turned loose Ballew and the pair of men with him out yonder somewhere."

Nye said: "You've been busy, Marshal."

Redleaf watched the big man moving among the trees, lost sight of him, and lifted his hat vigorously to scratch. He did not dwell upon the unique meeting or the big Indian's concern for the hold-outs; he concentrated instead on how he was going to convince his posse men they should go back down to that mosquito-inhabited wet meadow.

He started around the horse meadow southeastward, which was the direction Les Riley had taken. The dawn was cold; there was not a sound. Evidently roosting birds had detected the presence of men down below and had left the area. Those Indian horses seemed not to have picked up man scent, or, if they had, they were indifferent to it.

Les Riley rose twenty feet in front of Redleaf where he had been sitting in a wild grape thicket. He yawned, then said: "They should have come out here by now."

Chet looked elsewhere among the trees and undergrowth as he spoke. "Someday I'll tell you why we are going back down to that wet meadow, but not right now. Can you find the others?"

Les stared for a moment before answering. "Yeah. But they've put in a lot of time on this manhunt, Chet. They're going to want to know why we're going back empty-handed."

"Tell 'em the outlaws cut back."

"Did they?"

Redleaf continued to avoid his friend's gaze. "They could have. Round up the others and meet me back where we left the horses."

Riley watched the lawman passing back among the trees and spat, hitched at his britches, and turned to find the other posse men.

The sun was rising by the time Redleaf's companions came around the clearing to where he was waiting. That Virginian with the Adam's apple asked Chet pointblank if he knew for a fact that the men they were hunting had cut back.

Even Les Riley stood motionlessly awaiting Redleaf's reply. Chet's answer was curt. "They lost their horses, and being livery animals my guess is that the animals will start back."

The Virginian squinted. "An' you figure they'll try to track 'em down and catch them?"

"Something like that. Let's get mounted up."

The Virginian did not move. "Marshal, I'd like to know how you know them bastards lost their horses."

Chet answered while moving toward their saddle stock. "I heard horses going south last night. It wasn't those animals out yonder and it wasn't our horses, so that left the other ones."

The Virginian seemed to accept that. So did the other men, at least until they'd been on the trail for a while with sunlight beginning to bring warmth into the new day, then a raffish red-headed man eased up beside Riley and said: "This don't make sense to me. If they lost their horses, then seems to me we should be gettin' between them fellers on foot to keep them from finding their damned horses, an' that way we'd maybe catch 'em."

Riley did not argue. His response was offered tiredly. He did not understand this any better than the others did, but he had faith in Chet Redleaf. "If the marshal wants to do it this way, friend, then I guess we'll do it this way. All I give a damn about is that we find those men."

The red-headed man may not have been satisfied with that explanation, but he reined back and rode along, looking more bewildered than annoyed.

It was the Virginian who kept the topic alive. He was evidently garrulous by nature, and, with something he did not understand bothering him, he alternated between periods of loquacious complaining and scowling silence. Redleaf ignored them as he led the withdrawal back down through the timber. He was less worried about what they thought than he was about the possibility that Henry Nye might not be able to deliver the stolen horses and the men who had stolen them. If he failed, Redleaf was not only going to have a lot of explaining to do, but he was going to have to do it without mentioning Indians, and that, he told himself, presented the most difficult decision of his life—whether to tell the truth or to manufacture the biggest lie he had ever told.

When they reached the vicinity of the sump meadow, the sun was well aloft even though it did not penetrate the forest in very many places, and, while there was warmth, it was less than the sun's heat would be out in open country.

They did not go very close to the wet meadow because of the mosquitoes, but they were bothered by the hungry little insects even then. Until the heat eventually arrived, they were occupied in making big sweeps with their hats to prevent being bitten. The horses used manes and tails and stamping feet to protect themselves against all but the boldest mosquitoes. Gradually the insects abandoned the shadows and returned to the meadow. Their reason was a large band of deer that had come out of the northward forest in search of soft grass and water.

Chet lighted a smoke as did everyone else who smoked.

Mosquitoes did not like any kind of smoke. Eventually the posse men had sufficient relief to turn their attention to other things. Riley and the Virginian took the horses farther back in search of a grassy place. When they returned without the animals, the Virginian appeared to have been lectured about pestering Marshal Redleaf; at any rate he settled on the ground with his saddle for a pillow, tipped an old hat over his face, and went to sleep without saying a word. The other men also stretched out. They had been cold last night. They had not slept. This seemed to be an excellent opportunity to emulate the Virginian.

Les came over and dropped down near Redleaf. He rolled and lit a smoke and raised questioning eyes. "You got a good reason for this?" he asked.

Redleaf's answer was rueful. "It'd better be. If it's not, I might just as well saddle up and leave the country."

Les trickled smoke. "Indians?" he said casually.

Redleaf blinked. "What made you say that?"

"Those horses back up yonder. I was setting in the bushes real still and a couple of 'em came along, picking grass. Indian horses, Chet. One had cropped ears, the other one had somethin' braided into a few strands of his mane right up behind his ears. I couldn't make it out, but I've seen Indians' horses before that had those little braids."

Redleaf glanced among the trees where the posse men were either dozing or sleeping. "Henry Nye was up there."

"The hell!"

"Came out of the trees. There was a young buck, too. Nye said the Indians would try to capture the outlaws, but whether they could do that or not, they will steal their horses and bring them down here. I agreed to make a trade with them . . . they either catch the outlaws or set them afoot, and we'd come down here and wait."

Riley stubbed out his smoke. "Well, if they do it, that's not going to keep that feller from Virginia and the others from wondering how it happened."

Redleaf had already considered this and it bothered him less than what the outlaws would have to say about how they had been captured. "I don't know what Nye had in mind except for setting those men on foot. But I do know that, if he delivers Cuff, Fred, and Howard down here, it's not going to be any secret that they were caught by hold-outs, and that kind of talk will eventually reach the Army. All I promised was not to say I'd met any Indians up there."

Riley stood up and yawned. The heat was increasing even in the depth of the forest. "You don't have to worry about me saying anything. As far as I'm concerned, they can have this kind of country and more power to 'em." Les paused, gazing down at his friend. "How in hell do you get yourself into messes like this?"

For the first time in the new day Redleaf smiled. "I work real hard at it."

Riley turned to peer out through the timber in the direction of the soggy meadow. "Maybe it'd be a good idea if someone kept watch out there. It'd be a hell of a note if Nye's redskins brought those bastards down here and we were all asleep."

Redleaf agreed. "Yeah. That's my job."

"I can spell you off. I'll nap for a while, then spell you."

Chet nodded, and the freighter went back through the trees.

A band of blue jays came winging into the treetops, saw the men down below, and started their customary noisy caterwauling, which served as a warning to other upland wildlife that trespassers had invaded their area. Maybe the other creatures heeded the squawking, but the posse men didn't—except for Redleaf, who rose to pace among the trees because sitting still made him drowsy.

XIV

The Virginian awakened, raised his hat to look around, then sat up as Marshal Redleaf moved past. "Marshal, you hear anything?"

Chet stopped. "No."

The lanky mountaineer rolled over, lowered his head with an ear to the ground, remained like that briefly, then sat up squinting. "I guess I felt it," he said, and got to his feet.

Redleaf frowned. "Felt what?"

"Put your ear to the ground, Marshal. It's horses coming."

"From what direction?"

The Virginian raised a long arm. "Sort of northeast, I think. Listen."

Chet heard them, but very faintly. They did not appear to be traveling fast. In fact, if it had been only one horse, he probably would not have made enough noise to be heard, but it sounded like several horses.

He went among the men, rousing them. The Virginian stood a while listening, then faded back among the trees. He gestured for everyone else to do the same, and they did.

Les Riley reached inside his shirt to scratch as he watched the far side of the meadow. The sounds were clearly audible now. Les said: "I thought they'd be hightailing it."

No one commented.

It was not a long wait, but it seemed to be, before they could see movement over through the timber. Redleaf leaned against a large tree, relieved that Henry Nye's tomahawks had been able to steal the horses, and slightly disappointed when he could finally see all three animals because they were not carrying riders.

Riley noticed this, too. "Now we've got their animals, we can go back up yonder and hunt them down. You want to know something, Chet. I've been hungry so long my belly thinks my throat is cut."

One of the posse men wordlessly offered Riley a gnawed square of molasses-cured cut plug. Les looked at it, shook his head, and, as the posse man was pocketing the plug, Les shuddered. Just once he'd tried chewing tobacco. He'd been so sick he had thought he would die and had wished to hell he could.

That inquisitive red-headed older man hissed: "Yonder. See 'em? Three bays."

The horses stopped at the edge of the meadow, lowered their heads, and greedily cropped grass. The red-headed man muttered. "Wait. Them mosquitoes'll be along."

He was right. The starved animals began swinging their tails, shaking their manes and stamping, but not even biting mosquitoes could make them leave the meadow. Someone behind Chet in forest gloom muttered that it was a damned shame to treat animals the way those horses had been treated.

The animals were in full view across the little meadow. While they stood back in the semidarkness watching them, the Virginian said: "Couple of us could take ropes an' sneak around to that side and most likely either catch them or spook them on southward toward town."

Riley answered that. "Just shut up and wait," he growled. "Unless I'm wrong as hell, those outlaws will be tracking them because they can't get horses anywhere else."

That seemed to settle it for the Virginian as well as for the other posse men. Several knelt to get comfortable. The red-headed man had a question for Redleaf: "Marshal, if you heard them horses passin' southward last night, why do you expect it took them this long to get down here?"

Chet sighed. "They were hungry and most likely they had no reason to run all the way. Free-ranging horses sometimes take forever just to go five miles. You ought to know that, if you been around horses very much."

The red-headed man was rebuffed and remained silent. He was the one who had offered Riley chewing tobacco to take the edge off his hunger.

The horses were gradually grazing out toward the middle of the meadow, ravenously eating grass and fighting mosquitoes. If they hadn't been starved, they wouldn't have remained out there for ten minutes, not with clouds of stinging insects hovering above them.

Suddenly three men appeared among the farthest trees. They walked forth, then halted, wary as wolves but clearly anxious about the grazing horses. They were motionless for a long time before one of them, a burly, muscular man, stepped in front of his companions into the sunlight, swung his head, then said something as he walked out into plain sight of the motionless watchers across the glade. He had a bridle draped from one shoulder.

Redleaf looked at Riley. "Fred," he murmured, "the one that fake U.S. marshal said was named Fred Holden."

Les nodded without speaking. He was intently watching the other two who were still obscured by forest gloom.

Fred was attacked by mosquitoes, pulled his hat off, and swung it. This time, when he spoke, the hidden watchers heard profanity. Finally the other men stepped into the sunlight, splitting off to approach the grazing horses from both sides. Chet straightened up off the tree he'd been leaning against, and the Virginian said: "Now we can sidle around through the trees and come up behind 'em, Marshal?"

Redleaf shook his head in silence without taking his eyes off the outlaws. By sunlight he recognized every one of them. Several of the posse men murmured when they recognized Manion's store clerk.

The horses sidled away. They did not throw up their heads

and flee, but they moved away each time one of the outlaws started easing up to them.

Les Riley knelt and raised his Winchester to track the preoccupied outlaws who were softly talking their way closer to the horses. The red-headed posse man also knelt, so did the Virginian.

Redleaf grunted to himself. The outlaws on both sides and behind the loose stock were inadvertently driving the animals directly across the meadow toward him.

The loquacious Virginian softly said: "This is goin' to be like shootin' fish in a rain barrel."

Redleaf growled at him: "Don't you even cock that gun."

The Virginian removed his thumb from the hammer.

Out in the sunlight the outlaw called Cuff was chumming his way up to one of the bay horses. He had his back to the invisible posse man when he called to his companions. "Slow! Slow 'n' easy. I got this one about caught."

The animal had a gutful of grass. With his hunger appeased, he stood like a docile cow and allowed Cuff to stroke his neck, working forward from the withers until he could loop a rein around the horse's neck. He waited a moment before easing up his left hand to place the bit into the horse's mouth. His companions watched without moving until Cuff had bridled the bay horse and led it over close to the remaining loose animals, then Ballew and Fred moved in.

They had their horses. While the bridling was being done, the store clerk said: "I'd have given a lot of money to have had a rifle when those damned bears spooked them."

Fred was, as always, philosophical. "The hell with the bears, we got 'em back."

Marshal Redleaf waited until the last throat latch was buckled, then raised his Winchester in both hands, holding it belt buckle high, and walked out of the timber into filtered daylight.

The outlaws were turning to lead the horses eastward when Redleaf called to them: "Drop the reins and stand still!"

The outlaws stopped in their tracks. Only Fred twisted to look across the meadow. Riley walked forth as did the other posse men, all of them with fisted guns. Fred sighed and slowly opened his hand to let the reins drop. He spoke quietly to his companions but the words carried. "There's a whole damned army of 'em."

Cuff, the highly strung outlaw, fidgeted before slowly facing around. Howard Ballew neither looked around nor dropped the reins, but his shoulders sagged.

Marshal Redleaf hardly raised his voice as he said: "Which one of you has the gun? Toss it down."

Ballew had it shoved in the front of his britches. He obeyed the order but still would not look around.

Riley lowered his carbine, looked around for the Virginian, and jerked his head. Those two went off westward back through the timber to the grassy place where they had left the horses earlier.

Chet told the outlaws to turn around and walk toward him, and bring the horses with them.

A posse man said: "Hell, I never figured it'd be this easy."

Chet made a muttered reply: "We're not back to town yet."

When the outlaws halted about thirty feet away, they ranged looks among the posse men, then regarded Marshal Redleaf in stony silence. He sent two posse men to go over his prisoners for hide-outs although he did not expect them to have any, nor did they.

They looked tucked up and drawn out. Cuff and Howard were thoroughly dispirited and had every right to be. Fred hooked thumbs in his waistband, wagged his head, and said:

"You'd never have caught us if it hadn't been for them damned bears. They come in the dark and scairt the pee out of the horses."

Chet studied the outlaw, the only one of them he did not actively dislike. "Bears," he quietly said. "How many?"

"Hell, we don't know, but there was more'n two or three of 'em. They come out of the trees straight for the horses."

Chet nodded. Bears did not travel in packs, nor would they go anywhere near an area that had the sour scent of human beings in it, let alone deliberately stalk horses where there was man smell.

Riley and his companion returned, leading the posse horses. It did not take long to rig out and get astride for the ride back to lower country. The outlaws had to ride bareback, but that was the least of their problems. Because of the forest, Chet had his prisoners ride one behind the other in the middle of the column with posse men in front and behind them. He had no intention of losing them again.

Once or twice the men talked, but mostly they followed Chet through the timber on the downslope side in silence. When they could see sun-bright range land through the trees, Redleaf guessed it had to be about midday. He could not see the sun for another hour, by which time it was slanting away from the meridian. And it was hot when they finally rode clear of the uplands, starting down through the rolling low foothills in the direction of Mandan.

Spirits brightened a little when the men left the gloom behind. There was some talk of eating a horse, sleeping for a week, and even taking an all-over bath. The prisoners did not enter into the conversation until they had roof tops in sight, by which time it was midafternoon.

Mandan's tree shade was a respite after the long ride across treeless range land. Chet avoided the main roadway, halted out behind his jailhouse, herded his captives inside, locked them into the same cells they had previously occupied, which was beside the cell of their friend, the imitation U.S. marshal, and left them there.

As he was walking back toward the office, Fred called after him. "When do we eat?" Chet closed the heavy door, barred it from the office side, and went over to the water bucket, which others had half emptied.

The posse men took the horses down to the livery barn, then split up, half aiming for the café, the others aiming for Jack Hudson's saloon.

Les Riley sank into a chair at the jailhouse office and let go a rattling long sigh. "I've been keeping track. At a dollar a day you owe me about ten dollars."

Chet's eyes widened. "We haven't been after them for ten days."

Riley remained unperturbed. "Did you ever hear of something called overtime? That's what they pay on the railroad and in cities when you work a man past eight or nine hours a day. I said I've been keeping track."

Chet leaned back. "We're not through yet. We got the thieves but we didn't get Manion's money."

Les scowled. "Where is it?"

"I don't know. I'll get Howard up here and maybe he can tell us. But I'll make a guess. It's cached somewhere between here and that place where they camped up in the mountains."

Riley sat morosely until Redleaf returned with the store clerk, pushed him down on a wall bench, and asked pointblank where was Rodney Manion's $4,000?

Ballew was reluctant to answer until Riley leveled a finger at him. "Let me tell you something, Howard. If I've got to ride back up into the mountains again to find your cache, I'm going to come back and break your neck. And I'm not threatening you. I'm making you a promise." Riley lowered his hand. "And I'll tell you something else. I'm a freighter. I drive horses and mules from a wooden seat. You know why? Because I hate to ride 'em."

The store clerk considered Riley's angry face for a moment before switching his attention to Marshal Redleaf. "We been talkin' among ourselves. We got what you want and you've got the keys to let us out of here in the middle of the night."

Chet rocked forward to lean on his table. "Not on your damned tintype, Howard. The only two things I want now is Manion's money and for the circuit rider to get to town and sentence you bastards to prison and get all of you out of my sight. Now, one more time . . . where is Manion's money?"

The store clerk hunched forward, studying his hands. Riley shifted on his chair, gathered both legs, and gripped the chair with his hands, looking balefully across the room. He was ready to hurl himself at the man on the wall bench.

Ballew raised his eyes. "It's hid in a pouch behind Manion's desk at the store."

Redleaf stared. "Across the road?"

"Yes." Ballew saw their astonishment and straightened up on the bench. "That was Paul Scott's idea. I was to take it back to town after we got it, and hide it. Later, when the excitement died down, I was to fetch it to a meeting place. Paul didn't trust Cuff and Fred."

"But he trusted you?"

Ballew nodded. "We're related. We worked together a lot."

Chet's brows dropped. "That's his real name? Paul Scott?"

"Yeah, that's his real name. Why shouldn't it be?"

"Because I overheard you fellers up at your rendezvous mention a Paul Scott, so I knew the name before he showed up."

Ballew nodded. "Yeah. But we didn't know that. We didn't know you was out there listening."

Redleaf rose to take a pair of leg irons off a hook with which he chained Howard Ballew to the wall bench. He stood a moment, gazing downward, then jerked his head for Riley to follow him. As they were leaving the office, Redleaf said: "Go ahead and get loose, if you can. Those irons have held a lot of men."

Enos Orcutt was emerging from the café as Redleaf and Riley crossed the road. Chet beckoned to him, did not say why as he entered the General Store and, under the testy gaze of Manion's tall wife and another older woman who was having a list filled, marched back to the storekeeper's dingy office, walked in, and gestured for Riley and Orcutt to get on the far end of the massive old oak desk, and lift.

They could not lift the desk. It was too heavy for that, so they gruntingly see-sawed it until Redleaf could look behind it. There was a stained old canvas money pouch back there. He fished it out, using a long pole, opened it atop the desk, and, with the town blacksmith looking speechless, packets of greenbacks tied with red string tumbled out.

From the doorway someone gasped. Chet did not look around as he began stuffing the money back into the pouch, but Manion's wife moved resolutely forward and stopped the marshal with a firm grip on his wrist. The three men watched her lean down and examine the little packets, pick up several for a closer inspection, then hand them to Marshal Redleaf. "Is it the same money?" she asked.

Chet went back to filling the pouch. "Yes. Howard Ballew's over in the jailhouse. He told us where he'd hidden it."

Manion's wife reached with a firm hand, took the pouch from Redleaf, nodded brusquely, and marched out of the office. Up until now the blacksmith had not said a word, but, as the tall woman departed, he sank down upon Manion's desk chair and groaned. "It was here in town all the time? What kind of damned sense does that make?"

Redleaf's reply was as dry as an old cornhusk. "Pretty good sense, Enos. Stage robbers ride like hell after a theft, and lawmen go after them. Who would ever think to look in the very store of the man the money was stolen from? Come along, Les. We'll lock Howard in his cell and go get something to eat."

They left the blacksmith sitting there, looking bewildered. As they were approaching the café, Les said: "Finding the money like that was a blessing. I would have sworn we'd have to go back up yonder and maybe move a ton of boulders to find it."

Jack Hudson and the liveryman were already at the counter, eating. They looked up, nodded, and, as Redleaf and Riley sat down, the liveryman leaned around the barman to ask if what he'd heard at the saloon was true, that Chet and Les had brought in the escaped outlaws, plus one other outlaw who had already been locked in one of his cells. Redleaf looked down at the liveryman, ignored the question, and asked one of his own. "What d'you call that big mare of yours that I've been riding lately?"

The liveryman hung fire. He had not expected the question. "Sometimes I call her You Old Bitch, sometimes I call her Sow, and sometimes. . . ."

"How much do you want for her?"

The liveryman's eyes flickered to the barman before he answered. "Marshal, you don't want to ride no mare. They're. . . ."

"How much!"

"I don't like mares. I never liked mares. Thirty-five dollars and I'll throw in the halter."

"Thirty dollars and you keep the halter."

"Done. Mind if I ask a question?"

"Yeah, I mind. I'm hungry right now. I'll be down to pay you sometime before evening."

Jack Hudson had enjoyed the exchange. He finished eating,

dropped coins beside his platter, arose, and slapped Redleaf on the shoulder and walked out, leaving the liveryman sitting there in dogged silence to finish his meal alone.

Riley left after supper to visit the tonsorial parlor, rent a towel, the use of the bathhouse out back, and a bar of brown soap. Redleaf took pails of stew across the road, refused to talk to his prisoners, left the buckets under their cell doors, and returned to his office to roll and light a smoke, and to sit down on something that wasn't moving without having to listen to anyone or talk to anyone as daylight waned.

It was a short respite. Rodney Manion burst in, looking exuberant. He launched into a lengthy exclamation of gratitude that Redleaf listened to while smoking. When Manion was finished, Chet said: "Rod, I owe Les Riley fifteen dollars for the time he put in helping me round up the thieves and get your money back."

Manion flinched, then drew forth a wallet, unsmilingly counted out the greenbacks, placed them on Redleaf's table, and without another word or even a nod walked out, slamming the door after him.

Chet gazed at the closed door. "That's why people like you," he said to the departed visitor. "Because you're so generous and decent and all. You tight-fisted old son-of-a-bitch."

He settled back in the faint gloom of oncoming dusk, cocked his feet atop the table, and finished his cigarette. He was close to dozing when the roadway door opened again, but this time the visitor filled the opening, almost over-filled it. He nodded across the room, removed his hat, and beat clouds of dust from his clothing. As he was doing this he said: "Satisfied, Marshal?"

Chet smiled. "Yup. Plumb satisfied. Tell me something, Mister Nye. How many bears were up there, scaring those horses?"

The large Indian eased down into the chair Les Riley had vacated earlier. "None."

"I didn't think so."

Nye pushed out thick legs and eased back in the chair. "They have tanned bearskins with the hair on they use for some kind of hunting ceremony. To keep them believable, they rub bear scent on them each time they kill a bear to eat." Nye's dark eyes twinkled. "It worked. The horses left in a hurry, and, after they shed their bearskins, the tomahawks sort of eased the horses around until they smelled that green grass and water. Pretty clever, Marshal. Your outlaws did not see an Indian, and as far as I was concerned . . . and they were concerned . . . that was what mattered most. Incidentally they hid out and watched you capture your outlaws." Nye shifted position in the chair. "Would you say that maybe you owed those Indians, Marshal?"

Redleaf saw the big man's eyes resting on the $15 Manion had left on his table. He sighed, leaned, and pushed it to the edge of the table. "I'd say I owe them, Mister Nye. Will that help?"

Henry Nye's huge paw closed around the money as he stood up, smiling. "It surely will, Mister Redleaf. In the morning I'm going to take a pack string up there with supplies."

Chet cocked his head a little. "You better tell Manion it's supplies for the mine you two are going to work on. He doesn't like Indians very much. Well, hold-out Indians anyway."

Nye went to the door and smiled. "Odd thing about people, Mister Redleaf, they don't like one another unless there is a way they can make money off each other. You ever wonder about that?"

Chet shook his head. "Nope, never have. But it's something to think about. Good luck, Mister Nye." The large man winked and left the office.

Chet fished around for his whiskey bottle, had a couple of swallows, and locked up from out front before heading for the rooming house. Tomorrow it would be something else.

★ ★ ★ ★ ★

Prairie Town

★ ★ ★ ★ ★

I

Where Nature, in ancient times, had broken the back of the Sierras, had pushed back the monolithic slopes and scooped out a large valley, lay the town of Conifer. It had from its very beginning in the buffalo-hide trade days been a thriving place, for as soon as the buffalo were gone the Army came, which was natural and in a sense inevitable. Wyoming Territory's populous and war-like Indian nations, with an aboriginal economy based upon buffalo meat, buffalo hides, sinews, horns, and entrails, reacted violently to the deprivation of their basic and time-hallowed necessity. They stormed down from the peaks; they hid in ambush through the cañons; they attacked the destroyers of their economy as predictably as any other nation might have done. So the Army came to Conifer, established camps, commissaries, forts, and posts, all of which poured a steady stream of money into the locality's coffers, and what ensued for the cowmen, settlers, and merchants of Conifer Valley was a pleasant transition from the buffalo-hide business to the more progressive cash-and-carry enterprises of a growing community.

This same transition for the destitute Indians was not so noticeable, and again what was perhaps inevitable occurred. When the bedaubed, feathered Neolithics could not possibly make the transition from Stone Age to modern times in one generation, they vanished. It took a number of decades to accomplish this disappearance, but it happened, and all during those hair-raising days, as the savages were pushed farther and farther back into the mountains, as that good stream of paymaster gold flowed warmly into the economy of Conifer, the town grew, ranches were laid out, cattlemen brought their herds, and again, when the need for soldiers dwindled, this solidly established cattle trade once more came gradually to replace, with its gold, the diminishing prosperity occasioned by the Army's gradual withdrawal.

Altogether a period of sixty years was involved, and although the nation, and the world, peregrinated through troubled times beyond Conifer Valley and beyond the insular Sierras, actually the people of that section of Wyoming Territory were scarcely aware of anything except their own livelihoods, births, deaths, scandals, feuds, and fandangos.

A great war ripped the soft underbelly of the nation. The people of Conifer Valley were not involved. They were of course interested; when the stage brought month-old newspapers, everyone bid high for the privilege of reading the *latest* news. But none of the cowmen of Conifer Valley felt impelled to ride the thousand miles to get into that fight.

Once a band of trail-weary, shabby men in gray uniforms had briefly appeared in the valley, seeking horses. They had bought a herd and had departed southward. This had occasioned a brief flurry of excitement. It was Conifer's only first-hand knowledge of that distant war. But five years later, people scarcely remembered those leathery riders. They certainly did not recall any particular one of those men. But that was understandable for those Rebel cavalrymen had bivouacked apart from the town, had kept pretty much to themselves, and as though conscious of some grand destiny, as soon as they'd acquired their horses, they had left, heading back southward where momentous events, great and tragic, were in the making.

As storekeeper Jeff Stone had said shortly after those Confederates had left the valley: "Where a man's hearthstone is involved, he ain't at all the same man he otherwise would be."

Since those days Jeff had prospered. He had prospered before them, too, for old Jeff had opened his mercantile establishment during the hide-trade days and had grown right along with the rest of the town through all the intervening decades. He was a grizzled man whose legs troubled him. An itinerant medicine man had once told him the problem was centered in his knee joints, had something to do with calcification of the gristle. Whatever it was, though, Jeff sometimes suffered, usually in wintertime when Conifer Valley got cold with a yard of snow underfoot, while at other times, notably during the dry summers, he didn't suffer particularly, but he walked with a little jerky hitch to his gait. Still, when a man turned the corner past sixty years, he didn't expect everything to work perfectly, so Jeff was philosophical about his peculiar ailment.

He wore tortoise-shell spectacles, had several chins, a scanty thatch of nearly white hair, and a direct way of looking at life. He could scent a neat profit a mile off and he was somewhat of a power on the Conifer plains. Still there was one skirmish Jeff had never won. He hadn't actually lost it, but he'd never totally triumphed, either. That involved his wife Harriett, who was a large, handsome woman with a quick tongue and a quick temper. But Harriett was also a compassionate person; when the less fortunate came to her, Harriett's large heart had ample room for them. But she had her opinionated ways, too—Harriett Stone had no use for drunks, biting dogs, kicking mules, and gunfighters. She scorned the dance-hall girls of Conifer with the identical contempt she lavished upon men who used profanity in front of ladies. She was past fifty, solidly set in her ways, and, when Jeff came stumping home in the evenings, she had an ironclad rule; he could not sit down to the supper table without first vigorously washing and donning a coat. The little brush-fire encounters between these two solid and highly respected people of Conifer were legendary and Jeff had often said that, when a woman gets so fiercely set in her ways, it would be a mercy to everyone around her if she could be quietly put away. But then old Jeff had a way of bluntly making pronouncements that were never likely to be generally acceded to, so about all that came of them was whatever small, personal satisfaction he got out of making them.

Like the time he told Conifer's Town Marshal Hank Herman someone should force the town council to pass a law prohibiting the carrying of side arms within the town's limits. Hank, who was thirty years younger than Jeff, had logically pointed out that first someone would have to define the town's limits because no one ever had, and, while it was generally accepted that the town ended where the cow country began, there was nothing very definite about this. Jeff had let the subject lapse; he had his thriving business to occupy him. Hank had also let the subject lapse, but for different reasons. Hank, who was in his middle or late thirties, was a tall, lanky, durable man, proficient with his tied-down ivory-butted six-gun. He was a logical person with a predilection for Scotch whiskey and a dance-hall girl named Rita. He had been keeping the peace, more or less, in both the town and valley for eleven years. His authority actually did not extend beyond the town because he was elected as town marshal, not county sheriff, but as he'd said to Jeff Stone, before any actual delineation could be adhered to, someone was going to have to pin down the town's limits. Generally, though, the outlying cowmen accepted Hank's authority anywhere he chose to carry it because, like old Jeff, the cowmen had their own affairs to occupy all their time, didn't wish to become embroiled in something as devious and nebulous as the law, and behaved within the scope of what they considered to be elemental right and wrong.

Hank's office in Conifer was a lean-to built onto the ancient log jailhouse as a sort of afterthought. Originally the jailhouse had been a military stockade with three iron-bound oaken doors set in the front of a massive log wall. Behind each of those forbidding doors was a cell ten feet long by ten feet square. In the upper center of each huge door was a tiny barred opening. Because these three cells took up all the room, Hank's office had been built along the southward road front with a very narrow little passageway leading to the cells. The whole building smelled musty, was inadequately ventilated, and in winter the place had been frigid until Hank had installed an old Army wood stove, while in summertime it was torturously stifling. Hank had often commented that he could sweat out the most perverse drunk in twenty-four hours in the summertime, and during the wintertime he could, by simply not firing up his iron stove, reduce the most obdurate outlaw to a chattering wreck within the same length of time.

There was very little lawlessness in the community. The worst crime in ten years had been the axe slaying of a half-breed gunman by a girl at Rube Burrows's saloon that was four doors northward and on the same side of the roadway as Jeff Stone's mercantile establishment. But that hadn't been much of a crime as far as the law was concerned. The girl never denied her guilt. Where the real problem came in was after her hearing, trying to arrive at some way out of hanging the girl for murder. Not a red-blooded cowman on that jury had agreed to vote her guilty until the circuit-riding judge had given his solemn oath he would not pronounce the death penalty, which hadn't been an easy concession to wring out of the judge because the legal statutes made hanging the mandatory penalty for cold-blooded murder. On the other hand, such was the nature of those rough-tough cattlemen in court that day, that, if the judge had broken his word, they would have solemnly and righteously lynched him. The girl had been sent to the Territorial Prison at Casper, the judge left town on the evening coach, and Hank Herman hadn't had a comparable crime since. Ordinarily his jailhouse was empty. Now and then some berserk drunk trail hand might shoot up Burrows's saloon or race his horse up and down the main thoroughfare, firing at windows, or there might be a real Donnybrook when the riders of competitive cow outfits hit town simultaneously, but other than these interesting but not very villainous events the countryside was moderately peaceful and law-abiding.

At least it had been until this summer, and it might have gone right on being peaceful, too, if Frank Leslie of the Snowshoe outfit hadn't come drifting into town from the westerly range with an intriguing tale that he told Hank and Rube Burrows over the latter's bar during the midday slack period at the saloon when gossip usually filled in the time for what few men lingered at the card tables or sipped ale out of the summertime sun blast. Frank Leslie was a man in his middle years who had an inherent propensity for being short, gruff, and frequently downright disagreeable. He was a big, raw-boned, powerful man with dark eyes, swarthy complexion, and a slash for a mouth. He was an old hand in the Conifer country, owned thirty thousand acres of west-country grazing land, hired five tough riders, and had a reputation for never avoiding a fight. He was respected but he was not very well liked. But like the other cowmen, Leslie rarely concerned himself with anything around the town. As operating owner of a big cow outfit running about nine thousand head of cattle, he didn't have time for much else. So, when he rode into town in the middle of the day, bellied up to Rube Burrows's bar where Hank and Rube were idly visiting, those two immediately knew something was in the wind.

Leslie didn't leave them wondering long. In his forthright, blunt way he said: "Marshal, I got a riddle for you."

Hank nodded, said nothing, and waited. He didn't care much for Leslie, either. Rube drew a glass of ale and set it before Leslie, then leaned on his bar top, also waiting. The cowman gulped ale, set the glass aside, ran the back of one gloved hand across his bear-trap mouth, and looked squarely over at Herman. "This here's a big valley," he pronounced. "A prairie, actually, because you can't see from one end of it to the other, nor from one side of it to the other. Eighty miles long and eighty miles wide, they say." Leslie drank the rest of his ale, belched *sotto voce,* and blew out a big breath. "Things happen here us fellers in the west end never hear about. Things happen out our way you fellers here in town never hear about." Leslie put his bold, muddy stare on Hank. "You agree with that, Marshal?"

"Yeah," murmured Hank. "I agree with it."

"Well, now, yesterday I was on my north range near the foothills and come onto a fresh camp."

Beefy Rube Burrows felt let down. "What's so unusual about that?" he asked. "Hell, is that your riddle, Frank?"

"Nope, that's not my riddle. My riddle is this . . . in the first place that camp was hidden in a little draw with trees all around it so's no one'd accidentally stumble onto it. In the second place there was a fresh-killed yearling steer hanging on a tree there . . . with a fleshed-out fresh hide pegged on the ground . . . with my Snowshoe brand on it plain as day."

"Ahhh," muttered Rube Burrows, and rolled his eyes over at Hank Herman. "That's rustling, by God."

Frank Leslie nodded gravely but he didn't seem as indignant about this as Hank thought he should, so the marshal still leaned there, saying nothing and waiting.

Burrows refilled their glasses. For the length of time this took big Frank Leslie leaned pensively upon the bar, staring into space. When Rube set the glasses up again, Leslie didn't touch his. He didn't look around at Hank, either, but he was obviously addressing the lawman when he said: "An' in the third place, there was a dead man lying in that camp."

Rube Burrows's eyes sprang wide open. He had his ale glass halfway up; it stopped six inches from Rube's lips and hung there.

Leslie twisted from the waist to stare sardonically at the lawman, his muddy eyes dark with bleak irony. "What d'you think of that, Marshal?" he asked.

Hank, annoyed by Leslie's theatrics, said roughly: "What did you expect me to do . . . faint? How long's he been dead and who is he?"

"Never saw him before in my life," answered the cowman. "And I'd judge he was killed yesterday. You want to know how? By a bullet in the back, smack dab between the shoulder blades."

"Any of your riders on that part of the range yesterday to hear the shot?" Herman asked.

Leslie wagged his head. "Never had any reason to ride up there. Yesterday, I was just makin' a sashay through the trees on my way home when I stumbled onto the camp."

II

Saloonkeeper Rube Burrows was a large man, running mostly to fat now, although he'd obviously at one time been brawny and powerful. He was as homely as a mud fence with a big bulbous nose that frequently glowed like a huge ripe tomato. He was a raffish man whose close-set small pale eyes could upon occasion look coldly right through people, and, while Rube had his friends in town, and out in the bunkhouses and cow camps, he also had one implacable enemy—Harriett Stone. She bristled at the very sight of Rube and loathed him as proprietor of his Trailhand Saloon, dispenser of alcoholic beverages. Rube had one weakness; he loved gossip. It didn't have to be true gossip or even fresh, unretouched gossip. All it had to be was salacious or titillating, or, as now, startling gossip, so he gently replaced his ale glass upon the bar top and hung there, watching raw-boned, slit-lipped Frank Leslie, saying nothing until after Marshal Herman had asked about the identity of that dead man.

Then Rube said: "Frank, it's got to be a band of rustlers working the northwest country. They had a falling out an' one of 'em got shot by the others."

Leslie listened to everything Burrows said, lifted his glass, and drank deeply, set the glass back down, and shook his head. "More than just rustlers," he said gruffly. "Rustlers'd have hit my herd and lit out. These fellers killed a beef to eat. They camped up there in the trees several days without doing anything. Then . . . after all that . . . they had their fight and left one of their men lyin' there, shot in the back. Naw, Rube, not just rustlers. They're up to something else."

"Well, they broke the law. They killed one of your critters."

This, to Hank Herman who had been listening, thinking, and saying nothing, was the crux of the whole thing. Whoever those strangers were, they had unlawfully killed a Snowshoe beef. That's all they'd done thus far, in his sight, and it annoyed him the way Rube was attempting to make something big and ominous out of the butchering of one beef. He finished his ale, turned to Leslie, and said: "I'll be out for the body as soon as I can get a rig and drive out there. One more question, Frank. Any sign showing which way the others might have gone?"

"Nope," said Leslie. "But if you want to track 'em, I'll loan you a 'breed who rides for me. He could track the devil over a lava bed."

Hank nodded and walked on out of the saloon, stepped through sidewalk traffic, hiked on across to Pat Malone's livery barn, and called for a horse and buckboard. Malone himself emerged from the combination harness room and office, sucking a stalk of meadow hay, ran a caustic look up where Hank stood half in sunlight, half in barn shadow, and grunted. Pat was a short, broad, oaken man with the stubbornness of an ox, the disposition of a transplanted Irishman, and the short-windedness of a sedentary person who ate and drank much more than was good for him. He was no relation at all to Rita Malone, who worked over at Burrows's saloon in the gaming room, although they both shared the same last name. No one could have actually made that mistake, either. Pat was red-necked and rosy-cheeked. His eyes were sky-blue and his hair was rusty red. Rita, on the other hand, was dark and alluring and mysterious in the way some Indian or Mexican women are alluring. The name Malone no more fitted Rita than the name Gomez would have fitted Pat, but Rita had never explained how she'd come by the name and not even Hank, who perhaps knew Rita better than anyone else in Conifer, had ever asked about that.

"What rig?" growled Pat as he stepped along toward Hank. "What you need a rig for, anyway? Someone break a leg or something?" Pat sucked his blade of hay and halted to shoot a skeptical gaze upward at the marshal. "Last time you got a rig, the danged town council come over here in a body to demand an explanation of the bill I submitted. They figured maybe you was taking Rita moonlight ridin' an' charging it to. . . ."

"For fetching a back-shot stranger to town," said Hank coldly, interrupting that garrulous flow of words. "And if you don't want to give me the rig, I'll go borrow Jeff Stone's outfit."

Malone's working jaws grew suddenly still, his baby-blue eyes steadily widened, and eventually he whispered: "A stranger shot in the back? You mean killed, Hank?"

"Yes, I mean killed. Now are you going to get that wagon, or aren't you?"

"Sure. Sure, I'll get it. Where'd the killing take place? Who done it?"

"The rig," snarled Marshal Herman. "It's a long way out and a long way back, and I want to be in town before midnight."

Malone turned and walked off, shouting for someone named Alfie to come help him. Alfie was a derelict who had drifted into Conifer two years previously and had attached himself to Pat Malone. When he was sober enough to be useful, he worked around the livery barn. When he wasn't that sober, he slept it off up in the hayloft. He was about fifty years old, and, despite the fact that Pat Malone never sullied their happy relationship by offering Alfie money, somehow the old coot always had the price of a quart, which was a minor mystery in itself but, since no one cared a hoot about Alfie, no one made a point out of the source of his funds, either, and this included Hank, who watched old Alfie come tumbling out of the hayloft on unsteady legs and go scuttling out to the side corral for a harness horse.

Someone crunching through roadway dust to the livery barn's entrance behind him brought Hank twisting around. This was Lincoln Moore, the local stage line agent, a stork-like, bald, emaciated man of extreme timidity and deference. He and Hank were good friends, although just why this should be no one had ever figured out. Moore was so soft-spoken and careful about what he said people invariably ignored him after the first meeting. He wore steel-rimmed eyeglasses and peered through them from very round, very wet blue eyes. He was the direct opposite from the town marshal in nearly all things. Still, they were friends and Hank's annoyed look atrophied as Lincoln walked on up to him, saying in that mumbling way of his: "Figured I'd ought to look in on the new teams they sent me from down at Cheyenne. Bill of lading called for six horses or three teams." Lincoln squinted on down the dingy lane where Alfie and Pat Malone were rigging up a wagon for Hank, watched this carefully for a moment, then said deferentially: "You going riding, Hank?"

"Got a dead man to pick up and fetch to town, Lincoln. Some stranger who got himself dry-gulched up on Frank Leslie's westerly range."

"No," whispered Lincoln, bringing his watery eyes instantly back around. "Murder, Hank?"

"Just about got to be, Linc. He got it between the shoulders."

Moore dissolved into a cringing silence and moved out of the way as Pat led the harnessed horse up and halted, handed Hank the lines, and said: "If you figured you needed any help, I got nothing to do the rest of the day."

Hank climbed to the seat, adjusted the lines, set his foot upon the brake lever, and shook his head. "Routine drive out there and back," he said, giving the evened-up lines a little flick. "Probably nothing anyway. Couple of fellers had a falling out, one turned away when he should've known better . . . and that settled his hash for him."

Hank drove on out into bright midday sun smash, tilted forward his hat, puckered his eyes, and lined out his course westerly. By his best estimate he had five hours of driving ahead of him to get to Frank Leslie's place, locate the corpse, load it up, and head back. He could perhaps make better time on the return trip, so, with any luck at all, he thought he'd make it back into town by midnight or a little later. He considered Leslie's offer of that half-breed tracker. He also, somewhat grumpily, wondered why Leslie hadn't brought that corpse on into town when he'd ridden in himself to report the killing. But he gave that up after a while because he couldn't blame a man for not doing what he didn't feel like doing. Anyway, this was his job, not Frank Leslie's job, and, finally, because Frank was contrary by nature; even if the idea had occurred to him, he probably wouldn't have done it.

As soon as Hank got beyond town, the world of Conifer Valley spread out around him in all its majestic summertime shimmer and vastness. It was, as Frank had said in Rube Burrows's place, a vast plain, a huge prairie. The gaunt old surrounding mountains stood eternally roundabout, cutting the Conifer country off from all the rest of the world, making everything that happened here of importance to the people in the valley and likewise making everything that happened beyond the mountains something impersonal and vague and far-away, exactly as that war had been, years before, impersonal and far-away.

There were plenty of people in the Conifer country who had first seen the light of day here and who would die without ever seeing the light of day any place else. Then, too, there were people like Rita Malone who had come from that other, unknown, or at least little-known, world, and who were perfectly content to remain in the valley and forget everything they had known or experienced or felt some place else. Hank was such a person himself. He'd come to the Conifer country as a stripling youth, cruising for timber in the employ of a lumbering company. He'd stood on a peak one day, looking down into this other world, and he'd never gone back. There were others who'd come onto the plains the same way; in fact, it had only been within the last twenty years, since it was safe to do so, that people had begun raising families hereabouts. Prior to that time men and women came full-grown to the Conifer country.

There was an indefinable sense of safety, of security, in these hidden and apart places of the West where people put down their roots. After a few generations of inbreeding, things changed, the quality of the people deteriorated, even the livestock became less vigorous, but for the first and sometimes even the second generation there was always the strength of pioneering blood to sustain them, and the good shielding of the mountains to give their existence the protective insularity it required in order that the land could be worked, the creeks dammed and diverted, the log houses erected, and the small, sometimes trivial, sometimes vital facets of their lives worked out within the pattern of their vast privacy.

Hank rode along toward the Snowshoe range, thinking these soporific thoughts and drowsing under a brilliant yellow summertime sun, sometimes springing erect to see where he was, sometimes bouncing along, head on chest, fast asleep. A dead man might be waiting at the end of Hank's trail, but actually corpses were not exactly a novelty in the Conifer country. Ones shot in the back were decidedly unusual, but if the riddle was good enough, he'd never find the killers and no one would much care anyway, since the dead man was a stranger. He drowsed along, thinking that this whole thing was going to be routine, strictly routine. He'd bring the man in, they'd duly bury him, and that would be that.

III

It was late afternoon with the sky reddening off in the distant west when Hank bumped on into Frank Leslie's ranch yard, and at once two rangy, rough-looking men sauntered over to lean upon the wagon and casually greet Conifer's town marshal. One of these was Henry Helm, Frank Leslie's range boss, an imperturbable, rangy, sun-darkened man of Hank's own age who had survived flashfloods, gunfights, even two marriages, with nothing more to say regarding any of them than a disdaining grunt. It was said of Henry Helm that when he died and went to hell, walking over the devil's red-hot roadway wouldn't elicit anything more from him than one spat-out cuss word. The other man was Frank Leslie's top hand; he was known only by one name—Starr. Whether that was his first or last name no one knew, and no one cared. Starr was a smiling, affable man with jet-black eyes, Indian-straight black hair, and a high-bridged, slightly hooked nose. He wasn't Indian. In fact, he wasn't even part Indian, but he looked more Indian than most Indians looked. He had a savage temper, too, but it took a lot of gouging to anger him, which was just as well, everyone agreed, because once Starr cut loose everyone with a lick of sense who was within gunshot range, when this occurred, headed for the tall timber. Generally, though, Starr only went berserk when he'd been drinking, and as he leaned there, gazing amiably up at Hank on the wagon seat, he seemed the most inoffensive man under the sun.

When those casual greetings were over, Hank said to Henry Helm: "Saw Frank in town and he told me about a dead man out here somewhere. You fellers know about it?"

"We know," replied Helm, and turned to point with a rigid arm due north over into the hazed foothills. "See that pine snag standing out against the north slope? Well, about a quarter mile this side of it down in a little swale is your dead man."

Henry dropped his arm, leaned upon the wagon wheel again, and made a little clucking sound with his tongue. He regarded Hank briefly, then said: "Frank tell you they butchered a Snowshoe critter?"

"Yeah, but it didn't seem to be bothering him much."

Starr smiled broadly. "One critter out of maybe nine, ten thousand wouldn't bother Frank. What might bother him, though, is if whoever those fellers are, they're skulkin' around hopin' to make up a drive, and head out of here some fine moonlight night."

Hank accepted the tobacco sack Henry offered him, looped his lines, and set the foot brake as he went to work making a cigarette. "Maybe," he conceded, "but I got the impression from listening to Frank back in town that he didn't think those fellers were rustlers."

"Neither do we think that," said Henry, taking back his makings and going to work with them himself. "We got it figured they're here for some special purpose and it doesn't have anything to do with other folks' beef." Henry leaned into the match Hank held down, inhaled, exhaled, and leaned back to shoot a critical gaze out over the countryside toward that old snag pine where the dead man was. "We figure it's got something to do with robbery, Hank. Maybe they're skulkin' around up there in the hills, waiting to hit one of the ranches. You know, a couple of fellers could sit up there on the peaks with field glasses and watch everything that happens down here on the plain. Maybe, when they saw everyone ride out from this ranch or one of the other places hereabouts, they'd come down and do a little plunderin'."

Helm trickled streamers of smoke upward from his nose and mirthlessly smiled up at Hank. His inference was amply clear. This was a big country. There were a number of large, wealthy ranches in it. The town of Conifer had no bank; very few cow towns did have banking institutions in them. It was common practice for prosperous cattlemen to hide their cash, sometimes in iron safes, sometimes in carved stone vaults, and sometimes in a hollow tree or under a loose floorboard. But robberies of the big cow outfits were rare. For one thing there was always someone around, a few quick-triggered riders, an owner or his kinsmen with handy shotguns, or at least a big dog to warn of the approach of strangers. It was, generally speaking, easier and safer to hold up a store in one of the towns than it was to rob a ranch where everyone went armed and eyed strangers with courteous alertness.

Hank nodded. This was a distinct possibility and one that he'd encountered before, not often, in fact not often at all, still, he'd known of it to happen. "I'll ride out in a day or two," he said, and unlooped his lines. "Maybe I'll borrow that 'breed rider you've got to do the tracking. Frank told me about him, said he was pretty good."

"That'll be Sam Hawk," stated Henry Helm, and straightened up off the rig as it began to move out. "He's plenty good."

Hank waved. Helm and Starr waved back. Those two stood for a while silently, smoking and watching as Hank tooled his rig northward over the empty prairie. They didn't head back for their bunkhouse until Hank was a long way off and growing smaller in the fading light.

Out upon the plain itself, the immense valley floor, that golden sunlight remained a constant force, but over near those towering mountain slopes there was a mistiness that softened the harshness of naked rock, mellowed the rugged reach of vast distances, and eventually, as Hank passed into the first tier of trees, cooled out the late-day warmth. He had no trouble getting to that old snag pine where it stood amid a luxuriant stand of purplish trees. He tied up near the base of that old landmark and went walking carefully around until he came to a slight depression in this quiet world of tree shadows and pine scent, and there he saw the pegged-out hide of a freshly butchered beef. There, too, he saw the relaxed form of a man, lying full length with an odd flatness to him that had no counterpart among the living.

He walked over and stood, gazing downward. There was the little dark puncture between the dead man's shoulders exactly as Frank Leslie had described it. That settled two things—one, how the man had died; two, that he had been murdered. Hank toed the man over with his boot, looked into the unshaven, gaunt, long-jawed countenance of a man in his early forties who he'd never seen before, and sank to one knee to rifle the dead man's pockets. He came up with a Barlow clasp knife, a cud of hard-twist chewing tobacco such as one rarely saw in the Northwest, a few silver coins, and a flat packet of folded paper currency. Beyond that the dead man had nothing on him. Nothing that would identify him or nothing that would give Hank any idea what the man was doing in the Conifer country.

He stood up, shuffled back and forth around the little camp looking for signs that would give him some clue about the others who had been here, and came up with one quite obvious fact. From the boot prints and other indications, he read from the ground that there had been four men here. He even found where they'd had their horses hobbled, where they'd dumped their saddles, where they'd unrolled their bedrolls. Four men had come down here from the back-country mountains. They had not come to this spot overland where they certainly would have been seen. And they'd camped here three or four days before their companion had been killed and they'd then pulled stakes.

He walked on down to where the trees ended and the plain began. Hiked west a half mile and east a half mile, found no tracks where riders had emerged from the forest, and slowly went back to load up the corpse, thinking that the remaining three horsemen had not come down to the open country after the killing, but had returned to the mountains again.

He placed the dead man face-up in his wagon, climbed back to the seat, and clucked his livery animal around and back on down out of the trees. He had by now quite forgotten his earlier wish to be back in town before midnight, and bumped along, gazing over his left shoulder at the darkening uplands that stretched for a hundred miles northward, and drew steadily back away from the plain as he drove on eastward, until, down by Conifer, they were many miles off. To trail three riders in that tangled wilderness he'd need more than just Frank Leslie's half-breed cowboy; he'd also need the gift of second sight ever to find anyone up in there who didn't want to be found. Those mountains were a haven for all manner of wild game and all of it wasn't four-legged, either.

As evening shadows drifted in to settle smokily over the peaks and down into the visible valleys, Hank set his face toward town and let the livery horse pick his own way and his own gait. He had traveled a considerable distance with night pressing in around him when somewhere ahead he heard a horseman jogging along. Without knowing exactly why, but obeying an inner impulse, he halted, sat listening for a while, then clucked up the horse and started to drive southerly to intercept that oncoming rider.

Evidently the horseman had also heard Hank, for suddenly there was silence where before had been the quick, hard sound of shod hoofs striking packed earth.

"That you, Hank?" a man's gruff voice sang out.

"Yeah, it's me," Herman replied, recognizing that voice and steering straight for it through the darkness.

They came together after a while, the marshal from Conifer and Frank Leslie on his way home after a day and part of a night in town. They hauled up close by, regarded one another soberly until Hank said: "I got him in the back of the wagon." Then Leslie swung down, sauntered over, and peered down at the dead man.

"Yup, that's him," he said, stepping up beside the forward wheel. "Make anything out of it?"

"Not much. Like you said, he stopped one with his back turned, and he's a stranger. Nothing much in his pockets, a Barlow knife, some loose money, nothing to identify him."

Leslie inclined his head. "About like I figured. Did you stop by the ranch?"

"Yeah. Talked to Starr and Helm. They had a theory about maybe this gang hiding in the hills watching the ranches."

"Sound reasonable to you?" asked Leslie, watching Hank's face shadowed by his hat brim in the gloom.

"Yes, it sounds reasonable, Frank," replied the lawman quietly, putting his words together slowly. "But something else struck me, too."

"Yeah? What? Rustling, maybe?"

Hank shook his head, looped the lines, jumped down, and led the way back along the wagon's side. With Leslie beside him, Hank reached over and pointed at the dead man's middle. "When you found him, Frank, he was face down and you didn't roll him over."

"Why should I roll him over? He was dead. That's all I had to know."

"Look close here, Frank. See that belt buckle, see those initials on it? C.S.A. You know what kind of a buckle that is?"

"Sure," muttered Frank Leslie, bending far over the sideboard to peer downward. "Confederate States of America. Rebel Army belt buckle. I've seen one or two of those things before, Hank." Leslie leaned back and turned to frown at the marshal. "Feller's got to use something to hold his pants up, doesn't he?"

"Sure," agreed the marshal. "Sure he does. Only I wonder how many fellers who weren't Reb soldiers'd use a buckle like that? Sure wouldn't be any ex-Yankee soldiers."

Leslie shrugged and started back over to his horse. He seemed impatient now. "All right, this one was a Johnny Reb during the war. What does that tell you?"

Hank kept staring downward. "Maybe nothing," he murmured. "And then again . . . maybe something."

Frank Leslie swung up, settled across his saddle, and put a skeptical gaze downward at Hank. "It's your riddle now," he said. "Go ahead and make whatever out of it you've a mind to. Only, Hank, if one more head of my cattle gets butchered, I'm goin' up into the hills with my crew and find me some hungry ex-Rebs and have a hang-rope party." Leslie kneed his horse out. "See you again!" he called, and went loping on toward his home place.

Hank got back onto his wagon seat, flicked the lines, and headed straight as an arrow for town. It was past 10:00 P.M. now; in another couple of hours, more or less, Rube would be closing up his gaming room where Rita Malone had her little cage, where she sat night after night making change, cashing chips, taking the house's cut of ten percent out of all winnings, and keeping an eye on the green cloth-covered tables.

He thought he could make it if he pushed the horse a little, so he did. He went bouncing along over the soft-lighted prairie with his grisly companion stiffly jolting back there on his rough bed of scuffed floorboards.

Conifer showed up finally as a necklace of orange lights low down upon the empty plain. He kept his gaze upon it, kept his thoughts upon voluptuous Rita, trying to concentrate on what might lie ahead for him in her company. But it wasn't Rita, finally, who won out, it was his dead companion and the stirring semblance of a bizarre notion in his head. Who were those four men? Why had they come to the Conifer country from some distant place, to kill one of their companions? Why were they taking such great pains not to be seen, and, finally, why had they come here at all? As Frank Leslie had said, Johnny Reb belt buckles weren't any great rarity. They were far from being common, but every now and then a man appeared who wore one.

The war had been over a long time now. Mostly men no longer wore the appurtenances of their respective sides. But, while shirts and trousers, boots and forage hats wore out, belt buckles didn't. They were like the resolve that had once motivated their owners; they were made of steel, and they lasted for many years afterward. Still, most men Hank had known who'd been in that fight had been content to forget, or, if not forget exactly, then at least to say nothing—wear nothing—that would remind other men of what had cost them, at the very least, several years out of their lives. But here was a man who apparently hadn't wanted to forget. What other reason would motivate a man to wear his old Army belt buckle? And what was in Hank's mind now was the unique notion that perhaps that very belt buckle had been the cause of the ex-Reb's death, because there were also ex-Yankees who couldn't, or didn't want, to forget. To men like that, a Reb belt buckle could bring back in a rush all the old animosities, all the old resentments.

He was still exploring this avenue of thought when he came down into town from the north, rolling along over the stage road. Occasionally outward-bound riders loped past, scarcely heeding Hank and his wagon. The roadway had its usual coterie of boisterous riders and townsmen passing from saloon to gaming house to saloon. There were the hooting calls of cowboys back and forth and the spilled-out puddles of orange lamp glow in the roadway. When he plodded past Rube Burrows's place, he looked over, then swung on down to Pat Malone's barn, and turned in between Pat's two smoking carriage lamps on either side of the large, square, doorless opening.

Pat and Alfie were sitting on nail kegs just inside the entrance with their faces half lighted by a reflection coming past the harness room door. They got up and stood a moment, waiting for Hank to haul up and climb down, then they walked over and leaned to peer into the wagon. Alfie sucked back a quick, gusty breath, turned and walked stiffly and hastily away, the sight of that dead man badly upsetting him.

Pat, though, was undisturbed. He said: "Took you long enough getting back. Want a hand getting him out of there?"

Hank went around, dropped the tailgate, and nodded. "Got a dark corner we can put him in until morning?" he asked.

Malone nodded, caught hold, and between them they carried the dead man over beside a tie stall, set him gently upon some straw, and Hank stood gazing downward while Pat padded off and padded back, bearing with him a soiled old length of mustard-colored canvas that he flung over the corpse, hiding it.

"Know him?" Pat asked.

Hank said that he'd never seen the man before. He turned to cross over and enter the harness room. He had to sign a chit whenever he got a rig from Malone's barn. These chits were presented for payment to the town council. He was bending over Malone's desk, signing a blank form, when Pat walked in, leaned upon a rack of saddles, and waited until Hank straightened up to say: "Just lit a match and had a good look at him. Thought I recognized him when we were unloading him."

Hank squared around toward the liveryman. Lamplight highlighted their bronzed, tough faces for as long as they quietly stood regarding one another.

"That belt buckle clinched it for me," said Malone. "How good's your memory, Hank?"

"Fair. Why?"

"Recollect some years back a band of Johnny Reb soldiers comin' here to buy horses?"

"I remember. During the war."

"That feller out there was one of 'em. Give me a day or two and I'll recollect his name. He was the one who took delivery after their officer paid me."

"You sure of that, Pat?"

"I'm sure. I ought to be. It was me sold 'em the most horses hereabouts."

IV

After Hank left Malone's livery barn and before he hiked on up to Burrows's Trailhand Saloon, he had supper at a hole-in-the-wall café south of Jeff Stone's store, and drank a lot of coffee while he sat there deep in thought. Men ambled in, called rough greetings to him, and also ate. Most of them had departed long before Hank finally stood up, dropped a couple of silver coins, and walked on out into the cool night.

He kept telling himself the thing would be strictly a routine killing, that nothing would come of it if he didn't push it. A sensible lawman didn't make a lot of work for himself by probing into places where he had no actual business. A lot of men died every day in the West, were buried, and were forgotten. As long as killings didn't interfere with the lives and affairs of decent folks, no one got much of a sweat up over them. Every cow town had its boothill cemetery where the unknowns, the undesirables, and the unrequited lay peacefully moldering. Life went on, business prospered, comfortably settled people were not concerned, and smart lawmen like Hank Herman let sleeping dogs lie.

He turned and paced along northward up the sidewalk toward the Trailhand Saloon. It was after midnight but from the sounds up there and the stream of men passing in and out, Rube wouldn't be closing up for another hour at the least. When he pushed on past Rube's spindle doors, a blaze of hot light struck his eyes, bringing him to a quick halt until his night eyes became accustomed to that hurting brightness.

A cowboy on his way out said in a cheery voice: "Howdy, Marshal. Kind of late gettin' around tonight, ain't you?" The man's breath was overpowering from liquor. Hank mumbled something and edged forward toward the bar where he saw Rube watching him.

There were at least fifty noisy range riders and townsmen in the Trailhand this night. They were lined up along Rube's bar like crows on a fence. A few were standing along the wall here and there talking, joking back and forth. There was a cloud of bluish tobacco smoke that broke and eddied chest-high as men moved through it. The room was redolent of tobacco, man sweat, and horse sweat. On the right hand side of the bar's curving toward the wall was a doorless opening. Through there was Rube's gaming room, and, while there was no restriction at all concerning the amount of noise men could make in the saloon, there was a very definite unwritten rule about being quiet in the card room.

As Hank passed on over toward that doorway, Rube Burrows moved down behind his sweating bartenders to intercept him. He made it, nailed Hank at the little trap door where bar and wall met, and beckoned him over. Hank went, but not very willingly. He knew Rube Burrows's avid curiosity too well not to anticipate the questions that came the moment he leaned upon that little bar top trap door.

"Have a drink on the house," said Rube, setting a bottle and two glasses between them. "You get him all right?"

"I got him," replied Hank, carefully measuring out his shot glass full.

"Who was he . . . you know?"

Hank lifted the glass, tossed off his liquor, and shook his head as he replaced the glass. "Just a stranger," he said. "Business is good tonight, Rube."

But Burrows had his teeth into something; he wouldn't be put off by attempts to change the subject. "Have another drink. Was he really shot in the back?"

Hank pushed both glass and bottle away. "Just like Frank said . . . right between the shoulder blades."

"Up close or from a distance?"

"Up close. Rube, don't worry about it. Tomorrow we'll bury the feller. If you want, you can be a mourner. I think you'll be the only one."

"Wait a minute," said Burrows as Hank started to turn toward that card room doorway. "What'd he have on him? There had to be something that'd give you a clue about him."

"A Barlow knife and a little money. No letters, no papers of any kind."

"Ahhh," said Rube, his little wet eyes turning canny. "The killer took care of that, I reckon."

"Maybe. Is Rita in the card room tonight?"

"Sure. Like every night. Hank, how come you don't want to talk about this murder? You know what I think? I think this one's troubling you some way or another. I think you know something you're not mentioning."

Hank turned his full attention to Rube. He leaned across the bar top with his unwavering look, and he softly said: "Rube, you've got a good business here. I'd guess it'd keep a man plenty busy just minding it." That was all Hank said. He drew back, turned, and walked on into the card room.

Behind him, Burrows stood watching for as long as Hank was in his sight, then he slowly turned and slowly ran a thoughtful gaze out over his noisy, smoky saloon, his little eyes gradually coming to an unaccustomed brightness.

Hank walked among the green-topped tables, returned a nod here and there as he made toward the back wall, and felt the change. The same low-hanging waves of tobacco smoke hung chest-high and the same kind of men were at the gaming tables as also filled the yonder barroom, but here there was scarcely any movement, scarcely any sound at all. Once in a while someone would stand up, walk over to the little grilled cage where Rita Malone sat, and either cash in or buy more chips, but even these infrequent transactions were accomplished with very few words.

Hank saw Rita looking out at him from her liquid-dark eyes before he was halfway the length of the room, saw how she put her head slightly to one side as though measuring him or skeptically seeking to interpret the expression of his face. He smiled at her and drew in alongside her little cage where a small fortune in money was arranged in neat piles beside red and blue and white poker chips.

Rita had an aura to her that was instantly felt; it was a kind of sloe-eyed fatalism. Her face was smooth and her gaze was unwavering. She seemed to look upon people as though apart from them, as though she challenged them to break her quiet composure. She was dark, with the golden flesh of Latin blood. Her ebony hair caught lamplight, imprisoning it. Her mouth was long and straight and heavy, with the lips lying gently together without pressure. That seeming fatalism went still further; she seemed to be a person who, having experienced her share of life's cruelty, had made some kind of a pact with herself never to allow life to hurt her again. When she smiled, as she now did at Hank, her teeth were white, small, and perfect, and her face softly glowed. She could have been anywhere from eighteen years old on up to twenty-one or -two. Her body was solidly compact with the high breasts and flat stomach of physical strength and stamina. She was a woman whose presence acted upon every man, bringing up in him whatever was worst or best in him.

She said: "You're late tonight." She kept steadily considering Hank's face. "What is it?"

He told her of the dead man over at Malone's livery barn, keeping his voice very low as he spoke. She heard him out, showing nothing in her eyes or her expression. When he finished, she gently lifted her shoulders, let them fall, and said: "It happens. Every day it happens somewhere. Why does this particular one bother you?"

"Are you sure it does bother me?"

"I'm sure," she murmured. "After three years I know how things affect you. This one troubles you. Why?"

He looked out over the tables, heard the little soft rustle as chips and cards fell upon those green cloth table tops. He knew most of the men sitting around there slouched and easy, only their eyes showing spirit from time to time, showing temper and life, showing sometimes avarice, triumph, or disappointment and disgust.

"Because," he murmured finally, thinking of Frank Leslie's word, "it's a riddle."

She kept watching his bronzed profile but for a long while she was silent. A lanky cowman came up, nodded at Hank, murmured something, and pushed some crumpled bills through at Rita. She counted out chips and pushed them back. The cowman nodded again, and walked back to his table. Rita smoothed out the bills, placed them under a little weight, and turned back toward Hank.

"There is something in every man," she whispered, "that one day comes out. I've lived long enough to know how this is. With you, it has not yet happened. Maybe this is the time for it to."

He looked down at her, feeling the pull of her as he always did when they were close. Feeling all the powerful hungers of all virile men.

"Sometimes men go half their lifetime and never have to face themselves as they really are. I think it's even possible for some men never to have to see themselves in their true light at all."

He said: "I don't know whether I like you in this mood or not, Rita."

She shrugged and faintly, gently smiled up at him. "A woman learns her lessons in this life, bitterly, Hank. She learns, if she has any sense at all, never to trust her heart until she's found a man who knows himself."

"What does that mean?"

"I've waited three years to know the kind of a man you really are. What are the things you believe in. What are the things you'll react to. In all those years you've remained almost a stranger to me. Oh, I know when things bother you, when they anger you or make you laugh. But I think now, finally, I'm going to find out what, exactly, you believe in." She paused to consider his wooden expression, then she said: "As a lawman you have this riddle . . . this dead stranger over at Pat Malone's barn. It's eating away at you, this riddle. I think now, after three years, I'm going to see you react according to your beliefs, about something, and, Hank, it's been a long wait."

"It's routine," he muttered, looking away, then back again. "Someone bushwhacked him. Tomorrow we'll bury him in boothill and that'll be the end of it. Strictly routine, Rita."

A shadow of doubt crossed her face and was instantly gone. "I wonder," she said. "Will you permit it to be just routine?"

"Well," he muttered a trifle grumpily, "why shouldn't I?"

"I don't know, Hank. Maybe you should, if that's how you want it. But I wonder whether you will or not?"

"And if I don't, then what?"

"Then, *querido*, you will be facing what you really are. What you believe is right and what you believe is wrong. You will make it possible after three long years of waiting, for me to know the kind of a man you really are."

"I'll be damned if I understand all this," he said, beginning to frown at her. "Are you saying that the reason you've never given me the answer about our marriage is because you've wanted to be sure of me?"

"Yes. That's exactly what I'm saying."

He stood there a long while, gazing in at her, his thoughts crowding up and bringing him down to troubled confusion. Then, without another word, he turned and walked on out of the card room.

She watched him go, looking neither piqued nor disappointed, looking instead hopeful and a little sad.

He went back out to the bar, hooked both elbows upon it, and beckoned for a drink. He had two straight shots of rye whiskey, then left the saloon and stood a moment upon the plank walk's edge, staring glumly over at Malone's livery barn.

It was early morning with a chill in the air. Mostly the roundabout hitch racks were empty now. Even the noise from within the Trailhand had considerably diminished, and what noise there still was lacked that spontaneous conviviality it had formerly contained.

He stepped down into the empty roadway, paced on over to Malone's barn, and walked as far as the combination harness room and office. Pat was sitting in there nursing a cup of black coffee and scowling over some fly-specked ledgers on his desk. He swiveled around as Hank entered, looked up, and pursed his lips in a heavy nod.

"Wondered if you'd be back or not," he said.

Hank went to a nail keg and sat down. He reached up to push back his hat and put a stormy look over at Malone. "Seems like you're not the only one wondering about me tonight," he grumbled.

Malone let that go past. He said: "Let me guess, Hank. You came back here to ask me not to tell anyone what I know about that dead feller out there. Right?"

"Right."

"You still goin' to bury him tomorrow?"

"Yes, I'm still going to bury him. What of it?"

"Nothing," said Malone, looking away from Hank's angry gaze. "Nothing at all. I just wondered. Sometimes a feller's got to do things he doesn't like to do."

"What does that mean, Pat?"

But Malone wouldn't be drawn into an argument. He stood up, yawned prodigiously, and stretched with both arms thrown up over his head. "Late," he muttered. "Didn't mean to stay up this late." He dropped his arms, turned, and regarded Hank a moment, then bent from the waist, pulled out a desk drawer, and brought forth a rolled up length of dark, shiny old leather. "You better keep this down at your place," he said, handing the thing to Hank. "I took it off your friend out there under the canvas. It's his Johnny Reb belt. No point in leavin' it on him for everyone to see . . . and wonder about."

Hank unrolled the belt and sat for a long moment of silence, gazing at the initials on the buckle. As he began carefully to roll up the belt again, he said: "Pat, what is it you and Rita expect of me?"

"Nothing," said Malone smoothly. "It's your decision, Hank, not mine or hers. You bury him and forget it or you stir up a hornets' nest an' find out why he was killed and bring the murderer to justice. Either way it's your decision." Malone went as far as the door out of his office before saying: "See you tomorrow."

Hank walked on out to the roadway shortly after Pat Malone had left the barn. Around him Conifer was turning drowsily quiet. Even the lights over at Burrows's place were out now. He waited a while to see whether or not Rita would walk out. She didn't, so he turned and hiked along toward his dark jailhouse, carrying that rolled-up belt in his left hand.

V

It was 11:00 before Hank got back down to Malone's barn, and, because there was a rush of early day business occupying Pat, he walked on around where the dead man lay, meaning to give Malone time to finish his other business before calling upon him to rig up a wagon and lend a hand at hauling the corpse over to boothill. The mustard-colored canvas was there, exactly as it had been the night before, only now it lay perfectly flat. There was no corpse beneath it at all. Hank stood there, looking down and feeling stupid as he lifted a corner of that canvas and looked under, let it drop, and straightened back up again. The dead Johnny Reb was gone, vanished, disappeared.

Dead men didn't walk away. When they were total strangers they weren't even spirited away. He leaned upon an edge of the adjoining tie stall, staring at that flat old soiled piece of canvas, wondering whether or not Pat had moved him, and knowing very well that Pat had not or he'd have also moved the canvas. Alfie? No, Alfie had turned green last night just at sight of the stranger. Then who—and why?

Behind him Malone's voice rose over a number of lesser sounds calling boomingly out to someone to have a good trip. Hank turned and gazed over where the last of Malone's customers was driving on out of the barn. He could see Pat's pugnosed red profile. It was, as always, partially cheerful, partially pugnacious, but wholly forthright and candid. "Pat," he said softly, "come over here."

Malone turned and hiked on over. Alfie stood out there in the center of the barn's long runway looking uncertain. He finally whipped around and went scuttling toward the loft ladder.

"Who took him?" Hank asked bluntly, motioning toward the flat piece of mustard-colored canvas.

Malone stopped dead still, staring downward. He bent, lifted the canvas exactly as Hank had also done, peeked under it, and dropped it to draw upright and twist half around facing the marshal. His expression would have been ludicrous any other time. His eyes were perfectly round. "Where is he?" Pat whispered.

"That's what I'm asking you."

Malone swung back to stand stiffly staring at the canvas. "A joke?" he muttered, beginning to pucker up his creased forehead. "Is this someone's idea of . . . ?" He broke off to turn and bawl upward: "Alfie! Alfie, come down here!"

Alfie came tumbling down the loft ladder. He didn't cross

over, though; he stopped at the base of the ladder and ran a soiled hand under his leaking nose. His eyes were brimful of unshed tears.

"Alfie, after I left last night did anyone come around?"

"No. Not that I heard, Pat," whimpered the old alcoholic. "It was quiet as a church in here last night."

Hank said suspiciously: "Alfie, did you slip out and go for a bottle after Pat and I walked out last night?"

Alfie wobbled his head in a negative fashion. "Didn't have to, Marshal. Had my own bottle up in the loft. Stayed up there until Pat showed up a couple hours ago."

"Well, who the hell stole that danged body?" Malone demanded angrily, and turned to stare wonderingly at the canvas again. "Who'd want such a thing?"

"I dunno," mumbled Alfie, and turned to reach for his ladder with both trembling hands.

Hank watched the derelict scramble back up through the overhead hole into the haymow. He stood for a while, staring up where Alfie had disappeared, then he faced Malone again and the two of them looked dumbly back and forth.

"No burial party now," remarked Hank. "Listen to me, Pat. If you know anything . . . tell me."

Malone swore and stamped up and down in the runway, his red face getting redder. "What the devil would I pull such a trick for?" he eventually demanded, halting five feet in front of Hank and bristling with indignation.

"I don't think it was any trick or any joke," replied Hank. "I can't imagine why anyone would want to steal that body, but I don't think it was for a joke at all."

"Then why?"

"I don't know, Pat, but I'm sure going to find out."

"How? Hell, he was a stranger."

"Not to someone he wasn't. Not to the feller who put that

slug in his back, and not to whoever stole his carcass out of your barn."

"Maybe it was the same man both times."

"Maybe," assented Hank, and moved off toward the roadside doorway where morning sunlight struck the roadway and bounced back up to hurt his eyes, forcing him to squint. "But you want to know something, Pat? I don't believe that. I don't think the man who shot him was in town last night . . . or early this morning . . . to make off with his body, for the simple reason that he didn't have to worry about that dead feller at all. He couldn't have talked and there wasn't anything on him to implicate his murderer. So why would a feller ride all night long to get down here from the mountains, just to steal his carcass?"

Malone walked as far as the roadway with Hank. But there he halted. "A damned lousy riddle," he pronounced, and, when Hank put a caustic look back at him, Pat bobbed his head up and down defensively. "Well, it sure is a riddle, isn't it? What you lookin' at me like that for?"

"I'm getting sensitive about that word is all, Pat."

Hank stood a while in deep thought. Around them both, the activity of Conifer made its discordant sounds. Across the roadway over in front of Stone's mercantile establishment a freighter was unemotionally cursing his mules for not backing straight so that he could unload his cargo at the plank walk's edge. Two boys and an ambling dog went past, their shrill voices raised in quick, nonsensical argument, and two range riders jogged southward side-by-side, looking youthful and reckless and completely irresponsible.

"Pat, keep all this under your hat," Hank ultimately said.

"I will. Of course I will."

"Have you remembered his name yet?"

Malone wagged his head. "No, but last night I recollected some other things about those fellers."

"What, specifically?"

"Well, for one thing they kept to themselves, had a camp west of town near the foothills, their officer's name was. . . ."

"West of town in the foothills?" asked Hank, suddenly interrupting Malone. "Do you know where it was?"

"Sure I know. I already told you, I sold 'em more horses than anyone else hereabouts. In fact, that's how I got my start in the livery business . . . with the gold they paid me."

Hank walked back and stopped close to Malone, his gaze hard and bright. "Was their camp on Frank Leslie's range, by any chance?"

"Yes. Now that you mention it, their camp was on Frank's range. But not as far out as you found that corpse. It was. . . ."

"How do you know where I found that corpse, Pat?"

"Oh, dammit, Hank, use your head. You were gone nearly all day. You had to have driven at least fifteen miles out. After all, I didn't come down in the last rain."

"All right. Could you show me where their camp was?"

"Yeah. Even after all these years I'd know that spot. They picked the spot real good for holdin' a band of loose stock." Malone cocked his head to one side. "What's in your mind? You figure those fellers are campin' at that same place again?"

"I don't know. I'm beginning to wonder why, if it's the same bunch, they'd come back here after all these years, and why, after soldiering together all through the war, one of them'd suddenly decide to kill another one of them."

Malone made a derisive grunt. "*Humph!* If you had the answers, you wouldn't have any riddle left to sweat over."

"You busy now?" Hank asked, coming to a quick decision. "Could you ride out right now and show me that camp site?"

Pat hedged. He looked worriedly down into his barn. He glanced briefly up at the sun to estimate the time of day. "Guess I could," he said with no great enthusiasm. "But, Hank, none of this'll help you find that danged body, will it?"

"I've got a feeling I'm not going to find that body, Pat. But I've got to start unraveling this mystery somewhere, and that Reb camp site's the only lead so far. Unless. . . ."

"Yeah, unless what?"

"Nothing. Let's saddle up and get going."

Malone stood fast. "Whoa up," he said, turning yeasty. "Just a gol-danged minute, friend. You start keepin' secrets from me an' I'll start playin' the same game with you."

Hank threw a prickly sort of hostile glance at Malone that rolled off the stocky liveryman like warm water. "I'm the law," he said, "and you're the liveryman. You stick to beating on your own anvil and I'll stick to beating on mine."

"Not this time you won't," said Malone mulishly. "It looks to me, Hank, like I'm in this with you whether I like the notion or not, an' when fellers get back-shot, I don't aim to get involved at all, unless I'm going to be kept plenty well informed. Now, what was it you were about to say?"

"Pat, this can land you in a heap of hot water, if it's the kind of trouble I'm beginning to think it might be."

"I've been boiled a time or two before," said Malone stubbornly, still not moving an inch. "Come on, out with it."

Hank glared and hesitated. He knew Pat Malone as a shrewd, sometimes grumpy and truculent man who'd been many things in his lifetime from a buffalo hunter to an Army scout to a rough-string rider for the big cow outfits. He also knew Pat to be as close-mouthed as a clam, so he said finally, with obvious reluctance: "Gold, Pat. You said they paid you for those horses in gold."

"I did, and what of that? In those days no one trusted Yankee money too much, but Confed shinplasters . . . hell, you could fill a wheelbarrow with them and they still didn't equal one little five-dollar gold piece. Ask Jeff Stone. He refused to sell those Rebs supplies and shells except for gold."

"Jeff, too?" murmured Hank.

"What d'you mean, Jeff, too? Of course Jeff. There was a dozen of us hereabouts had dealings with those Rebs. They hung around here for nearly a month. What's that got to do with . . . ?" Malone's voice trailed off into a long, long hush and his baby-blue Irish eyes suddenly widened to a full and wondering roundness. "No," he whispered, "you're not thinkin' it's the gold they carried?"

"That's exactly what I am thinking, Pat. But I'm also thinking that, if someone here in town knew those Rebs were back in the country, skulking around in the mountains where they hid out during the war, whoever that someone is, he's probably also thinking the same thing. Gold. Gold coins they buried somewhere hereabouts just in case they might've gotten captured by some Yankee patrol after they headed back south with those horses they bought."

Malone let his breath out in a long, soft sigh. He stared for a full minute over at the marshal before turning, beckoning Hank along beside him, and walking down into his barn runway again. Alfie was nowhere in sight, so they rigged out their own horses and rode on out, but instead of leaving town by the front roadway, they passed down the barn into the back alley, turned northward, and rode as far as the first intersecting, east-west roadway. Here, Pat Malone swung left and led them out of Conifer with the midday sun across their shoulders.

They passed women in their backyards hanging out clothes. They also saw old men pitching horseshoes in a vacant lot, and some boys encouraging a big old speckled mongrel to dig out a badger's hole. All the sights, sounds, and smells of the town rode with them all the way out to the last few tar-paper shacks where the indigent, the wastrels, and the shiftless hangers-on lived. After that lay the immensity of open country with the mountain slopes far off northward, but circling on around the valley toward those far upper reaches many miles off where Frank Leslie's range got lost in the distance, and neither of them said a word.

Pat kept angling over toward the far-away foothills. He rode as a man would ride who knows exactly what his destination is. Hank went along at his side, watching those same hills, thinking some peculiar thoughts, wondering about something that made no sense to him at all, such as stealing a dead man's carcass, but saying not a word.

VI

It struck Hank that the thing both Rita and Pat Malone had been wondering about had somehow been taken out of his hands. That decision he'd been resisting was now being made for him. Or so it seemed as he rode along with the noonday sun beating down from above, warming his back and side and shoulders. He couldn't call that mysterious slaying a routine affair now even if he wanted to. For one thing, there wasn't going to be any burial. For another, the laziest, most indecisive lawman on earth couldn't help but be intrigued by the theft of a dead body. And finally he didn't want to call it a routine killing anyway; there was something here that worried a man's conscience; if he chose now to look the other way, for as long as he afterward lived he'd always wonder.

It seemed actually to take the pair of them much longer than it did to reach the foothills, and as a matter of fact had Malone kept going straight north it would have taken them longer because north, as well as southward from Conifer, the mountains were miles away. But Malone angled along westerly over onto Frank Leslie's range, struck the hills about nine miles from town where they began to curve around toward the valley's west end, and he finally halted a half mile out and pointed to a small cañon where wintertime run-off had sluiced out a sunken little pocket of land perhaps twenty acres in diameter with trees surrounding it and open to the southward.

"That's where they had their camp," he said to Hank. "In that little cañon there."

"Good spot," observed Hank, riding on.

"Good enough," agreed Pat. "They rigged a sort of rope corral around among the trees back there so's the horses could only get out one way, southward. They had their camp across the southward opening, and that sealed off the cañon. I thought at the time whichever one of 'em figured that out was no greenhorn."

"How many were there, Pat?"

"Seven. That one you found shot was their sergeant." Malone bit his lip, darkly scowled, then blew out a mild curse. "Almost had his name. It was on the tip of my tongue. But I'll think of it."

"Who was their officer . . . you remember that?"

"Yeah. Captain Saint George. Captain William Saint George. He was a tall, handsome feller who didn't say much. He knew horses, though, and the others seemed to look up to him. I remember the day I delivered his horses and got paid. I said something about the war to him, an' by golly he just stared at me, didn't say a word, just stared. Acted like he figured I was lower'n a worm for not takin' a hand in it."

"And the others?"

Malone shrugged. "Looked like a bunch of mountaineers. Raw-boned, sun-browned men, armed to the teeth and plenty able to care for themselves. You know, in those days there were still a few war parties of Indians around. I thought at the time that seven men didn't make a very big party to drive a herd of horses through the mountains with Indians skulkin' around. But after I'd made a trip or two to their camp, I began feelin' sorry for any Indians who'd jump that bunch. They were tough men, Hank. Tough and capable. I figure, maybe if the Confederacy'd had more like Saint George's detail, they just might've won their war."

Hank halted again at the entrance to that grassy place with its surrounding tree fringe, dropped both hands to his saddle swells, and sat there gazing around. Malone also halted, but he talked on as recollection brought back to him many details of that nearly forgotten camp and its inmates.

"Yonder, to the right there, was where Saint George had his bedroll. About a hundred feet off from the other fellers. About where we're standin' is where the picket line was. There was always two, three of them loafin' down here, watching the prairie southward." Malone suddenly smiled broadly. "I remember now . . . that sergeant's name was Harold Burris. Sergeant Harold Burris. He was the oldest of the bunch except for one other man, that other one always stayed over by the captain. Sort of an orderly or something, a dog robber or a swamper around the captain's camp. He never had anything to do with me. When I brought the horses up here, he was like the captain's shadow, stayed back out of the way, and never even spoke to me. He was a man in his forties, if I remember correctly, sort of skinny and worried-seeming all the time. Of the whole bunch I figured him to be the least worthwhile, but even he looked pretty rugged, if it came to a scrap."

Hank listened to all this reminiscing while running his scanning gaze out and around. The little cañon seemed now never to have been disturbed at all. Until Hank got down, paced slowly over to the trees, and upon several of them found ancient rope burns in the soft bark, he wasn't entirely satisfied that there had ever been a camp here. But after seeing those old burns, he walked up near the far ending where the northward hills stood almost straight up, and there he halted.

"Come here, Pat," he called softly. Malone didn't dismount. He rode his horse up and halted. Hank pointed just beyond the first fringe of pines. "What's that look like to you?" he asked.

Malone squinted, grunted down out of the saddle, and walked ahead a hundred feet, halted beside a ragged old bull pine, and said: "I'll be damned. A hole." He turned. "Hank, by golly you just might be right. Someone's sure as the devil been digging up here. And not too long ago, either."

Hank walked on up to the edge of that hole and stood gazing thoughtfully downward. He pushed at the crumbly edge with his toe; moist earth broke away.

"Maybe two, three days ago," he said quietly. "No more'n that, Pat."

Malone knelt and ran a hand into the loamy earth, withdrew it, and reached up to toy with his watch chain. He didn't speak or move for a long while. Neither did Hank Herman. They were thinking the same thought but from different approaches.

"What do you make of it?" Malone asked, after a while.

"They did bury something, Pat. Or at least someone buried something here."

Malone got back upright, stooped to dust his knees, kept considering that hole in the ground for a moment or two longer, then he said: "Three feet deep by maybe three feet wide. Hank, you could bury a hell of a lot of gold in a hole that big."

"That's what's bothering me. Maybe it wasn't gold, after all."

"What, then?"

But Hank shook his head. "Damned if I know, Pat. But one thing's reasonably clear. Those Rebs did come back. After all these years, they did return."

"One of 'em did, anyway," agreed the liveryman, "and whoever he brought back with him must've gotten greedy and plugged him in the back."

"I'll gamble that all four of them were part of that original bunch of seven men."

"What happened to the others? There'd be three more."

Hank turned away from the freshly dug hole and leaned upon a tree. "It's a long way south from Wyoming to where they had to go with those horses, Pat. Texas would've been the nearest Southern state. But even if Indians didn't account for the other three, and even if they all got back to wherever they were to deliver those remounts, there was still a year and more of hard fighting before the war ended after that. From what I've heard a few men say who were there, mortality among cavalrymen was dog-goned high. Three out of seven would be about right, I'd guess, Pat."

Malone also stepped away from the hole and stood somberly gazing southward out over the great prairie beyond. He seemed to be considering a number of things for as long as he was silent, then he said: "All right, something happened to three of 'em, and the other four are part of the original bunch. Now then . . . where are they, what are they lookin' for, and why was Sergeant Burris shot?"

Hank didn't reply for a while. He stepped back out of the trees, went slowly pacing back to his horse, caught up his reins, and stood looking around this quiet, afternoon-shaded place. Not until Pat Malone, back in his saddle again, came walking on down where the marshal stood, did Hank say: "I'll tell you something, Pat. I'm not too concerned with where those four men are right now. I'm not even too concerned with why Burris was killed. What's got me puzzled is what those men buried around here some place, and who else besides them knew about it."

Malone looked long at Hank from the height of his saddle before saying: "You mean to tell me you think someone right here in our town dug that hole back there?"

Hank turned, stepped up over leather, and nodded over at

Malone. "I think it's entirely possible. Look at it this way, Pat. If four Reb soldiers buried something here, or somewhere around here in these foothills, would they hang around as long as these four men have, even butchering a beef to eat while they hung around even longer, or would they come here in secret like they've done, dig up whatever they hid here, back during the war, then head right on out of the country?"

Malone reached up to remove his floppy old hat, scratch his head, drop the hat back down again, and sit over there on his horse, staring hard at the ground for a while without speaking. Finally he brightened, saying to Hank: "But they got it. They dug it up out of that hole back there in the trees."

"Nope. Pat, that camp over near Frank Leslie's place showed that they'd been there several days. Maybe a week. Now, men who knew what they were here for wouldn't need a week to dig it up. They wouldn't even have to make a camp right here. You said yourself it's an ideal camp site. Look around you. They can see in every direction except northward. No one could sneak up on them . . . even if anyone knew they were in the country and wanted to sneak up on them. But they still wouldn't have to camp here, if they knew where that buried stuff was. All they'd need would be maybe one day to rest their animals, dig up whatever was hidden here, and light out. No one would ever have known they were here."

"All right," growled Malone. "What are you drivin' at?"

"Those Rebs didn't dig that hole back there, Pat."

"Who did?"

"Someone else. Someone from town maybe, or one of the local ranchers."

"Who? Just name me who?"

"I can't."

"You're thinkin' maybe it was me because I knew those fellers back during the war. Dog-gone you, Hank, I got a notion to. . . ."

165

"I wouldn't be talking like this if I thought it was you, Pat. I know it wasn't you."

"How do you know that?"

"Dammit, use your head. That hole back there was dug no more'n three days ago. For the past three days you haven't left Conifer. I saw you around town every one of those days, and for a week before that, so it couldn't have been you."

Malone's expression of irritation began gradually to disappear. "Hey, wait a minute," he breathed quickly. "Wait just a darned minute, Hank. I think we got the answer. Go back to town and quietly ask around. Whoever rode out of town and was gone all day within the last week, packin' a shovel, will be our man."

"One of our men," corrected Hank. "There'll be the four Johnny Rebs, too. But I think we're on the trail now, Pat. I think, too, that whoever dug this hole might also be the man who can tell us how Sergeant Burris got shot." Hank canted an assessing eye at the lowering sun. "Let's head for home," he said. "It'll be dark by the time we get back."

They rode on out onto the prairie saying nothing more for a long while. The shadows of early evening came down off mountain slopes like shrouds to put a graying haze over everything. Visibility was limited and the great depth of silence they passed through was so totally without sound that their cooling-out world might have been uninhabited except for the pair of them.

They were still several miles out when Malone said: "I've been tryin' to recall everyone those Rebs had business with in town. They bought the horses from me. They also bought a few head from Frank Leslie. They bought grub and ammunition from Jeff Stone, and I remember seein' liquor in their camp, so I reckon they also visited Rube's saloon. Outside of me, that leaves Stone, Leslie, and Rube Burrows who'd recollect them.

And if you include me, then that makes four of us who might've dug that hole back there."

"There'll be more," opined Hank, slouching along looking ahead where Conifer lay low upon the gloomy plain. "Seven men don't stay in one place a month without bumping into at least a dozen people, one way or another."

"Yeah, I know that," responded Malone. "But I'm trying to limit it to folks who just might know these fellers had something worth hiding."

Hank looked around. "Know what I'm thinking, Pat? I'm thinking that not all those seven men knew they had something worth hiding. Otherwise, they wouldn't be wandering around in the mountains like they're doing . . . they'd have already dug it up and ridden back wherever they came from."

"That officer," said Malone quickly. "That Captain Saint George. He'd have known."

"Yeah. And the dead sergeant. I'm gambling that he also knew."

"Would that be why someone shot him, Hank?"

"He was worth a lot more alive than dead. At least until they found their cache."

Malone rolled up his eyes, tilted his head, and in an almost prayerful voice swore at the faint-twinkling overhead stars. "When I figure I'm almost out of the woods," he afterward complained, "something comes along and darkens the whole cussed picture for me again."

"One thing for you to remember," said the marshal as they came within sight of town. "Keep quiet about all this. Don't even talk in your danged sleep, Pat."

"You know me better'n that."

"Yes. But it doesn't hurt trying to impress you with the seriousness of what we know, either. And one more thing. You're in this up to your ears right along with me now, and whether you like the idea or not, starting tonight you'd better start wearing your gun again."

VII

Hank didn't see Pat Malone again until the following evening after their ride up to the old Confederate camp, and then it was by accident. He was making his final rounds of the day and stopped at Rube Burrows's Trailhand Saloon for a nightcap, and there stood Pat over at the free lunch counter, making a sandwich of liverwurst, onions, pickles, and rye bread. They exchanged a glance, but Hank ordered his drink and ignored Malone, who took his sandwich and a glass of beer on over to a corner table.

Rube was his usual garrulous self this night, but for some reason he neglected to ask about the dead man beyond muttering something about missing the burial, which Hank didn't reply to. The saloon was not as crowded this night as it had been the evening before. Some of Leslie's riders were in town, though, and Henry Helm sauntered over to lean upon the bar beside Hank and ask casually if Hank had found out anything about the dead man. Hank said he hadn't and changed the subject. He and Helm spoke desultorily for a few minutes, then Snowshoe's range boss drifted on back where his own men were lounging along the far end of the bar and Rube said: "Leslie must be gettin' soft-hearted, letting his men come to town in the afternoon like this."

Hank nodded, understanding by this remark that Rube meant, in order for the Snowshoe riders to hit Conifer before midnight, they'd had to have left the ranch not very long after midday. It was that long a ride.

When someone called Rube away, Hank finished his drink and strolled on into the card room. Rita was there behind her little grille with her chips and money neatly stacked. She smiled out at him as he walked over and leaned there, looking around the room. "Not much business tonight," he said, considering the three games, two of poker, one of faro, in progress.

Rita shrugged. "The middle of the month is never very good. Look at Mister Stone over there at the faro table. He's been playing steadily for two hours."

Hank looked and smiled as an errant thought struck him. "If Miss Harriett knew he was squandering money in this den of iniquity, she'd skin him alive."

"She's ill," said Rita. "I asked him how she was when he bought chips. He said she wasn't feeling well."

Hank gazed indifferently at the other players, brought his gaze around finally to Rita, and said softly: "You didn't wait for me to walk you home the other night."

She seemed near to smiling when she answered. "You were mad at me that night."

He shifted his stance, looked out over the room again, and said: "No, not mad, just a little annoyed. You sounded like some kind of a preacher with all your talk about what lies inside a man."

Rita steadily regarded Hank from her liquid dark eyes without speaking for a while. He tried to guess what her grave look meant, didn't succeed, and said: "Tonight, maybe?"

She smiled with her heavy lips. "After closing time, yes. I'll wait for you on the sidewalk."

He nodded. With no other place to go and in this pleasantly hushed atmosphere standing there beside Rita Malone, he didn't care whether he ever moved again or not.

She said casually and conversationally—"Look at this."—and held out a dark, rough-looking small coin. "To make sure it was a gold twenty-dollar piece I had to scratch it with another coin."

Hank didn't reach for the coin. He simply stood there, staring, with his heart suddenly pounding so loud in its dark cavern he thought Rita would also hear it. The coin she was holding out to him was almost black. Its normally smooth surface was badly pitted and its rounded edges were eroded. It looked like it had been lying underground for a long time. Hank's expression did not change at all as he pushed a hand into one trouser pocket, dredged forth a handful of coins, selected a shiny $20 gold piece, and reached over to drop it into Rita's palm, taking the eroded, pockmarked coin.

She smiled, saying dryly: "That wasn't a very good exchange, *querido.*"

He still didn't say anything. He turned the eroded coin over and over in his fingers. Its symbols were discernible but its date was not. He scratched it, with Rita's dark gaze on him becoming slowly concerned and slightly troubled. Finally she said: "What is it, Hank? You're pale as a ghost. What's the matter?"

He fisted the old coin and threw a quick, hard look out over the room. When he spoke, he didn't raise his voice above a whisper and he didn't look around at her. "Where did you get this? Who gave it to you?"

"Mister Stone. Why? Is it counterfeit?"

"No. No, it's not counterfeit."

"Then what is it, Hank? Why are you troubled? It's only a coin someone buried. Lots of people bury money. Someone just didn't take very good care to see that the weather didn't affect this one."

"Yeah," he murmured. "Are you positive Jeff Stone gave it to you?"

"I just told you that he did. Of course I'm positive. A coin like that one is unusual enough to be remembered."

He stood there, gazing over where the merchant was playing faro. Stone looked flushed and upset. As Hank watched him, he removed his spectacles, vigorously polished them, put them back on, and scowlingly concentrated upon his game.

"Hank, tell me what it is," said Rita, her voice becoming slightly sharp with insistence. "Has Mister Stone become involved in something illegal?"

He shook his head, pulled his gaze back around, and said: "Listen to me, Rita. He's losing at the faro table. When he comes over to buy more chips, keep the money he gives you separate from the other money you have here. You understand?"

"Yes, of course. Will you tell me what this is about?"

"Sometime, yes, but not right now. And Rita . . . I won't be able to walk you home tonight after all."

Those beautiful dark eyes lingered on Hank a moment after he'd said this. Then Rita did an unusual thing; instead of showing pique, she smiled. "That's all right," she murmured. "Hank, I'm glad."

"Glad?" he echoed, looking surprised.

"Yes, glad. Never mind why."

He stared in at her. A cowman came stalking over, grumbled something at Rita, and pushed some paper currency in at her. She counted out chips, passed them back, and the cowman stalked back over to his poker game again. He hadn't seemed to notice Hank standing there at all.

Hank was standing in quiet thought all through this transaction, but when the cattleman had departed, he said: "Tell me, Rita. Have you ever seen Stone in here before tonight?"

She shook her head at him, pulled up her lips in a wry small smile, and said: "No, but when he mentioned that his wife wasn't feeling well tonight, I thought this was probably the first decent chance he'd had to gamble in a long time, and let it go at that."

"Thanks," said Hank, and walked on across the room, out into the yonder barroom, and kept right on going. When he was out upon the plank walk again, he spied Pat Malone, standing out in front of his livery barn, smoking. It had not been his intention to show Pat the eroded gold coin, but now, on the spur of the moment, he walked on over, took Malone's arm, and without a word led Pat back to the doorway of his office. There, he released Malone's arm, opened his right hand, and held it out palm upward.

Pat scowled at the coin, bent slightly from the waist to study it, but made no immediate move to take the coin. Finally, as understanding slowly came, Pat took the coin, stepped on into his office, and held the thing up to the light. He afterward gravely handed it back and put a hard look over at Hank. "Where'd you find that thing?" he asked.

Hank told him. He also told him about Jeff Stone gambling over at Burrows's card room, and Pat put down his cigarette, sat down, and ran a hand through his thatch of rusty hair.

"Jeff don't gamble," he said. "I've known Jeff Stone more'n ten years and he don't gamble."

"He's gambling tonight, Pat."

Malone wagged his head. "He's upset then." He raised sober eyes to Hank. "You reckon that's part of the Reb cache, that old rusty coin?"

"I don't know. I do know it sure picked a bad time to show up if it's not part of that cache."

"Maybe Jeff got it at his store. Maybe some old gaffer had that thing salted down somewhere like most of those danged cattlemen do with their money."

"Maybe," agreed Hank. "Maybe not, too. I want you to do something, Pat. Keep this coin for me." Hank put the coin upon Malone's desk. When the liveryman screwed up his face to protest, Hank said: "I don't want to be carrying it and I'm not in my office enough to risk leaving it there. Besides, if anything happens to me, I want someone else to know what's going on."

"What could happen to you?" asked Malone, getting slowly

to his feet. "What else have you stumbled onto?"

"Nothing at all. As a matter of fact, until I saw you a while back over at Rube's lunch counter, I didn't know a blessed thing more than we both knew yesterday . . . which wasn't very much. But now I'm beginning to wonder about a few things."

"What things, for instance?"

"A fresh grave somewhere around town, for one thing."

"Huh? You mean . . . his?"

Hank nodded and stepped to the door. "You keep that coin, and, as soon as I can, I'll be back." He passed on out of Malone's office, strolled ahead to the roadway, and carefully adjusted his hat as a cover for the long gaze he threw northward and southward along the roadway.

It was late now, close to midnight. Before very long Rube would be locking up for the night. He hadn't had many patrons in his establishment anyway, so Marshal Herman turned and sauntered along southward toward his jailhouse. But he didn't enter when he got down there. Instead, he stepped back into his recessed doorway and leaned upon the siding, looking northward up toward the Trailhand Saloon.

It was nearly 1:00 A.M. before the last stragglers shuffled on out of Rube's bar up the roadway. One by one the lamps were put out inside the saloon. The last patron to walk on out into the cool night was the emporium owner.

Hank drew up off the doorway wall, watching Stone closely. He seemed in no hurry to head for home. In fact, when he finally dumped his hat upon the back of his head and stepped forth, he turned northward instead of southward, which would have been in the direction of his home, and went slowly pacing along the yonder plank walk.

Hank let Stone get almost to the first intersecting roadway before he also moved out northward, but upon the opposite sidewalk. There was very little light brightening the main thoroughfare now. It was entirely possible for a man to stalk another man without being detected at it, as long as he kept enough nighttime darkness between them, which Hank did.

Jeff turned east at the nearest roadway and at once faded from Hank's sight. The marshal hastened along, cut diagonally across the road up near Burrows's saloon, did not catch sight of Rita Malone, standing there, watching him, and swept along to the intersecting turn-off. Here he paused briefly, then stepped on around.

Jeff Stone was several hundred feet along. He hadn't increased his pace at all and he seemed to Hank to have no particular destination as he ambled along. He acted like a man whose gambling losses might be deeply troubling him. But Hank knew enough about Stone's financial condition to know losing $40 or $50 at Rube's faro table wouldn't cause him undue pain.

Stone walked all the way out to the easternmost limits of town. Even after the wooden plank walk ended, he stepped down into the dust and went treading along, still with his head hung in that dejected or upset attitude. He passed the last tar-paper shack far out, then turned and paced along southward. Now, Hank knew, he was finally walking in the correct direction to reach his residence, and, thinking that this was surely the older man's destination, he slackened his own gait just enough to make out Jeff Stone on ahead, but without getting close enough for the merchant to see or hear him.

Finally, where the easterly terminus of his road loomed ahead, Stone slowed still more. When he came at last to his own street, he turned and started ahead toward his house, but now he was barely moving along at all. Hank halted where the plank walk began, leaned upon a picket fence, and watched.

Stone's house was a white-painted structure of two stories. It was one of the best residences in Conifer; one of the very few that had both an upstairs and a downstairs, and also one of the few that was painted. There was a light in the back of the house that reflected along the side wall and dwindled where it came on across the yard. Hank watched Jeff pause at his gate, put forth a hand, and stop dead still without opening the gate. He stood out there in the soft starlight, gazing up at his house. Hank couldn't possibly see his face but he could, and did, make out the older man's slumped posture, and it struck him as very unusual. Normally, even with his bad knees, Stone was an erect, self-assured man. In all the years Hank had known him, he'd never before seen him in a gambling room, or looking as dejected and troubled as he looked this night.

Stone twisted, shot a slow look eastward up toward the dark shadows where Hank blended in, turned, and glanced westward the same way. It struck Hank that Stone was looking for someone, that all his walking hadn't been chance at all, that he'd expected to see someone out here in the night.

That was the last thought Hank had for a long time. Something exploded at the base of his skull, a million violent lights erupted behind his eyes, and he felt himself falling.

VIII

Dawn was a pale streak upon the eastern rim of the world when Hank opened his eyes, pushed a hand upward to fend off some sharp object that was gouging him, found this offensive object to be a pointed slat off a fence, and planted both his elbows down hard to lever himself upright into a sitting position. His head felt as though he'd just come off a week-long drunk. Each time he exerted himself, the throbbing became particularly intense. He got to his feet but only by degrees. And he was cold, so cold his teeth chattered and his body shook.

He stood for several minutes looking around, orienting himself with the time and the place, permitting realization to come gradually. While he had been trailing Jeff Stone, someone else had evidently also been trailing him. He felt disgusted with himself for never once looking back. The longer he stood there deeply breathing, gingerly exploring the pulpy lump at the base of his skull, the more some elemental facts began to form up into a kind of pattern within his mind. Stone had been seeking someone. He remembered coming to that conclusion. Evidently whoever had struck Hank down had been the person Stone had walked through the night expecting to meet, and evidently the reason that unknown person had never approached the merchant was because he'd spied Hank following Stone.

He groped along a hundred yards through the still, cold predawn with one hand passing lightly along fence pickets. When he came even with the Stone residence, he paused to cast a glance inward past the gate. There was no longer any light showing; the house was as still, as dark and gloomy as every other house on this back street.

He continued along as far as the intersection of Stone's street and the main north-south roadway of Conifer. Here, too, the silence and emptiness was solidly uninterrupted. He crossed over to his jailhouse office, walked on in, lighted his lamp, and crossed to the desk to ease down gingerly upon a chair.

For a half hour he didn't move, but, as the pain began to lessen somewhat, he went to a washstand, dipped a towel into cold water, and put the soggy thing upon his head injury. After that he sat down again and composed himself to wait out the diminution of his headache, and also to think some bitter thoughts. He still knew nothing, and in fact, search though he might, he could not come up with a single crime Jeff Stone or anyone else had committed, except for the person who had sneaked up and struck him down, and even that, painful though it was—and humiliating, too—constituted no great crime, only a minor one. Striking an officer of the law wasn't punishable by much of a jail stretch, and, even if it had been, he had no idea who had struck him. He had an inkling of why he'd been struck down, and this very reasonably led him to the conclusion that as soon as Jeff Stone opened his store, he would go over and make Jeff tell him who he'd been hoping to meet the night before. After Jeff told him that, he'd go after that person, arrest him, and have the man who had assaulted him. With any luck he'd also have something else, too, some answers to the mystery of the eroded gold coin, and perhaps, if his luck held, at least a partial explanation of the other knotty problems that were plaguing him.

He made a pot of coffee on the jailhouse stove, drank two cups of the black brew, and immediately felt considerably revived. Dawn was making the deserted roadway appear distinguishably gray outside now. Dark, still store fronts began to stand out noticeably, and a slab-sided mongrel dog went ambling down the roadway's center, his nose to the ground, the first sign of life in this new day.

Hank went over and washed. He even shaved, and afterward flung the wash water out the back-door into the alleyway. His headache was still there but it had become progressively less bothersome, and by the time he heard someone's stout boot falls approaching down the echoing plank walk out front, he could put his hat on and adequately cover the lump where he'd been struck by that fence slat.

It was Pat Malone who entered the office, his face still slightly puffy from sleep but pink from a recent scrubbing. "Saw your light when I was heading for the barn," he said to the town marshal. "Wondered what got you up before breakfast."

Malone wasn't wearing a gun and Hank made a caustic remark about this to which Pat gave an indifferent shrug and said: "What I need a danged gun for?"

Hank turned and removed his hat. Malone saw the lump. He

gasped and asked the obvious question. Hank explained what
had happened to him, and finished with the same admonition
he'd offered Malone the day before, only a little stronger this
time. "You'll probably be next, and without a gun you won't
stand much of a chance. Now, will you get smart, Pat, and put
the damned thing around you?"

Malone grinned impishly. "You were wearin' yours and it
didn't. . . ."

"Go to hell," growled Hank, gingerly replacing his hat. It was
a little early in the day for him to enjoy humor, particularly of
this kind.

Malone sobered. "What d'you figure it's all about?" he asked.
"Who'd be followin' old Jeff, and what's his part in this?"

"Dunno," muttered Hank, crossing to the desk and sitting
down there.

Someone knocked softly on the outer door. Neither of them
had heard anyone walking up so they looked at one another in
surprise. Pat stepped across, lifted the latch, and drew back the
panel. Rita walked in. She had a light shawl over her hair and
down across her shoulders. She looked up at Pat, moved past
him, and saw Hank at his desk. She stopped, gave Hank one of
her solemn looks, and said: "Why were you following Mister
Stone last night?"

Hank didn't at once reply. He stared at her for a full minute,
then he didn't answer the question, he asked one of his own. "If
you saw that, maybe you also saw something else. Who was following me?"

She looked puzzled. "Following you? All I saw was Mister
Stone walking northward, and after he turned the corner you
came along following him."

Pat eased the door closed, placed his thick shoulders against
the office wall, and steadily watched the lovely girl. He didn't
offer a word to either of them. He simply watched and listened.

"Why, Hank? Was it because of that old coin?"

"Partly," conceded Hank. "Partly just plain curiosity. Where were you?"

"On the sidewalk outside of Rube's bar. I saw you go across the road behind him." Before Hank said anything more, the beautiful girl reached into a pocket, brought her hand forth, and placed several small objects upon the desk in front of Hank.

He looked downward. So did Pat, and it was the liveryman who made the only sound in the room—Pat gasped. Rita had placed four more eroded gold coins on the desk.

"Mister Stone cashed them in for chips," she said, "after you left. He lost about a hundred and fifty dollars at the faro table last night."

Hank bent over to consider those coins. None of them was as eroded as that first coin had been, but each of them showed the ravages of lying in moldy earth for a long time.

As Pat stepped over, picked the coins up, and intently studied them Hank leaned back in his chair, eyeing Rita. "Did you show these to Rube?"

"No. He doesn't know I have them and I'll have to put them back when we open up this afternoon."

"No one besides we three know about them?"

"Well, we three . . . and Mister Stone."

Malone cocked a skeptical eye at Hank. "One other person probably knows," he said. "Your friend from last night with the fence slat."

Rita looked at Malone with an uncomprehending expression. Neither Hank nor Pat enlightened her. In fact, neither of them had anything more to say on the subject of the gold coins.

Hank got up, retrieved the coins, and handed them back to her. He shot a quick look outside where sunlight was just beginning to tint the town's topmost roof lines a soft shade of pink, and told Rita to go on home, that as soon as he could he'd come see her. She left, but had she been a less fatalistic person she'd have insisted on some answers to the questions that were undoubtedly in her mind.

"Now what?" Pat asked. "One thing is plumb certain. Stone's mixed up in this to his ears, and he's not the only one."

"Yeah," murmured Hank, walking over to a little barred window where he stood gazing out at the awakening town. "He's not the only one."

"And," said Pat firmly, "it was gold buried up there in that danged hole."

Hank shrugged. This seemed too obvious now for comment. "What I'd like to know," he murmured thoughtfully, "is how these people knew about that gold. You said yourself when those Rebs were here during the war buying remounts, they kept pretty much to themselves."

"That's a fact," confirmed Malone. "But like you said yesterday, in the month or so they hung around here, they'd have to bump into a lot of people."

Hank turned his back to the front wall and considered Pat from pensive eyes. "We've got to get some answers out of Jeff Stone. He's the only one so far who seems to have any answers. He just didn't all of a sudden get that many eroded old gold coins from his store customers."

Malone crossed to the door and lifted the latch. "What do you want me to do?" he asked.

"Nothing," stated Hank. "Go on up to your barn, buckle on your Forty-Five, and act like nothing has happened. I'll watch for Jeff to open his store, then I'll nail him."

"You'll let me know what you get out of him?"

Hank nodded and Malone walked on out into the first golden light of the new day, heading northward toward his place of business.

Hank stood by the window, looking out. He saw several

merchants open their establishments, saw a ranch wagon come bumping in from the south country with two hunched-up range men upon its seat. He also saw Rube Burrows come ambling along, none too bright-eyed, and open his saloon. But for as long as he stood there gazing out, he did not see Jeff Stone come along as was his custom for many years, and unlock the doors to his general store.

He was becoming impatient but not suspicious, when Jeff's oldest clerk came hurrying along a half hour late to open the store and pass quickly on inside. Then something came out of nowhere and struck Hank hard; for the first time since he could recall, Jeff had not appeared to open his own place of business. Something was wrong. He stepped to the doorway, passed on out, and went striding across the roadway toward Stone's emporium.

As he entered, there were already several women customers being waited upon by a younger clerk, and other shoppers came in even as Hank stood there in the early-morning gloom of the building, looking around. He didn't see Jeff at all, and in fact until he passed on back to the little rearward office, he didn't even catch another view of the man who'd opened the place this morning. But in the small office he found his man. The clerk looked up over bifocal spectacles when Hank walked in, his solemn gaze as round-eyed as the look of an old owl, and the man faintly nodded.

"Marshal," he said softly. "Good morning. Something I can do for you?"

"Yeah, you can tell me where Jeff is."

The old clerk dropped his gaze and stood up from Stone's roll-top desk where he'd been sifting through piles of papers, bills, invoices, ledger sheets. "His wife's sick, Marshal," the older man said in that same cornhusk-dry tone of voice. "He asked me to open up for him."

"You talked to him this morning?" asked Hank.

The clerk looked wonderingly upward. "Yes, I talked to him," he replied, sounding surprised that Hank would ask such a question. "He was at his house. He gave me the keys and asked me to. . . ."

"Is he coming down to the store later on?"

The older man shook his head. "He said he'd have to stay with Miss Harriett until the doctor got there. He said not to count on him showing up today."

Hank turned, went to the door, then faced back toward the clerk again. "Tell me," he said, "have you taken in a lot of old gold pieces lately?"

The clerk hung fire over his reply to this. He gazed owlishly up at Hank, then wagged his head. "We don't get much gold money any more, Marshal. It's nearly all silver and paper currency nowadays. Sometimes we'll get a five or a ten in gold, but it's a pretty rare occasion. Of course, during the war. . . ."

"Thanks," said Hank, cutting the older man off and walking on out of the office.

He passed back through to the yonder sidewalk, and there he paused as two bearded riders rocked past, both of them stained with the dust and wear of travel. He turned when a recognizable voice hailed him and saw Rube Burrows striding along. Rube had that hard brightness to his gaze that Hank had come to know so well after all the years of their acquaintanceship.

"Hey," he said as he slowed and halted, "you know old Charley Dumphy, the gravedigger?"

Hank inclined his head. He knew Charley, knew him well, in fact, because Charley was a periodic drunk; as regular as clockwork Hank jailed him three times a year until Charley sobered up.

"Well, he was just in my place bellyachin' because someone went and borrowed his lowering contraption, got it all dirty, and then tossed it down in Charley's front yard."

Hank kept looking over at Rube. The device Rube was speaking of was a set of ropes attached to blocks for the lowering of coffins into deep graves. Hank had seen Charley use the thing innumerable times.

"Borrowed it?" he said.

Rube broadly grinned. He raffishly dropped an eyelid and raised it. "You don't have to play games with me," he said in a conspiratorial whisper. "It's all right with me if you didn't want anyone to know you was buryin' that dead feller you found out on Frank Leslie's range. Only you sure better not let Charley find out it was you borrowed his lowerin' contraption or he'll sure bawl you out for not cleaning it up afterward."

"Oh," said Hank quickly, "I'd never let Charley find out, Rube."

Burrows chuckled. "How come you to bury him like that, Hank . . . in the night an' all?"

Hank cleared his throat and spat out into the roadway playing for time. He smiled over at Rube and ultimately he said: "Well, to tell you the truth, I wanted to save the town the expense of a professional job. You know, Charley works by the hour and he works damned slow."

Rube bobbed his head up and down, winked again, turned, and went hustling back toward his saloon. Hank didn't move for as long as Rube was in sight, and even afterward he lingered a moment with his upset thoughts before turning southward and walking along toward the intersection of Jeff Stone's street corner and the main roadway. But he didn't swing eastward there toward the Stones' residence; he crossed on over and kept right on walking southward toward the far end of town, beyond which a quarter mile stood the sagging old paling fence around Conifer's boothill cemetery.

IX

The grave was there all right, far back under some ancient locust trees, and it was obviously fresh although someone had painstakingly worked at making the sod appear as though it hadn't been disturbed. But it was a near physical impossibility to dig a man-size grave, re-cover it, and not leave plenty of traces around. There was no headboard and Hank hadn't expected to find one. He stood in tree shade, considering the replaced squares of grass and thinking that he'd finally found Sergeant Harold Burris who had been spirited out of Pat Malone's livery barn. All he had to find now was the man—or men—who'd planted Burris here, the reason why they'd stolen his body in the first place, where they'd hidden it between the time they'd stolen it and the time they'd buried it, and finally why Sergeant Burris had been shot.

He left the cemetery walking thoughtfully back toward town and was almost to the intersecting roadway leading off toward the Stone residence, when he saw Pat Malone, with a six-gun belted around him, leaving the jailhouse. Pat paused under the overhang to turn and run a searching glance up and down the roadway. When he saw Hank, saw that Hank had also seen him and was crossing over, Pat stepped back and leaned upon the rough log exterior of the jailhouse, waiting.

When those two came together, Pat said with an ironic expression: "We got visitors in town."

Hank looked up the roadway and back to Pat's face again. "Where?"

"Over in Rube's place. But before you go look 'em over, come with me an' look at their horses and outfits."

Malone wouldn't utter another word as he beckoned, turned, and paced up to his barn. He was silent even after he led Hank to adjoining tie stalls and nodded at the travel-stained animals hungrily eating there. "Their horses," he explained, "been ridden danged hard lately." Pat turned and pointed at the public saddle rack. "Those first two rigs are also theirs. Take a good look, Hank."

Hank walked over and looked. One of the saddles was old and scarred, and where the saddlebags and bedroll had been lashed aft of the cantle were three dim letters carved into the leather.

"C.S.A." stated Pat quietly. "That mean anything to you?"

Hank straightened back, said nothing, and moved along to examine the second saddle. It was a nondescript Texas A-fork outfit with the rigging exposed, with brush scratches on it, and a limp old carbine scabbard slung under the right stirrup leather.

"Look," said Pat, and upended that scabbard, trickled some moldy earth out of the thing, and let the scabbard fall back. "Know what the owner of this rig's been using his saddle boot for? No danged carbine, Hank. He's been usin' it to hold a shovel, and the dirt off that shovel fell down inside the boot." Pat stepped back, looked straight up at Hank, and planted both his heavy fists upon his hips. He was clearly very self-satisfied and triumphant. "Satisfied about the strangers?" he demanded.

Hank didn't answer the question. He said: "Did they both have beards?"

Pat nodded, still looking bleakly triumphant. "Both had beards an' both been ridin' hard and long."

"There's still one missing," murmured Hank. "There were four of 'em before Burris got killed. Then there were three. Now there are only two of 'em."

Malone shrugged. "Gold'll do that to men," he opined. "Especially large enough amounts of it. You'll probably find Number Three lying face down up some lousy gulch like you found Burris."

Hank turned and walked up to the roadside doorway. He halted there to gaze across at the Trailhand Saloon. Behind him

Malone said: "I watched 'em walk over and go inside. Unless they walked out when I was down at the jailhouse lookin' for you, they'll still be in there."

"Pat," said Hank quietly, "didn't you recognize either of 'em? Yesterday I got the impression from the way you remembered things, you'd know those Rebs if you saw 'em again."

Malone wagged his head. "It was a long time ago. But with those beards I wouldn't even attempt it now. Durin' the war they were a lot younger, and clean-shaven."

"Yeah," muttered Hank. "That'd account for the whiskers, wouldn't it? They'd know someone in Conifer might remember 'em." Hank paused, rubbed a hand unconsciously over his chin, then said: "Something you can do, Pat. Walk on over there and keep an eye on those two. I've got to go see Jeff Stone, then I'll be along and take over with our Reb visitors."

Pat looked pained. "I'll do it if you figure it's plumb necessary," he said. "But I'd rather not. You see, Alfie's gone and I don't like to leave the barn untended."

Hank looked around. "Alfie? Where's he gone to?"

"Don't know. He wasn't here this morning when I got back from your office. I reckon he's out on a tear somewhere, the runny-nosed old bum. If I paid him any wages, danged if I wouldn't fire him."

Hank turned back to considering Rube's saloon again. He had it in mind that those two strangers were not in Conifer because they needed a drink of whiskey at Rube Burrows's place. He also had it in mind that he didn't want those men walking up on him while he was interrogating Jeff down at Stone's house. He didn't know exactly what danger was near, but he felt certain that for some reason he did not yet fathom there most certainly was danger. A lawman's sixth sense warned him that two of that mysterious band of riders were in town to bring some problem they shared with Jeff Stone, and perhaps other local people, to a head; that same sixth sense warned him that violence was building up in his town.

Pat said: "Tell you what I can do for you, though. I can go over to the hotel and get Rita to go to Rube's place and keep an eye on those two. In fact, if they've been on the trail as long as they look like they've been, I got a hunch Rita could keep 'em quiet over there for as long as you need."

Hank's troubled expression vanished. "For a pug-nosed Irishman," he said to Malone, "sometimes you actually show a little smidgen of real intelligence. You go do that, and tell her to keep 'em there for at least an hour. I'll be through with Jeff by then . . . with any luck."

Malone nodded and started to move past. As he went by, Hank added: "By the way, I know where Sergeant Burris is."

Pat spun around. His face mirrored quick, hard interest. "Where?" he asked.

"Buried under the locusts up in boothill. I've got a hunch that Jeff knows about that, too. I've also got a hunch that whoever belted me with that danged fence slat last night had a hand in the burying. Don't ask me how I got those notions. I couldn't explain it. Now go on."

Malone hesitated briefly, seemed to be about to say something, but in the end he merely inclined his head and went scuttling on across the roadway where late morning traffic was steadily building up.

Hank also walked southward, but he didn't cross the road until he was down almost to his jailhouse where the intersecting roadways came together. There, as he shuffled through roadway dust, he heard some catcalls up the northward roadway and turned to look. Frank Leslie with two of his men was jogging southward from the upper plains down into town. Some other range men who had recognized them from the plank walk had called hootingly out to them. It was early for Leslie to be in town, but more unusual he rarely rode in with any of his men. Hank speculated briefly on this, but put it out of his mind as he walked on over to the opposite plank walk, stepped up, and kept walking eastward down the side street toward the Stone place.

It was now 10:00 with the sun warming the roadway, brightening the far-away peaks, and reflecting bitterly off minute particles of mica in the air that forced people to squint their eyes nearly closed against the painful brightness. Conifer's only doctor was closing the gate leading to Jeff Stone's house when Hank came striding along. The doctor's horse and buggy were standing at the sidewalk's edge, and, as Hank came up, the medical man put his bag upon the seat, turned, and nodded at Hank.

"Fine morning," he said.

Hank was laconic about that. "How can you appreciate something like that, Doc, when you spend all your waking hours looking at swollen tonsils and listening to folks groan about their ailments?"

The doctor smiled. "It's not so hard, Hank," he replied. "When you leave the sickbed and walk out into the sunshine, you just forget about one and concentrate upon the other." The doctor paused, shot a look backward, and said: "Anyway, some ailments aren't really serious. They're mostly in people's minds."

"You mean Miss Harriett's troubles, Doc?"

"Yes."

"What's ailing her?"

The medical man reached inside his coat, drew forth a cigar, bit off the end, poked the thing between his teeth, and lit up. He drew back a big bubble of smoke and savoringly let it out, his expression turning wry. "Nothing," he said. "Not a blessed thing. She's upset about something. Got a bad case of the nerves. Now, if it'd been you in her shoes, I'd have prescribed a big slug of rye whiskey. But not Harriett. I've known her thirty years, Hank. If I'd recommended a whiskey sedative, she'd probably have jumped out of that bed and thrown me bodily out of the house." The doctor paused again, considered his cigar, flicked ash off it with his little finger, and looked up, still with that wry expression. "You know, her paw was quite a drinking man, Hank. You look surprised."

Hank was surprised. He'd lived in the Conifer country all his life and had never heard anyone mention Harriett Stone's father before. "Didn't know the old gent," he said.

"You wouldn't have known him," stated the doctor. "That was down in Texas, boy, thirty years ago. I knew the whole family and the old gent was made of cast iron and rawhide. He drank his whiskey with his meals. I recollect Hattie sitting there at the supper table looking no more put out about that, in those days, than you or I'd look now. But after she married Jeff and came up here to Wyoming, why she changed so much I scarcely knew her myself, when I came up here to open an office. She's death on demon rum now. On gambling, too. On just about anything grown men do for relaxation. Don't know what happened along the way, but she sure got a lot of hard-set opinions formed in her mind between those days and these."

Hank made a rueful face. "I know about her opinions, all right," he said. "She's been after Rube Burrows's scalp for ten years."

The doctor chuckled, turned, and climbed up into his buggy, eased around, and sat down. "Rube's harmless," he said, clamping his teeth down upon that cigar and unfurling his lines. "He's a nosy old granny but he gives fair measure at his bar and doesn't stand for any shady deals in his card room." The doctor winked at Hank; he was a man in his late fifties, shock-headed and stocky. He was both liked and respected in the Conifer country.

"You know, Hank, Harriett's paw used to gamble every Saturday night regular as clockwork. He was quite a feller, old man Burris. Quite a feller."

Hank reached out and caught the cross brace of the medical man's buggy. "What did you call him?" he said breathlessly. "Just now . . . what did you say Harriett Stone's father's name was?"

"Burris. Old Sam Houston Burris. Knew him well. Fine old Texan he was. Well, Hank, go do your visiting. I've got two more calls to make before I can head for home. See you again."

Hank stepped back, watched the doctor flick his lines, cluck at his horse, and go driving westward up toward the main north-south roadway. He was still standing there like he'd taken root when the doctor's rig turned right and went dustily on up out of sight, and even afterward he didn't move right away. He acted like a man who'd just been kicked in the stomach by a mule.

X

Jeff answered Hank's light knocking at the front door. He was dressed as though for the store except that he had no necktie on. He stood in the doorway looking out at Hank through his spectacles, offering no greeting, no invitation to enter the house, and looking neither surprised nor chagrined at the identity of his caller.

Hank said: "Sorry to hear about Miss Harriett, Jeff. Hope she's feeling better."

Stone faintly nodded. "I'll tell her you called, Hank," he murmured.

"You do that," said Hank, watching the older man's face. "Jeff, step out onto the porch with me a minute, will you?"

Without a word Stone came on through the doorway, eased the panel closed, and moved over where several chairs stood.

Still without speaking, he motioned for Hank to sit down. He eased himself down into one of those chairs and kept watching the lawman.

Hank didn't sit, not right away. He said, thinking to jar the older man with bluntness: "Tell me why you secretly buried Sergeant Burris, Jeff."

The only indication of astonishment Stone showed was a quick, brief blinking of his eyes, and a slowness in replying that indicated to Hank that he had to organize his thoughts before answering.

"What makes you think I did it?" he asked, obviously hedging, playing for time.

Hank took a chair, spun it around, and dropped down with both arms across the chair's back. "Come on," he said. "Jeff, that was the wrong answer. You should've asked me who Sergeant Burris was."

"All right, who was he?"

"Your wife's brother, I'd guess."

Stone removed his spectacles, squinted through them, drew out a pocket handkerchief, and began to polish them. "Are you sure about that?" he asked.

Hank said truthfully, "No, but I aim to find out today, Jeff, and you can make things a heap easier for both of us if you'll quit beating around the bush."

"All right," Jeff said quietly, replacing his glasses and looking through them at Hank. "Harold Burris was my wife's brother. Now you know. What of it?"

"Like I asked before, why did you bury him last night in secret?"

"I didn't."

Hank, with a dawning suspicion that Stone was being truthful, found himself suddenly adrift in a sea of questions. For as long as it took to select the proper one to ask next, he and Jeff

Stone steadily regarded one another.

"But you knew he was dead, Jeff," he eventually said.

"Yes, I knew. That's what's bothering Harriett. She hadn't seen her brother in something like twelve years, Hank. I had the job of tellin' her he was dead."

"How did you know that?"

Old Stone looked out into the empty roadway speaking softly: "Frank Leslie came into my store yesterday to buy some Winchester ammunition. He said he'd just left you up at Burrows's saloon, said he'd found this dead man in the hills north of his place and that you'd taken a rig and gone out to fetch the body back to town." Jeff drifted his troubled gaze back to Hank's face before going on. "That's how I learned about it."

Hank gently wagged his head at Stone. "Dead men are common enough," he murmured, staring straight at Stone. "What interested you in this particular one?"

Stone didn't answer that right away, and, even when he spoke again, he evaded that question. He said: "I saw you come back into town and drive into Malone's barn. Later, after you'd left, I walked over, found that canvas back beside the harness room, lifted it . . . and recognized my wife's brother."

"Jeff," said the lawman quietly, easing back off his chair, "you're giving me part answers. What made you wait until after midnight to slip over and have your look at that corpse?"

"Well . . . I knew Burris was coming here."

"Yeah? And you knew he wasn't coming alone, didn't you?"

Stone inclined his head with evident reluctance. "I knew," he murmured so faintly Hank hardly heard him speak.

"How did you know?"

"He wrote us that he was coming."

"Where's he been all this time, since the war, Jeff?"

"In Texas. That's where the family is . . . or at least that's where what's left of it still is. The war thinned out the Burrises.

Harriett and Harold were the only ones left, except for some shirt-tail kin."

"Why was he coming to Conifer, Jeff?"

Stone shook his head solemnly. "I can't tell you that," he said.

Hank reached up to push back his hat. "All right," he said. "Tell me this . . . why was he killed?"

Stone shook his head again. "I can only guess about that. Like his burial. I can only guess about that, too. Listen, Hank, let sleepin' dogs lie. Don't stir this thing up all over again. The war was a long time ago."

"Dammit, Jeff, I'm not trying to stir anything up. All I'm trying to do is square up a murder and get some answers for the record."

"You're not going to get them from me, Hank. Besides, there's been no law broken. At least no law that I know of."

Hank plunged a hand into his pocket, drew forth that eroded gold coin, and held it out. "Where'd you get this thing, Jeff?"

The older man scowled downward at Hank's palm. "How should I know?" he said irritably. "We get all kinds of coins at the store."

Hank looked sardonic. "You'd know, Jeff, and so would your chief clerk at the store, and he told me this morning that you fellers hadn't gotten any coins like this in a long time."

Hank put the coin back into his pocket and resumed his leaning-forward position across the chair's back. For a long moment he awaited some word from the troubled-looking older man, and, when none came, he said: "Have you been out of town within the last three, four days, Jeff?" Then, before Stone could reply he also said: "Don't play games with me. I can verify whether you have or not."

Jeff heaved a quiet sigh and looked back out into the quiet roadway again. "I haven't been out of town. If you doubt that,

193

go ahead and ask my clerks at the store."

"Then," said Hank, "I'll tell you something, Jeff. Someone dug a hole up where those Reb soldiers had their camp when they came here during the war to buy remount horses, and I'm guessing there was a cache of gold coins buried up there. I'm also guessing that somehow or other you wound up with that cache. That's where this coin came from. That's also where those other coins you lost at the faro game in Rube's saloon last night came from."

Stone got up out of his chair. "You're wrong," he said. "Hank, leave it lie. No law's been broken. Stay out of it."

Hank also stood up. "I can't stay out of it," he said. "As for no law having been broken, Jeff, your brother-in-law was murdered. That's not only a crime, it's a pretty danged serious one."

Jeff kept looking over at Hank for a long time before he spoke again. "Why, all of a sudden, have you turned into something you've never been before?" he demanded. "Hank, I've known you a good many years. You've always been an easy-goin' feller who'd rather look the other way than get involved in a lot of trouble. Why, all of a sudden, have you changed?"

Hank, placing this question in the same category with something Rita had said to him the night he returned to town with dead Harold Burris, made a little frosty smile at the storekeeper. "I reckon the time comes in every man's life, Jeff, when he has to take a stand. He can back up and look the other way just so long, then he's got to make himself look squarely at the things he believes in. I don't believe in murder. I don't give a damn where the chips fall this time, Jeff. I'm going to buck the tiger to the limit until someone answers for your brother-in-law's killing." Hank lifted one hand, tapped Stone lightly on the chest with an extended finger, and said: "If you won't co-operate, maybe Miss Harriett will. It was her brother. She had to think a lot of him or she wouldn't be abed with grief like she is now. Maybe you aren't interested in seeing his murderer roped, Jeff, but I've got a feeling she might be."

"No, Hank," said Stone swiftly, his voice firming up with strong resistance for the first time since they'd been talking. "No. You leave my wife out of it."

"All right. Then tell me about those two men who rode into Conifer this morning."

Stone's eyes suddenly became very still. "Two men?" he murmured.

"Yeah. One of 'em has C.S.A. carved into the cantle of his saddle. It's almost illegible but it's there, Jeff. They're both bearded men and pretty well travel-stained. Are they two of the three men who rode here with your brother-in-law?"

"I don't know."

"The hell you don't, Jeff. What're you looking so sick about all of a sudden? Where's the third one? Did the others kill him, too?"

"I tell you, Hank, I don't know what you're talking about."

Hank removed his hat, struck it against his thigh, and made dust fly. He was losing patience with Stone, but he curbed this growing irritation. Out of all the questions he'd asked, he'd come up with only one solid fact. Stone had not known those strangers were in town, and he very clearly was afraid of them. Everything else he'd told Hank had only seemed to add to the confusion.

"Hank, I'm asking you as an old friend to let it lie."

"I can't let it lie, Jeff. Murder isn't something you can sweep under the rug. As for friendship . . . you haven't demonstrated very much of it here this morning yourself. Now you listen to me, and you listen good. I'll give you until this evening to come around to my office with the answers to this mess. If you don't show up, I'll be after you with a warrant for your arrest on the grounds of complicity. And one more thing, Jeff. Just who did you expect to meet last night when you went walking around town after you left Rube's card room?"

Stone's troubled gaze suddenly grew still upon Hank's face. "Did you follow me last night?" he asked, sounding more surprised than worried.

"Yep. I followed you. Who was he, Jeff?"

"Sorry, Hank."

"All right. You're going to be a heap sorrier if you don't think this over and come to the jailhouse by tonight with all the answers," said Hank, and turned, walked to the steps, and started on down toward the roadside gate leading out of Stone's yard. He was through the gate and turning right to head back uptown when Stone called softly to him from up on the porch.

"Hank, are you certain only two men rode into town?"

For a moment Hank looked back without speaking. This matter of the strangers seemed to have bothered Jeff more than anything else. "I'm sure," he said. Then he took a long chance and also said: "That other one . . . that third one . . . he's probably around, too, but being sly about it. You know, Jeff, if I were in your boots, I think I'd start carrying a gun, because, if what I'm beginning to believe is right . . . those ex-Rebs are here to kill someone, probably you."

Stone showed no more reaction to this statement than he'd shown to some of Hank's other remarks; he simply stood up there on his porch, gazing owlishly down where Hank was beginning to move again, and showed nothing, either in his stance or in his expression.

Hank swore under his breath and hiked along to the distant meeting of this side road and the main thoroughfare. As he turned the corner, heading northward, he nearly collided with someone hurrying southward. He nimbly side-stepped and looked around. It was Pat Malone and he said a trifle breathlessly: "I'm glad I found you. There's been some kind of a ruckus over at Rube's place. Come on."

Malone didn't allow Hank time even to shoot a question at him; he plucked at the marshal's arm and went hurrying back northward up the sidewalk in the direction from which he'd obviously just come hurrying along.

It was now high noon with a pale yellow sun directly above the town, with piling up heat striking out in the dusty roadway, and with a kind of lethargic somnolence everywhere except up in front of Rube Burrows's saloon, where several men, including rough Frank Leslie, were standing out on the plank walk talking.

As Malone and Hank came up, those idlers looked at the lawman. One of them in that bunched-up crowd said: "You better step easy in there, Marshal. Couple of curly wolves showin' their fangs."

XI

As Hank pushed past Rube's spindle doors, he caught sight of two lanky, bearded men with their backs to the bar, gazing straight out across the nearly empty room where Henry Helm and the rider known only as Starr were facing them across an upended table. Behind the bar, Rube Burrows was standing motionlessly, his homely face twisted with uncertainty and what looked to Hank like an expression of amazement.

Pat halted at the doorway but Hank strode on in. He was careful, however, not to step between those four men, and until he was well to the left of the bearded men, over in the direction of Rube, he didn't turn. But when he did, that was when he saw the two knives sticking in the wall no more than a foot from Starr's head, one on each side of the dark, Indian-looking Snowshoe rider.

Hank recognized the lanky bearded men, but when he spoke

it was to Helm and Starr. "Clear out," he said shortly. "Go on, you two . . . walk out of here."

Helm seemed to lose a little of his tightness. He said: "Sure, Marshal, only I don't like the notion of showing my back right now."

Helm was watching those two tall strangers as a man watches a pair of close-lying, coiled rattlesnakes. So was Starr, except that the swarthy, dark-eyed range rider had a disbelieving look on his face and he neither blinked nor spoke.

Hank twisted from the waist, wordlessly held out his hand toward Rube, and, as Burrows bent to scoop up a sawed-off shotgun from under the bar and hand it over, Hank said, bringing that murderous weapon to bear upon the strangers: "All right, Henry. You too, Starr. Outside."

The Snowshoe men gathered themselves up, turned, and stiffly marched out through Rube's swinging doors. For ten seconds after their departure, and with the barroom totally silent, Hank kept the riot gun upon those tall strangers. There was no one in the room excepting those two, Hank, and Rube Burrows. The outside noises of the town came in, but until Hank placed Rube's backbar weapon upon the bar top, making a slight, hard clatter as he did this, there was not a sound in the barroom.

"All right, fellers," said Hank to the big bearded men. "What was it all about?"

The nearest of the two men turned and put a calm, soft gaze over at Hank. "Nothing serious," he drawled, and completed his turn. "Better set 'em up, barman," he said to Rube. "Include yourself and the marshal here, too. He doesn't look so bad, but, barman, you sure look like you could use a drink."

The second bearded man also turned, but this one leaned sideward upon the bar in such a fashion that he could see from the corner of his eye whether anyone came through the roadside doors or not.

"Rube," said Hank as Burrows reached for a bottle and four glasses. "What started it?"

But Rube had not lived to get halfway into his forties by being vociferous at times like this, so he only shot Hank a reproving look and said: "Starr . . . you know how he sometimes gets . . . downed three or four straight shots, an' bumped one of these fellers. There was a few words . . . I wasn't standin' too close, Hank. . . ." Rube lifted his shoulders apologetically and let them fall.

The nearest lanky stranger said: "He took a swing at me, Marshal. I ducked under it and pushed him off. He went for his gun. I knocked him down, kicked the gun clear. He jumped up, run over to his pardner . . . that feller you called Helm . . . and made a grab for Helm's holster. My pardner here pinned Starr to the wall with a knife on each side of his head. That's all there was to it, Marshal, except that Mister Helm stood up like maybe he figured to buy in . . . so we told 'em to go ahead and die hard, if that's the way they wanted it. Then you walked in."

This lanky, gray-eyed, very calm, and drawling man slowly and genially smiled over at Hank. He seemed not the least disturbed by what he'd just come through.

"I reckon that half-breed-lookin' feller's had enough. Drink up, Marshal. Right nice of you to drop in when you did. I sort of had it figured, if we killed those two, that mean-lookin' cuss outside and his friends out there wouldn't have let us walk out of here alive. Much obliged, Marshal. Drink up an' have another one."

Hank didn't touch his glass. He swiveled his head to gaze at Rube. Burrows scarcely moved at all but he solemnly bobbed his head up and down, indicating that the tall stranger had told it exactly as it had happened.

Hank downed his drink, set the glass aside, and ran a look up and down the two bearded men. They were both over six feet tall. They were heavy-framed but slab-sided with the solid angularity of frontiersmen. Their eyes were calm and confident. What the rest of their features looked like Hank could only roughly surmise because of the dense, dark beards they wore. There was a difference between them; one seemed at least six or seven years older than the other, but in dress, mannerisms, even in speech and movement, they were alike.

The younger one made a motion for Rube to refill Hank's glass but Hank put his palm over the glass, saying: "Thanks just the same. One glass of Rube's rye whiskey a day is enough. They tell me miners use the stuff instead of explosives to melt rocks with."

The younger stranger smiled, showing even, large white teeth. He turned, left the bar, strolled over where those two big wicked knives were sticking in the wall, rocked them loose, and, when he faced back around, Hank could not see where he'd put them. He had a tied-down six-gun and a worn old leather shell belt, but there were no scabbards and no visible knives. As the stranger came ambling back to the bar, Hank said: "You know, in Wyoming, folks take a pretty dim view of knives."

"I don't blame 'em, Marshal," drawled the younger man, leaning back upon the bar again. "I don't like 'em too well myself. Thing is, when a feller don't want to kill someone . . . like that black-lookin' cowboy, for instance . . . knives sometimes work out a heap better'n guns."

Several of those outside range men drifted on back into the saloon. Frank Leslie was among them. Hank saw Leslie put a smoky gaze upon the two lanky men as he dropped down at a table. With him were Starr and Henry Helm. Neither of those two even looked over at Hank.

Leslie called out: "Rube, a bottle and three glasses over here!"

There was something brittle in Frank's voice. Hank heard it.

He also recognized the symptoms when he gazed over at Leslie's face. The west country cowman was building up to trouble. Hank said to the pair of bearded men: "Take a little walk with me, boys, outside in the sunshine. The air in here needs some clearing." He was standing away from the bar when a soft voice spoke behind and off to one side of him. He turned. Rita was standing in the card-room doorway. "Later," he said to her, and jerked his head at the tall strangers.

The three of them started on across the room. At the door Pat Malone still stood, quietly and efficiently looking around. Several more riders drifted in. The room was beginning to fill up again with its early drinkers and loafers. As Hank stepped around that table, watching the Snowshoe men, Frank Leslie lifted his smoldering gaze to the marshal's face. He seemed on the verge of speaking. Hank didn't give him a chance. He said: "Later, Frank. Just sit easy for now."

Leslie didn't say a word. Also with him at the table Starr and Henry Helm glanced upward as the two tall strangers went past. Those four men gazed steadily at one another until the strangers were past, then all the roiled tension began to dissipate. Over at the bar Rube sang out: "Drinks on the house, boys."

Hank stepped out through Rube's swinging doors, halted, and half turned, awaiting his companions. When they also emerged, he let out a long breath, considered the tall men critically, and stepped on down into the roadway's dust. "Across the way," he said, and added nothing to this by way of explanation. The strangers dutifully followed on over to the first store front south of Malone's livery barn where several benches stood, and finally halted as the lawman came fully around facing them. The eldest of those two, a man in his late forties, thinly smiled.

"Good maneuvering, Marshal," he said to Hank. "For a second back there I thought the mean-looking one at that table was going to make trouble."

"He's capable of it," said Hank dryly, meaning Frank Leslie. "You see, a couple of days ago some riders butchered one of his Snowshoe beeves at a little camp up in the foothills. He didn't like that."

"Can't exactly blame him," murmured the elder man, watching Hank's face closely.

"There's a little more," said Hank, returning that steady regard with a look just as close, just as intense. "Those butchers also left one of their friends lying dead up there . . . back-shot."

"Is that so?" said the older bearded man, his tone silky-soft. "Marshal, what exactly did you walk us over here to say?"

Hank stood there, gazing straight at those two. He took his time coming to a decision, then he said: "Who buried him, boys, and who shot him?"

Neither of the strangers showed any surprise. The older one said: "Marshal, we got no idea what you're talkin' about."

Pat Malone came strolling over. Pat had his gun on and he wore it with the aplomb of a man who was no novice with weapons. He halted just before stepping up onto the plank walk, cocked his head skeptically to one side, and said: "Hank, Frank Leslie's makin' war talk over there."

"I expect he is," said the lawman dryly. "Pat, take a real close look at these two."

Pat gently inclined his head. "I already did," he said, and put his candid gaze straight up at the older of those two strangers. "How are you, Captain? It's been a long time."

The bearded stranger stood like stone, gazing back at Pat. "You sure you haven't made a mistake?" he asked quietly.

"Plumb sure, Captain, plumb sure. When you and your friend rode into my livery barn, I had my doubts, but not now I haven't. You're Captain William Saint George, even with that beard. You remember me, Captain?"

The gray-eyed, handsome man stared at Pat for an interval of total silence before finally saying softly: "I remember you, Mister Malone. I remembered you the moment I rode into your barn and dismounted. Yes, you're right, it's been a long time."

Malone drifted his gaze on over to Hank. "Captain William Saint George," he said. "Formerly of the Confederate States Army. Captain, this here is Hank Herman, marshal of Conifer and generally the law for these parts."

St. George nodded gravely to Hank. "Pleasant meeting you," he said, and a little ironic twinkle appeared in his eyes. "Especially when you walked into that saloon right when you did."

Hank didn't return that faint smile. He said: "All right, Captain, I've been looking forward to this meeting. Now I'd like the answers to some questions, if you don't mind."

St. George might not have heard for all the indication he gave of it. He motioned toward the younger, equally as tall and lanky man with him. "This is Dave Pemberton, gentlemen. Also late of the Confederate States Army."

Pemberton nodded but said nothing. He kept his eyes on Hank as though expecting something unpleasant to come from that quarter.

"Why was Sergeant Burris killed?" Hank asked without any additional preliminaries. "Who shot him in the back, Captain?"

St. George regarded Hank stonily without at once answering. Ultimately though he said: "Marshal, do you propose to arrest me?"

Hank frowned. "Not right this minute I don't."

"In that case," said St. George, "thanks for walking into the saloon over yonder when you did, and . . . good day, gentlemen."

St. George was moving when Hank said: "Hold it, Captain. It's not going to be that easy. I'll arrest you if I have to, and

Pemberton along with you, unless you give me some answers."

St. George was at the edge of the plank walk when he halted and turned back. "Are you sure you want to know who killed Sergeant Burris?" he asked thinly, his eyes darkening and his lips drawing out thin.

"Dead sure," said Hank.

"All right, Marshal. Then you go on over to that saloon and ask that mean-looking man who walked in after our altercation with those two cowboys."

"Frank Leslie?" asked Hank incredulously.

St. George nodded, jerked his head at Dave Pemberton, and hiked on over to the hitch rack in front of the Trailhand where the two of them briefly halted, briefly spoke, and split up, St. George heading southward to Stone's store, Pemberton stepping northward as far as the edge of the shade out front of Rube's saloon, where he settled his wide shoulders against the building front, crossed both arms across his chest, and stood gazing over where Malone and Hank still stood watching all this.

"Trouble's coming," breathed Pat. "Pemberton's takin' sentry watch over there."

Hank stepped backward to the bench and eased down upon it. "Leslie," he said quietly. "They're waiting for Frank Leslie to walk out of Rube's place."

"You goin' to let 'em do it, Hank?"

Malone got no immediate answer to this. Hank sat there digesting what Captain St. George had said. He didn't actually believe Frank Leslie had killed Harold Burris and yet he could find enough supporting evidence to support the possibility. For one thing Burris had been shot on Leslie's range. For another, if Leslie had stumbled onto that butchered Snowshoe beef and Burris at the same time, being a violent, quick-tempered man, it was entirely possible he'd have called Burris. But whatever else

Frank Leslie was, Hank did not consider him a bushwhacker. If he and Burris had fought, Burris might have died, but he wouldn't have been shot in the back. That wasn't Frank Leslie's way.

Hank looked over where Pemberton was standing, his long frame in its travel-stained attire blending with the front of Rube Burrows's saloon. He swung his attention southward to where Captain St. George had disappeared into Jeff Stone's store. He had to make a choice between covering two places at the same time, so he stood up and said briskly: "Pat, you sit here and wait until Saint George comes out of Stone's store, then go down there and tell that old gaffer who is Jeff's chief clerk I said for him to tell you exactly what the captain wanted. Then go on back to your stable and I'll see you there after a while."

"Sure enough," agreed Pat. "And what'll you be doing? Stopping Pemberton's scheme to precipitate a massacre when Frank and his boys walk out over there?"

"Exactly."

"Well," said Malone, also gazing over at Pemberton and getting back the same kind of a stare from the lanky, bearded ex-Confederate, "if you want my opinion, Hank, this is entirely too neat to be accidental."

"That," confided Hank shortly, "is exactly what I'm thinking. Pemberton wouldn't tackle Frank, Henry Helm, and Starr by himself. I'm guessing that third one's around here somewhere, lying low with his carbine up and ready. I'll give you odds they planned it like this before those two even rode into town, just in case someone recognized them, or made trouble. Somewhere around here there's a rifle zeroed in on whoever starts for either Pemberton or Saint George."

"It was zeroed in on you 'n' me about ten minutes ago," agreed Pat dryly. "Which is as close as I like to come to gettin' blasted outen my boots without even knowin' it was likely to happen."

"Move out when Saint George leaves the store, Pat," ordered the marshal, and stepped forward out into the roadway, heading across to the Trailhand.

The roadway had its usual midday traffic passing in and out of town. There were a few riders passing along, too, but mostly this traffic consisted of wagons in from the outlying cow outfits, some freighters grinding along through pulverized dust, and the usual passers-by on foot, generally women with sunbonnets on and carrying market baskets on their arms. Altogether the scene was a homely, peaceful one, unless a person happened to sight lanky Dave Pemberton standing over there with his bearded, hard-set face and his narrowed eyes shaded by his hat brim.

Pemberton watched Hank all the way across the road. When the lawman stepped up onto the plank walk, heading straight for Rube Burrows's spindle-doors, his intention obvious, Pemberton stirred, but he did not move to make an interception as Hank half thought he might. Instead, he followed Hank with his eyes until the marshal was lost to his sight when he entered the barroom.

XII

At the sight of Hank coming through Burrows's front door, the lively talk in Rube's saloon dwindled down almost to a whisper. Frank Leslie was still sitting with Helm and Starr at the same table. All three of them watched Hank. He briefly regarded them, then passed over where Rube was leaning across his bar talking to some cowboys. Rube drew upright, padded southward to where Hank halted, and leaned over again.

"There's trouble building," said Hank quietly to Burrows. "I want a little help from you."

"Sure," said the barman. "What, specifically?"

"I'm going to herd Leslie and his riders out of here through the back alley door, Rube. I want you to go out there and have a good look around."

Rube made no immediate move off the bar. He puckered up his eyes and thoughtfully considered Hank's face. "There were only two of those lanky fellers. Why don't you let Frank's crew teach 'em some manners?"

"I've got my reasons. You going to do like I asked or not?"

"Sure I'm going to. Nothing to get fired up about." Rube eased upright, gazed over where the Snowshoe men were steadily watching them from over near the door, and said: "It's got somethin' to do with that stranger you secretly buried, hasn't it?"

"I didn't bury him, Rube, and someday someone's going to grab that nosy big beak of yours and twist hell out of it, for your sticking it where it's got no business. Now go on out back, make darned sure there's no sniper lying in wait back there, and, when you come back, I'll be over at Frank's table. You just nod to me if the route is clear."

Burrows turned and shambled off. Hank waited a moment for the desultory conversation to start up again, then he strolled over, spun out a chair at Leslie's table, and dropped down astraddle it. Leslie, Henry Helm, and Starr stared at him.

Leslie said: "If I'd come up a couple of minutes sooner, it wouldn't have ended like that. Who the hell do those bushy-faced brushpoppers think they are, anyway, pickin' on my riders?"

"Ask Starr," said Hank dryly. "One of 'em could've pinned his ears to the wall."

"We don't need any preachin' from you," snarled dark and troublesome Frank Leslie.

"You aren't getting any preaching, Frank, you're getting sound advice. Get up from this table and walk out of here . . .

through the back alleyway door."

"What! You think I'm runnin' out because a couple of . . . ?"

"You're not running out, Frank. None of you is," said Hank coldly, breaking into the angry rush of words from Leslie. "You're going to walk out of here like I said. Then you're going south to the first roadway and walk west on over to my jailhouse. I want to talk to the three of you."

Leslie's jaw hung slack as he intently watched Hank's face. "Are you tryin' to arrest us?" he eventually said. "Hank, by God, this town's never had a. . . ."

"It's got one now," said Hank brusquely. "It's got a lawman who'll arrest you or anyone else if he has to."

"Arrest . . . ? What the hell for?" said Henry Helm, jarred out of his heretofore silence by dawning understanding of what Hank and Frank Leslie were talking about. "Hank, you can't be serious about arrestin' Frank an' us."

"Serious as I've ever been in my life, Henry," replied Hank, and caught movement over at the bar where Rube had returned and was standing, nodding his head up and down. "Now the three of you get up, do like I just told you, and don't do anything foolish."

Frank Leslie didn't move. Neither did the other two. Leslie said: "Hank, so help me you're askin' for serious trouble."

There was no mistaking the threat and the promise in the cowman's voice. Hank heard this and heeded it. "Get up," he snapped. "Get up and make it look real natural as you cross over and go out the back door into the alleyway."

"Listen," said dark, Indian-like Starr. "If you figure we ain't got the guts to walk out that front door just because them two. . . ."

"Shut up, Starr. Frank, you lead out. Get up now and move or you'll wish you had."

Leslie's thick shoulders rose a little, curved inward a little as his hands below the table top gently moved. He was glaring wrathfully at Hank; he was ready to fight and willing to do so.

Hank's expression was sardonic. "Don't try it," he warned. "I'll cut you in two from under this table, Frank. I've had my gun trained on your belly ever since I sat down here. Now get up!"

Leslie's nostrils noticeably quivered and his shoulders stopped moving. For two long seconds he dueled Hank with his fiery eyes, then very slowly and stiffly he stood up. Both Helm and Starr followed their employer's example. When Leslie stepped back, turned, and started walking on across the room, the other two followed after him.

Hank was the last one to arise and he didn't have his six-gun drawn at all. As he moved out, his eyes crossed with the wondering regard of Rube Burrows. Hank dolorously wagged his head. It had been a close thing, back there at that table.

Leslie was the first to hit the alleyway. Next was Starr and the final Snowshoe man to leave the Trailhand by this unorthodox route was Henry Helm. Hank jerked his head sideways. "Walk south like I said," he ordered. "And no monkeyshines, keep those right hands swinging easy-like."

Leslie uttered a sizzling oath. "You think you're preventin' a gunfight, don't you?" he snarled without looking back.

"No, Frank. I think I'm keeping you from being killed."

"Hell," spat out Leslie. "Those two . . . we'd eat up five like 'em for breakfast."

"Well, there're not five of them, Frank, but there are three. All you met were two of 'em. The third one's hiding out somewhere. He'd cut you in two the second you stepped out that front door into the roadway, and you'd never even see him."

Starr and Henry Helm swung to stare incredulously. Starr

said: "Three of 'em, Marshal? You mean it's some kind of a trap?"

"Yeah," growled Hank. "Slow down, Frank, we're getting near the end of the alley. Now turn right and, when you hit the roadway yonder, step out and keep right on going until you're at the jailhouse. Walk on in and remember what I said . . . no monkeyshines."

But now Henry Helm was suddenly turning suspicious. "Hold up, Frank," he said to Leslie who was several paces ahead. "If there's a hide-out gunman around in the roadway somewhere, how do we know we aren't bein' led right out to him?"

Starr muttered something about the possibility of this, too, and Hank snorted at them both. "Hell, a minute ago you were ready to chew up dragons and spit out scales. Where'd all that fire go, fellers? Frank, keep moving."

Leslie did, even swaggered a little as he swung right and walked straight out into Conifer's southward main roadway. He looked northward, up toward the Trailhand Saloon. So did the others, including Hank, but they were quite some distance southward, and to compound that no one expected them to show up where Hank herded them on across and into his jailhouse.

They were probably seen by Pemberton. Perhaps even by Captain St. George, too, and conceivably by that unseen third ex-Rebel Hank felt certain was somewhere close by watching, but no one called down to them. In fact, as nearly as Hank could determine when he hesitated at the jailhouse doorway for a searching look northward, no one was paying the slightest attention to them.

"Well," snapped Frank Leslie to Hank, when the latter stepped in, closed the door, and put his back to it. "Now what . . . you simpleton? Do you know what you've accomplished? You've made the three of us look like fools before the whole blessed town."

Hank rested his hand upon his holstered gun. "Maybe I did, Frank," he replied, giving Leslie glare for glare. "But one thing I didn't make you look like . . . a murderer."

Leslie's fierce look faded. He very slowly locked his jaw hard, hooked both thumbs in his shell belt, and stared. He was waiting. He was ready to fight, willing to fight, but he was waiting for Hank to say all of it before he went into action. Off to one side stood Henry Helm and Starr. Those two were gazing over at Hank as though he'd just said something too preposterous for credence, as though they marveled at his irresponsibility for making such an incredible statement.

"You told me about finding Burris and your butchered beef, Frank. You even rode all the way into Conifer to tell me what you'd found out there. Why didn't you make it more believable, Frank? Why didn't you just say you caught a rustler butchering a Snowshoe critter and shot him? I'd have believed that, at least until I'd seen that hole in his back."

Leslie's swarthy face got shades darker as blood poured in under his cheeks. His eyes, instead of showing fire, showed a very lethal opaqueness. They got milky and flat with a hard glaze to them. Frank Leslie was going to try to kill a man now.

"I could believe all of it except the shooting of Burris in the back, Frank. That I had a tough time swallowing. Why did you kill him?"

Leslie said quietly: "Are you through?"

Hank nodded. "I'm through."

"Then by God, you'd better go for your gun, Hank. No man calls me a murderer like you just did. No man."

Hank drew in a thin breath and let it back out. He knew, standing less than fifteen feet apart and being probably equally as swift with guns, neither he nor Frank Leslie was going to walk away from this.

"Sure," he said, "I'll draw on you, Frank, but, first, tell me why you shot Burris in the back."

"I didn't shoot him in the back, you dirty son-. . . ."

"Rope that kind of talk, Frank. Do you know a man named Captain William Saint George? He told me you killed Burris."

Leslie's glazed-over stare suddenly widened. "Saint George," he whispered. "William Saint George? He was there?"

"Frank, behind that beard on the older man in Rube's place this afternoon is Captain Saint George."

Leslie seemed now to be losing a lot of his starchy stiffness. He kept staring unbelievingly at Hank. "You're a liar," he whispered. "Saint George is dead. He was killed at Sabine Pass during the war. I read it in a newspaper eight years ago. Saint George is dead."

Hank shook his head. "That was him in the saloon this afternoon. Frank, I don't know why you killed Burris, but I can tell you this, just from talking a few minutes to Saint George and Dave Pemberton . . . they know you killed Burris and they aren't going to let it go past. Now you'd better tell me why you did it."

But Frank Leslie, the hardened range man whose reputation for brawling and being disagreeable was a legend in the Conifer country, didn't say another word. He turned, groped to a chair, and sank down upon it.

Hank looked at him. So did his two riders, Helm and Starr. Those two looked speechless and bewildered. They eventually ran an inquiring look over at Hank, but he ignored them.

"Why, Frank?"

Leslie sat there, looking blankly straight ahead at the yonder wall. A little muscle in the side of his left cheek twitched. He acted as though the others were miles away, as though he were entirely alone with some consuming private thoughts.

"Did you know Burris was Harriett Stone's brother, Frank? That he'd written Jeff and Harriett that he was coming here?"

Leslie looked up with an effort. "Harriett Stone's . . . brother?"

Hank inclined his head. "That's right. There were four of them . . . Burris, Pemberton, Saint George, and one other. They were in the hills. You knew that. You had to know that, Frank. The tracks were at their camp where you shot Burris."

"No," said Leslie hoarsely. "I only saw Burris. I didn't see any tracks. I didn't look for any. I rode onto him peggin' out that hide. I didn't even recognize him when he jumped up and went for his gun. I beat him to the draw but missed with my first shot because my horse shied. He spun around trying to aim. That's when my second slug hit him . . . in the back."

Hank waited a moment, then looked at Starr and Henry Helm. "Go on back to the ranch," he told those two. "I'm locking Frank up for tonight." Hank sounded tired. "It's more for his own protection than because of the Burris killing. Go on back, you two."

XIII

A half hour after Starr and Helm left the jailhouse, Pat Malone came in. He seemed mildly surprised to see Frank Leslie sitting across the little office unarmed and looking upset, and, although Malone was obviously anxious to talk, he did not do so until Hank urged him to, saying that Leslie wouldn't interfere with whatever they had to say to one another because Hank was going to lock Frank up in one of his jail cells.

"What for?" asked Pat, bewildered.

"Murder. Frank's the one who plugged Sergeant Burris."

"Frank?" said Malone, looking astonished. "In the back?"

"He says Burris went for his gun and whipped around as he fired, that the slug caught Burris in the back by accident."

Pat stood, staring over at Leslie, who was slumped over on his chair paying neither of the little room's other two occupants the slightest heed.

"Out with it," said Hank. "What was Saint George doing over at the store?"

Malone swung toward Hank but he still looked strongly doubtful. "He asked where Jeff was."

"And?"

"That old gaffer who is Jeff's head man told Saint George that Jeff hadn't shown up today, that Miss Harriett was ill abed an' Jeff stayed home with her."

Hank got up out of his chair but Malone, anticipating his reason for this, said: "Never mind. I went round to Jeff's place an' Saint George wasn't there. I went back to my barn and both their horses were gone. I reckon they rode on out of town while I was asking questions at the store. Anyway, they aren't here. I even looked in up at Rube's place."

Hank stood silently thoughtful. If the ex-Rebels were gone from town, then it meant they had a camp somewhere close by, because he was certain they'd be back and before too long. He was convinced that St. George was on the track of that buried money, had traced it here to Conifer, and would therefore return.

"Well?" said Pat, becoming impatient. "What's next?"

"For you, nothing. At least not until tonight. Then I've got a feeling you and I'd better stake out Jeff's house. Maybe Saint George doesn't know yet that Jeff knows about that money, or maybe he's already found that out. But either way, he's going to try and see Jeff. We know that because he's already tried to see him. What's worrying me now is what he'll do to Jeff when he does meet him."

"Yeah," murmured Malone. "So you an' I'll be on hand tonight when he comes back . . . if he comes back."

Hank turned and put a wondering glance over at dejected Frank Leslie. "Frank," he said, "I'm going to lock you up to keep them from killing you. Maybe you're involved in this some way. Right now, I neither know nor care, particularly, but I don't want any more killings in town. You understand?"

Leslie nodded and looked up. "Are you plumb sure that Burris was Harriett Stone's brother?" he asked. Hank nodded, and Pat Malone looked startled but he didn't interrupt when Hank said: "I'm sure of it. Tell me something, Frank, why didn't you tell the truth about that killing?"

"You saw where that slug hit Burris," said Leslie. "Who'd ever believe it happened like it did? Even now, after I've told you the truth, you don't believe me. I got a standin' in the country. I got investments here. What'd folks say if they thought I bushwhacked a man? Even a danged stranger . . . but now, if Burris was Harriett's brother instead of just an ex-Confed drifter. . . ." Leslie wagged his head back and forth and dropped his eyes again without finishing his last sentence.

"I didn't say I didn't believe that's how it happened, Frank," retorted the marshal. "But I've got plenty of reason to believe Saint George and his friends won't believe it, so come on, I'm going to lock you up."

As Leslie arose and allowed himself to be herded on through to Hank's cell room, Pat Malone eased down on a chair and sat quietly until Hank returned. Then he said: "Did Jeff bury him?" He meant Harold Burris. "That's got me plumb puzzled."

Hank tossed down the key ring to his cells and humped up his shoulders, let them fall, and said: "Damned if I know. He says he didn't."

"Do you believe him?"

Another shrug from Hank. "I'll tell you this much, Pat. When Jeff told me that, I looked at his hands. He's soft as punk wood, you know that. The hardest work he's done in years is count money."

"Well, what of that?"

"No blisters, Pat. No ingrained dirt in his hands and no blisters from digging a hole."

Malone's eyes gradually brightened. "Then he didn't dig that grave."

"I told you . . . I don't know whether he did or not."

Pat got up, shaking his head. "I got to get back," he mumbled. "Alfie hasn't shown up yet an' the barn's unattended."

Hank turned, opened the door for Malone to pass through, and said: "I'll walk on up there with you."

They left the jailhouse, which Hank carefully locked from the outside, and sauntered northward up through dazzling sunshine to the livery barn. There, as they turned in, Pat let off a loud oath and called shrilly at a vague shadow down through the barn's gloomy interior.

"Alfie, confound it, where you been?"

The shadow shuffled forward almost to where that hurting sunlight struck inward, but stopped short to stand, peering forward and making sniffling sounds. Alfie didn't say anything; he just stood there, looking more unkempt and disreputable than ever.

Hank felt pity for the hostler as well as disgust. Alfie had obviously been on one of his shattering drunks. Pat darkly scowled, turned toward the office door, and muttered: "Oh, forget it. Go out back and wash up, then go on up into your loft an' sleep it off."

Alfie shuffled away as Hank followed the liveryman into the office, then both of them stopped dead still and staring. Rita was standing in there with dingy shadows around her.

She said—"Hello."—and faintly smiled past Malone at Hank. "I'd just about given you up."

Malone moved uncertainly aside. He was an unmarried man with most of the inhibitions of his middle years still with him. He strongly admired beautiful women, but was quite at a loss as to how to act, what to say, even how to look, when he was unexpectedly confronted by one. But that didn't matter. Rita clearly wasn't the slightest bit interested in Pat Malone. She moved slightly to go over closer to Hank and say: "I went to the saloon as Pat asked me to, and I didn't have any trouble at all getting the younger of those two bearded men to smile at me. The one called Dave. But the other one . . . the really handsome one . . . he just stood there, studying me as though I were something from another world."

"To him you probably were," murmured Hank, feeling those masculine hungers rising up in him at her nearness, the way they always did when she was near. "Did you see the argument start?"

Rita inclined her head. "I saw it, and afterward I heard them tell you about it, too, from the card-room doorway. But they overlooked two minor details, Hank. The one called Dave let Starr go for his gun deliberately, before he knocked him down. I don't think I ever saw a man who could move as fast as Dave can in my life. And the handsome, older one, when Starr and Helm were going to fight them from over by the door, that one said . . . 'Either one of you touch your weapons and you'll get what your boss gave a friend of ours, a slug in the back.' "

Malone's jaw sagged. He stared at Rita, then slowly looked up at Hank. "There's your proof," he said softly. "There was another one."

"Outside in the crowd of riders on the plank walk," agreed Hank. "I'll be damned. Well, it's a good thing for Helm and Starr they didn't try for Big Casino."

Malone backed up and eased down upon his desk top. "Cold as ice and calculatin' as they come," he said. "That Saint George must've been quite an officer. He doesn't miss any bets at all when he gambles, does he?"

"You'd try not to miss any too, Pat, if you were gambling with your life," replied Hank dryly, "which is exactly what he's doing."

"One more thing," said Rita. "I was going down to the café when they rode out of town. They went south, and. . . ."

"South?" blurted out Malone, screwing up his face. "That doesn't make sense. They got reason to ride north, not south."

Hank put a caustic gaze over at the liveryman. "You wouldn't expect anyone who thinks they might be trailed to head straight for their real camp, would you, Pat?"

Malone considered this and fell silent.

"What else?" Hank asked the lovely girl. "You were about to say something else?"

"Well, the same time they left town heading southward, *querido*, there was another rider heading northward out of town. I watched this one, too, because, you see, I know almost every man in Conifer, and that one also was a stranger to me."

"Lots of men ride out of town," murmured Malone.

"No," said Rita. "This was the only one riding north right then, and he. . . ."

"Had a beard," breathed Hank, anticipating Rita's next remark. She nodded up at him.

"Yes, *querido*, that one also had a beard."

Hank started to speak, suddenly froze motionlessly where he stood, remained like that for a long second, then whipped around with surprising speed, jumped out through the office door, and left Pat and Rita dumbfounded. Those two, hearing a scuffle out in the runway, went over and also left the office.

Hank was standing out there in the barn's gloomy center, holding old Alfie with one arm. The hostler was writhing and straining to get free.

Hank looked over at Malone. "Listening," he said. "I heard him move. He was standing flat against the office front wall, listening, Pat."

Hank gave old Alfie a rough shove over toward Malone. Pat wrinkled his brow and stared uncomprehendingly at the old derelict. He said—"What the hell, Alfie?"—in a mumbling and uncertain way. "I thought I told you to go up to your loft an' sleep it off."

The hostler's wet eyes swam from Pat to Rita and back over his shoulder at Hank. He seemed frantic to get away, seemed all unstrung by this totally unexpected occurrence.

"Alfie," said Pat gently, "you don't look like you usually do when you come off one of your rip-roarers." Malone stopped speaking but kept staring at the older man. Finally in a strengthening tone of voice he said: "What the hell have you been up to? Alfie, where have you been the last twenty-four hours? What've you been doin', you old soak?"

But Alfie only stood there, looking like a trapped animal without offering a word of defense.

Hank stepped up and halted beside the hostler. Without saying anything, he took Alfie's right hand and held it up to the weak light of this dingy place. The hand was soiled with ingrained dirt and it had blisters on the palm, small ones because Alfie's hands were accustomed to light manual labor, but blisters nevertheless. Hank dropped the hand and stared over at Pat, still saying nothing. Malone stepped back and leaned upon his office front, staring at his hostler. After a long time he whispered: "You, Alfie? It never occurred to me you could be involved. You buried him, Alfie? Why?"

While the emaciated, watery-eyed hostler still stood there, looking desperate but with his lips tightly locked, Hank said: "Alfie, make it easy on yourself. Listen to me a minute. My jail-house this time of year is like a sweatbox. I can hold you twenty-four hours without any charges, and, if I did that, believe me, you'd die a hundred deaths because it's hotter'n hell in those cells. It'd sweat you down to a pulp. I don't want to do that . . . so talk. Why did you steal Burris's body and bury it?"

Words broke past Alfie's lips in a hoarse rush. "He was dead, wasn't he? You fellers had no right to leave a dead man lyin' in a lousy livery barn with a dirty old piece of canvas over him like that. He deserved better'n that. He was a good man, a brave, true man, an' you left him lyin' in the dirt like he was a . . . a dead animal of some kind."

Alfie was panting, his watery eyes filled with tears and he dashed a hand along under his leaky nose as he flashed a wild-eyed, desperate, and defiant look around at Hank and Pat Malone, and even over at white-faced Rita.

Hank let his breath out in a long, soft sigh and gazed at Malone without speaking. Malone was staring incredulously at his hostler. Finally he whispered: "Alfie, by God, you were one of them. I know you now. I thought when you first showed up here that there was something vaguely familiar about you. You were Captain Saint George's orderly. You were the one who always hung back and kept to yourself. Good Lord, Alfie, you've changed."

Alfie sniffled and flung half around so as not to have to look at Pat Malone's staring eyes. He seemed to want to run away, seemed about to do so, too, except that Hank was there, barring any sudden movement he might make.

It was Rita who spoke next. She said in a very soft tone of voice: "Alfie, come over to Rube's with me. I'll make you a good warm meal. You need some decent food." She stretched out her hand to the quaking wreck of a man and touched him. Alfie stiffened at that touch but did not lift his head or speak.

Hank put a hand lightly, gently upon the old derelict's shoulder. "Alfie, you were one of Saint George's men who came here for remounts during the war, weren't you?"

Alfie barely nodded his head in confirmation of this. "And you knew Sergeant Burris?"

Another of those barely perceptible nods raised and lowered the drunkard's head. He sniffled and drew away from Rita's touch. "I knew him well," he murmured. "He was a fine man. Strong and true. He never said anythin' about it when I got drunk, just left me alone. He understood, did Sergeant Burris. He knew what it was like to see your home burned with your loved ones in it. He knew why a man drank. He was a fine man, a fine man."

XIV

For a little while there was total silence in the livery barn as each of those four people standing there in front of Malone's combination harness room and office considered their private thoughts. Outside, the brilliant sun brightly shone and people passed back and forth upon the yonder walkways. Wagons, riders, and buggies moved in and out of light and shadow, and occasionally men's voices, raised for one reason or another, floated mutedly inward, striking the awareness of those four people.

Hank said: "Alfie, what's it all about? Was it the buried gold that brought them all back here?"

"Yes, it was the money."

"But Alfie, why now? Why so many years after the war?"

"So many years," mumbled the hostler, at last raising his eyes to Hank's face. "The war was yesterday, Marshal. No. No, it was day before yesterday. Yesterday was the time it took Cap'n Saint George to find the others. Him an' me, we were together when it ended. He told me to come back here as soon as we got out of the prisoner camp, and stay here. To watch an' listen, and keep tabs, an' as soon as he could find the others he'd fetch 'em all here an' we'd dig it up an' divide it."

"I see," said Hank quietly, still with his hand lightly lying upon the old derelict's shoulder. "It took this long to find all the others, Alfie?"

"Yes. They were scattered an' the Cap'n, he got bad hurt by Yankee cavalry at Sabine Pass. He almost died. It took time for him to get fit again. It took more time for him to find the others. Two of 'em he never did find."

"Alfie," said Pat Malone. "Did the captain send you money?"

"Yes, when he was able he'd send me money in the mail. Him and Sergeant Burris both. Fine men, the pair of 'em. And now that dirty, black-lookin' Frank Leslie's went an' killed the sergeant. Murdered him, shot him in the back because the sergeant wouldn't tell him where it was hid."

Hank and Pat Malone exchanged a quick, startled look. Hank said: "Alfie, Frank Leslie says he accidentally shot Burris in the back. That Burris was going for his gun when Frank shot him."

"That's a damned lie. Excuse me, Miss Rita. I didn't mean to cuss in front of you. But that's a black lie. You ask the captain. Him and Dave saw the shootin' as they were ridin' back down through the forest. They tried to catch Leslie afterward but he rode like the wind for town. But they saw it, Marshal, and it was plain murder."

"All right," Hank said soothingly. "I'll ask the captain. But tell me, Alfie, how did Leslie know about the buried money?"

Alfie shook his head despondently. "I don't know," he muttered. "But he knew all right. He even went up to our old camp the night after he shot Sergeant Burris and dug around up there, figurin', if we were back in the country, we were after it, too, an' he figured to beat us to it. He knew all right." Alfie suddenly straightened up and his eyes flashed with the quick fire they had once showed often enough in the fury of battle. "But Leslie's days are marked, Marshal. He did a vile thing and Cap'n Saint George isn't the kind to overlook that . . . ever.

Neither am I. Neither is Dave Pemberton or Gifford Bragg. One of us'll get him for that. He won't. . . ."

"Gifford Bragg, Alfie?" asked Hank. "Is he the other one, the one who came to town with Pemberton and Saint George today?"

"Yes, Giff's the one. Canister tore out some muscles in his left leg. Giff limps because of that. But he's death with either hand, Marshal, when it comes to guns. And Giff was Hal Burris's pardner all through the war. Like brothers they were. You wait an' see. Leslie's days are marked now, damn him."

Hank stood quietly for a long time, putting pieces of this strange business together. He remembered, this morning, seeing Frank Leslie ride into town with Starr and Henry Helm, and he also remembered wondering why Frank brought those two with him because he'd rarely ever known Frank to ride to Conifer with his cowboys. Also, he knew now why Frank had gone to pieces when he'd learned that Burris had not been alone; he knew the instant Hank had told him the other former Confederates were also in the country, that he'd made a fatal error in shooting Burris. Finally Hank had the answer to who had dug that fresh hole up at the old cavalry bivouac he and Pat had found the day before.

Pat Malone, speaking to Alfie, caught Hank's attention and brought it back to the present. Pat was asking questions. He said: "Alfie, where does Jeff Stone fit in?"

"Mister Stone was our contact here in the Conifer country," responded the hostler. "He was a Southern sympathizer. He was the one we were supposed to see first when we arrived here. Sergeant Burris was his brother-in-law, an' as soon as we'd scouted the countryside an' found it safe for Confederate soldiers, Sergeant Burris rode in one night and made the contact. The very next night Stone come out to our camp. He told us who we dared trust and who didn't dast put no faith in.

He even told us Mister Malone here'd sell us horses, and Frank Leslie, too. He. . . ."

"He also knew about the gold you fellers were carrying, didn't he?" Hank broke in to ask.

Alfie looked around. "Knew about it," he responded. "Why, Mister Stone was our intermediary." Hank and Pat looked puzzled, and Alfie, seeing this, said: "You didn't know, did you?"

"Know what?" asked Pat.

"We didn't just come here to buy horses. We were on a secret mission for the Confederate government. We weren't just run-o'-the-mill Reb cavalrymen. Why, Cap'n Will Saint George was one of our best Intelligence agents. He was entrusted to deliver the operatin' gold to our agents on the West Coast."

Hank and Pat, even Rita Malone, still were gazing wonderingly at him, so Alfie smiled at them. It was the first time Hank had ever seen the old derelict smile; he thought it made old Alfie seem twenty years younger, as he surely must have once been, a good-looking, self-respecting man of principles and high ideals. "You still don't understand," he said. "All right, I'll explain. The Confederacy needed foreign troops, foreign alliances, but most of all we needed foreign armament. We couldn't get credit and we lacked the cash. But, if we'd gotten control of California's goldfields, you see, we could've financed our war with gold and won it. Anyway I think we could've won it. But there were Yankee sympathizers thick as fleas on a dog's back in California. They knew what we were tryin' to accomplish an' they had soldiers guardin' every road to the Coast. So, Cap'n Saint George was sent up here to Wyoming with the gold. He was to leave it with our contact in Conifer, and later, when they could safely do it, the secret agents from the West Coast were to come here, get the gold, go back, and buy or bribe their way into places of power so a road could be opened for an eventual Confederate invasion of California. Now do you understand?"

Hank understood; so did Pat and Rita. But not a one of them uttered a sound. What had just been disclosed to them was so daring, so feasible, so startling, that they simply stood there gazing at whiskey-soaked Alfie, the derelict.

Finally Pat said in a whisper: "The saints be praised. Alfie, just how much gold was there?"

Alfie shook his head. "I don't know. Even though I was the cap'n's striker an' he trusted me with his life, he never talked about the money with any of us. We knew what we were doing in Wyoming . . . using that horse buyin' as our excuse for bein' here . . . but we never talked about our real reason even among ourselves."

Hank said: "Did Captain Saint George give the gold to Jeff Stone?"

Alfie nodded. "That he did, Marshal. I know that for a fact because I helped pack it down here in the dead o' the night and take it down under Mister Stone's store and bury it there in the cellar while the others stayed outside on watch with their guns."

Hank walked around Alfie over to a nail keg in front of Pat's office and sank down there. For a while he sat and said nothing. When Rita walked over to stand close beside him, Hank raised his head and gazed at her.

"Now you know," he said to her. "Now you know the whole story. Why I was interested in that gold coin you showed me. Why I felt there had to be more than just a simple case of back-shooting to that killing."

She smiled down into his eyes. "You haven't mentioned the most important thing I had to know, Hank. That you weren't lazy and shiftless and content to drift along through life with nothing to hold to, nothing to believe in. That's what I've been waiting three years to find out about you."

He showed her an ironic faint light in his gaze and said: "Are you sure you've found out that I do have principles, Rita? How do you know I'm not looking for an easy way out of this mess right now?"

She brushed his bronzed cheek with her fingertips. "You're not, *querido*. A woman knows about things like that once she's seen her man in action. You're not looking for a way out at all. You're looking for a way to avenge one man's life and perhaps save a second man's life as well."

"Who's the second man, Rita?"

"Jeff Stone. Do you want me to tell you what you're wondering? You're wondering whether or not these bearded men won't also want to kill Stone if they discover that he doesn't still have all that money."

Hank looked over where Pat Malone was watching them and listening. Pat solemnly inclined his head. "She hit the nail flush on the head," he said to Hank. "And you're not the only one who's wonderin' about that."

Alfie shuffled his feet over where he stood a few feet from Malone. He was listening now, and at these remarks about Stone he became quietly alert. When he saw Hank cast a glance over at him, the hostler said: "He wouldn't do that. Mister Stone wouldn't do anything with that money."

No one said anything in rebuttal, but Hank stood up, slapped his leg, and looked down into Rita's eyes with his expression troubled and sardonic. "You'd better go now," he said to her. "I wish we could go buggy riding, Rita, but for the next day or so I reckon that's plumb out. And, Rita, don't say anything. Particularly don't breathe a word of this where Rube'll hear you."

"Trust me, *querido*," she softly said, stood upon her tiptoes, and planted a quick, light kiss squarely upon Hank's lips. She then dropped back down, turned, and walked on out of Pat Malone's barn.

Hank, with difficulty, swung back to the two men standing

there, watching him. To Alfie he said: "Have you seen Captain Saint George today?"

"I was here when he and Dave came for their horses. I talked to them last night, too, before they came into Conifer. I told them I'd taken care of Sergeant Burris and they told me they knew who killed him."

"Where'll they be tonight, Alfie, up at that old bivouac you fellers had during the war?"

The hostler kept watching Hank's face over a long interval of silence before he faintly shrugged and said: "I don't know, Marshal."

Hank nodded wryly. "And if you did know, you wouldn't tell me. Isn't that it, Alfie?" All Hank got was another of those non-committal little faint shrugs so he turned to Malone, saying: "Don't let him out of your sight, Pat. Never mind our other plans, the ones we discussed earlier at the jailhouse about staking out Jeff's place tonight. I'll take care of that. You just make sure Alfie hangs around town tonight."

Malone nodded, eyeing Hank wonderingly. "You got something new in mind?" he asked.

"Yeah. A long talk with an ex-Reb officer."

"Where'll you find him, Hank?"

The marshal gazed at Alfie again and didn't reply to Malone's question. "Want to help me prevent a killing?" he asked.

Alfie emphatically shook his head. "No, sir, Marshal. I not only don't want to prevent it, I'd like to be there when they come face to face with Leslie."

"I wasn't thinking of Leslie, Alfie. In fact, your Reb comrades aren't going to get a whack at Frank Leslie because I've got him locked up. I was thinking of Jeff Stone. You see, Alfie, I happen to know that Jeff doesn't have all that hidden gold left."

But Alfie wouldn't believe this. He said: "Marshal, you know how long I've been in this town, lookin', listenin', and watchin'

227

like Cap'n Saint George told me to do? Well, in all that time I've never seen Mister Stone act like a man who's spendin' more'n he makes out of his store. No, sir, I don't believe what you say about Mister Stone and our gold."

Hank shrugged, then said: "Tell me, Alfie, how did you fellers know Stone still had the gold, that he didn't give it to those wartime secret agents from California?"

"Because the war ended before those agents could get up here to collect it. Mister Stone wrote Sergeant Burris down in Texas he still had it. That's what started the whole thing. Sergeant Burris told Cap'n Saint George. The cap'n said, since there was no government left to give it back to, and because no one else knew about it or had any right or claim to it, he'd round up his old band and ride here, an' we'd divide it so's each of us could get a new start somewhere."

Hank ran this carefully through his mind, trying to determine whether or not these men had legal claim to that money. He decided that they did have, at least as far as he was concerned, and put this thought out of his mind. "Alfie," he said quietly to the hostler, "I don't mean any trouble for your captain or your comrades. All I want is to see a murderer brought to trial, and this whole mess legally settled. You can help by promising me not to interfere. Will you do that?"

Alfie nodded.

XV

Hank left Malone's livery barn, heading for the Stone place, but he didn't get that far. Glancing across the road as he reached the intersecting roadway leading east, he saw something that stopped him in his tracks. The door of his jailhouse was ajar. He distinctly recalled locking it from the outside when he and Pat Malone had left, earlier, to walk on up to the barn.

He stood over there, gazing at the shadows beneath his

overhang, beyond which stood the door ajar. There were no horses at his hitch rack, and in fact there was no sign of life across the road at all. Just that door hanging slightly open on its hinges. He turned and started slowly over. He had to pause and permit a dray wagon to go past. The driver nodded, and called a casual greeting. Hank responded, then stepped on past, moved up to his door, and paused outside, listening. There wasn't a sound coming from inside. He thought of his prisoner and his prisoner's friends with a sinking sensation behind his belt. It had never once occurred to him that Frank Leslie would attempt anything like this and yet he could not deny that Frank was a violent, tough, and resourceful man.

He pushed back the door, peered into shadowy, hot gloom, saw nothing, and stepped over the threshold. At once he saw his mistake. Henry Helm was standing behind the door with his six-gun out and cocked. Henry had obviously had that door open so he could watch the outside roadway from the crack between door and wall.

Henry eased the door closed, or nearly so, and flicked with his pistol toward the desk chair. "Sit down, Hank," he said quietly, "and don't make a sound."

Hank stood like stone, staring over at Helm. He made no move to obey and he said: "Henry, what the hell's wrong with you? Do you know this can land you in the territorial prison for ten years . . . breaking a prisoner out of jail?"

"I said sit down and I meant it." Helm tilted his .45 muzzle, let it align itself upon Hank's broad chest. "Hank, I don't want to shoot you, but I will if you make me do it. You've got my word on that."

Hank backed up to his desk chair and obediently sank down. Across the room the oaken door leading to his cells was half open. From down there came the soft, urgent sounds of men's voices.

"You're a fool, Henry," said the marshal. "I thought you had better sense than to let Frank talk you into something like this."

"Yeah," said Snowshoe's range boss dryly, "I guess you did, otherwise you wouldn't have just locked the front door and walked off."

"You'll never get away with it in God's green world."

"Sure we will, Hank. And we'll have what's needed to get away with it, too."

This statement brought the lawman's eyes back to Helm. He understood it to mean that Frank Leslie had promised his cowboys a cut in the hidden hoard of Confederate gold. He began to wag his head back and forth before he spoke. "Henry, change your mind before it's too late. Frank doesn't know where that money's hidden. He can't give. . . ."

"He thinks he knows, Hank. Furthermore, even if he doesn't know for sure where it's at, we all three know who's around here who does know, and when fellers take chances like we're takin', believe me, pardner, we'll have plenty of reason to sweat it out of them as do know."

Hank started to protest again, but at that moment he heard one of his cell doors creak open. This sound distracted him. It also distracted Helm, but the range boss only flicked his eyes toward the cell-block door for a second, then swung them back to Hank again, and now they were triumphant.

Moments later swarthy, powerfully-built Frank Leslie walked out into Hank's office with Starr two steps behind him. Evidently neither of those two had heard the conversation in the outer room because they both halted and stared, first at Hank, then on over to Helm and Helm's tilted six-gun.

Frank grunted, stepped over, yanked out desk drawers until he located his six-gun, opened its gate, spun the cylinder to make certain the gun was still loaded, dropped it into his holster, and put a sardonic look downward at the lawman. "You shouldn't have come back," he said.

"Frank, you're a fool if you think you can break out of here with impunity. Even a murder charge is preferable to what you're doing now."

"Yeah?" said Leslie, his dark eyes turning hard, cold. "First you got to make that murder charge stick, Marshal. Then you got to get me tried and convicted. But first off . . . you got to take me again, and next time it won't be so easy. Next time I'll be prepared for you."

Hank leaned forward, his expression intent. "Frank, I put you in here to save your neck. You ride out of town now, and I don't believe you'll last until tomorrow night. I already told you . . . Burris wasn't the only one of them around here. Saint George is here. So is that feller who can throw knives, Pemberton. So is a feller named Gifford Bragg, and Bragg's the one who was Burris's pardner. There's another. . . ."

"Marshal," drawled Frank Leslie, "did I ever tell you that you worry too much? Sure, when you said the others were back, it threw me for a few minutes. But after I got to thinkin' it over, I come to a conclusion you're goin' to have to admit is pretty logical. Those fellers will kill me if they can. We all know that now. Well, I'd be a fool to sit in your lousy sweatbox and wait for 'em to do it, wouldn't I?"

"They won't kill you in this jailhouse, Frank, but as soon as you head for Snowshoe, they'll know about it. Then, I think, they will get you."

But Leslie shook his head at Hank. "Uhn-huh," he said, shaking his head and grimly smiling. "You'd be surprised how much gunfire I can pay for with that Reb gold. And I'll do it, too."

"Hell, Frank, you don't even know where that gold is."

"Don't I? You sure of that?"

"Yes, I'm sure of it. If you'd known, you wouldn't have dug that hole up there at the old Reb camp site. It wasn't up there, and you don't know where it is."

Leslie refused to be shaken, though. He said: "All right, but now I know where it ain't, so that limits the field considerably." Frank jerked his head at Starr. "Tie him to his chair," he said to the Indian-looking cowboy. "Belt his ankles, too. We don't want him givin' us any trouble until we're clear of town."

Hank darkly scowled at Frank as Starr moved forward. "You idiot, you've got a fortune in land and cattle. What's so valuable about a few thousand in Reb gold that it's worth risking all this for?"

"You got the wrong slant on things," retorted Leslie. "Before I killed Burris, the gold interested me, of course, but after I killed him, an' after I learned them other Rebs were around, then it became a matter of me stayin' alive. A man'll do lots of things to save his carcass he ordinarily wouldn't do." Leslie turned. "Henry," he said to his range boss, "go around back and bring our horses to the front hitch rack. Walk easy an' keep your eyes peeled."

Helm leathered his weapon, cast a final, wooden look at Hank, and slipped out the roadside door. Starr, working silently at tying Hank to his desk chair, muttered to Frank Leslie: "Maybe we ought to bust him over the head, too. He could holler after we ride out of here."

Leslie smiled wolfishly at Hank but did not reply to Starr's suggestion. He instead said: "Marshal, you've always been a sleepy feller who drifted with the tide. Too bad you had to wake up this late in life, because, if you'd just go on bein' sort of shiftless, we could work something out. Maybe a couple thousand dollars in Reb gold would make you shiftless again. How about it? It'll make things a heap easier for you 'n' that Mex girl you took such a shine to." When Hank didn't answer this offer of a fat bribe, Frank Leslie shrugged. "Two thousand in gold is better'n a crack over the skull with a gun barrel."

Finally Hank spoke up, but he completely ignored Leslie's offer. Instead, he asked a question: "What's the truth about the Burris killing?" he asked.

Leslie's mirthless smile faded a little at a time until the cowman's dark and narrow face was expressionless. He seemed to be considering several ways to answer that question. In the end he didn't answer it at all. He said: "I've got five riders workin' for me. I aim to hire five, maybe even ten more men. I figure to split that Reb gold up between 'em and not take a cent of it myself. Marshal, for that kind of money I'm buyin' life insurance. To earn that money those fellers only have to kill Saint George, Bragg, and Pemberton. After that . . . they fade out. Drift on out of the territory. Then I'll surrender to you an' you can bring me to trial. Marshal, without a livin' witness, do you think you'll ever get me convicted for killin' Burris?" Leslie shook his head. "Not in this world you won't . . . and to save my neck it's not goin' to cost me a thin dime. How do you like that plan?"

"It's fine," said Hank dryly.

"Well, then, Marshal, cut yourself in for a share of it, an' we can get this whole mess cleared up in one lousy day. What d'you say?"

"No thanks, Frank. Maybe it's like you say . . . and evidently you're not the only one who's believed it up to now. Maybe I haven't been a real good lawman before. But murder is something I can't swallow. Murder and everything else you're figurin' to do. No thanks. If this is how you want it, do what you've got to do. But Frank, I feel sorry for Henry and Starr and those other three riders out at Snowshoe, and anyone else who gets mixed up in this with you, because they're sticking their heads into nooses the minute they kill those Rebs."

Starr finished tying Hank and straightened up behind the chair, looking steadily over at Leslie. Frank saw this look and understood it. He nodded. Starr drew his six-gun, raised it, and brought it down in a tight, savage little arc. There was a crunching sound of steel striking through a felt hat and down into the lawman's scalp and skull. Hank's breath burst out in a pent-up fashion, his body turned suddenly loose in its bonds, and he sagged unconsciously forward.

Leslie gazed a moment at the loose body in front of him, jerked his head at Starr, and stepped over to the doorway. Outside, Henry Helm was leaning with exaggerated casualness upon the jailhouse hitch rack with his back to the building and his eyes shaded by his hat brim intently watching the roadway traffic.

Leslie called forward: "All right, Henry?"

Helm called back without facing around—"All's clear, Frank."—and pushed lazily up off the rack, proceeded to untie their three animals, and, as the other two stepped swiftly out of the jailhouse, Henry handed them their reins. They mounted swiftly, and sat a second out there in bright, hot sunlight, surveying the town. Then Frank Leslie made his first mistake; instead of turning southward and jogging out of town down that way where no one would have paid him the slightest heed because only a little knot of people even knew he'd been jailed, Frank turned northward and went jogging up through the roadway traffic past the saddle shop, the apothecary shop, the livery barn, and the Trailhand Saloon, leading Helm and Starr to the upper stage road where they'd speed along for a mile before cutting west toward Snowshoe.

Alfie was raking down the wetted runway when those three riders eased past. He turned casually to glance out, saw those men, recognized Frank Leslie instantly, and held to his barn rake with knuckles that turned white from the straining, following Leslie, Starr, and Helm almost to the northern limits of Conifer. Then he tossed aside the rake, ran a hand under his

nose, and hastened to the livery barn office to say breathlessly
to Pat, who was sweating over his books, that Frank Leslie and
two of his men had just ridden past.

Malone didn't believe it, but Alfie's expression brought him
out of the office in a lunge. The pair of them crossed to the
outside walkway, and Alfie pointed up where those three riders
were just breaking over into a long lope as they rode clear of
Conifer's northward environs. Malone didn't say a word. He
spun and went lumbering southward down the plank walk,
weaving in and out of startled pedestrians, mostly women shoppers, until he got to the jailhouse. There he plunged inside—
and stopped in his tracks. Five seconds later Alfie came pant-
ingly inside, also, his thin chest heaving from that unaccustomed
exertion and his breath rattling in the silence as he and Malone
stared round-eyed at the sagging-forward, fluttery-breathing
lawman bound to his desk chair.

"Fetch a pan of water," said Malone, drawing forth a big,
wicked-bladed clasp knife as he moved to cut Hank's bonds.

"Where?" asked Alfie helplessly.

"I don't give a damn where!" roared Malone, his face fiery
with indignation. "Just get it. Look around. There'll be water
here somewhere."

Alfie shuffled forward, peering around until he found the
bucket of drinking water with its dipper. These things he took
over just as Pat sliced through the last ropes and Hank eased
forward out of the chair onto the floor. His hat fell off.

Pat said: "Look there. They sure hit him a good lick over the
head."

Alfie looked, sniffled, and nodded. "Above the place where I
hit him with that fence slat," he murmured.

Pat, holding the bucket of water, looked around. "You hit
him?" he asked.

Alfie nodded. "The other night when he was follerin' Mister

235

Stone. Never mind that for now, pour the water on him."

Pat did. He upended the bucket and handed it back to Alfie. "Go get some more. There's a pump out back."

Hank gasped, choked, spat, and coughed. He batted his eyes upward and groaned. Pat knelt to help him sit up. Pat looked enormously relieved.

XVI

It was several minutes before Hank could speak. A good deal of that water had run up his nose and he retched along with his coughing. But when he was able to, he cast a jaundiced look at Pat and heartily but weakly swore. Malone was delighted and, using his powerful arms and shoulders, got Hank back up into his desk chair.

Alfie came padding back into the office with another bucket of water. He looked dubiously at Hank and said: "I reckon we won't need this."

Hank said: "You're danged right you won't. What're you two trying to do, drown me?"

Malone motioned for Alfie to put the bucket back on its stand as he said to Hank: "Leslie's gone. We just saw him ride northward out of town with Starr and Henry Helm."

"Tell me something I don't already know," growled Hank, considering his drenched clothing. He put up a hand to his head and groaned. "Damn that Starr, anyway. You don't have to hit a man that hard to knock him out."

Alfie came shuffling up and sniffled. As though this reminded Malone of something, he said: "Hank, you never told me Alfie busted you with a fence slat."

Hank looked around at Alfie from eyes swimming with pain. "I didn't know it was Alfie who did that," he said. "Why, Alfie?"

"Well, you kept gettin' between Mister Stone an' me. I was supposed to see him, to tell him Cap'n Saint George wanted to talk to him. Only you were trailin' him an' you kept gettin' in the way."

"Did you ever get to see him?" Hank asked.

Alfie shook his head, but he didn't explain why he hadn't gone on after he'd rendered Hank unconscious to meet the storekeeper. All he said was: "I stuck a note in his hatband at the store when there was a heap of shoppers in there, sayin' for him to walk north from the Trailhand, that I had somethin' to tell him an' that I'd meet him as he walked along. Then you. . . ."

"Yeah," grumbled Hank, exploring his second lump. "You've already explained that. Then I got between the pair of you. All right, Alfie. I owe you one for that."

Hank gingerly stood up. He walked unsteadily over to the water bucket, wadded up a soiled little towel, plunged it into the water, and gingerly bathed his head with it. While he was doing this, he said: "Pat, Leslie's offering big money to his hired hands to kill the Rebs. In fact, what he's offering is that Reb gold. He told me right here in this office he means to hire as many guns as he can to make sure Saint George and his friends are shot down."

"Why?" asked Pat, looking perplexed. "How can he hope to find the money if he does that?"

"It's not the money he's worrying about. It's the Rebs. He's convinced that they'll kill him for shooting Burris . . . which I think is plumb right. But I'm not concerned with that, at least not right now. What I'm sweating about is what'll happen if Frank gets his hired guns, and happens onto Saint George and the other Rebs. It'll be a massacre if Frank has his way, and, if he doesn't, if the Rebs are on the alert, it'll be a bloody battle. Either way, I've got to keep it from happening."

"But how?"

Hank finished bathing his head and turned. As he did so, Alfie said meekly: "How, Mister Herman? How's Leslie goin' to find the cap'n and the others to kill 'em? He doesn't know where they are."

Hank blinked away some excess water from his eyes to see Alfie better. An idea firmed up in his mind as he did this. He said: "Alfie, dog-gone you, let's have it. Where are they?"

But Alfie went into one of those odd, uncertain silences of his again. He blinked over at Hank and shuffled his feet, and refused to say a word.

Malone glared. "Alfie, you consarned idiot, haven't you got it through your whiskey-fogged brain yet that Hank is for your friends and not against 'em?"

Alfie looked stubbornly crestfallen when he said: "Well, Mister Malone, all I know is that he had Leslie in his jailhouse, an' he let 'im go, an' they're our enemies, an' if Leslie hires a herd of fast guns, the cap'n an' the others won't stand much of a chance."

Hank made a motion to silence the sputtering curses of Pat Malone, walked back to his desk, and eased down upon one corner of it, looking at Alfie. "Maybe," he said, "I should just tell Leslie where that damned money is hidden. That'd save your friends, Alfie. At least it'd give 'em a little time to get a good head start on Frank's gunmen. What do you think of that?"

"You don't know where that gold is," retorted Alfie, looking weakly defiant and stubborn.

Hank sighed. "You got a bad memory," he informed the hostler. "Up in Pat's barn you told us you helped bury the money in Jeff Stone's cellar under the store."

Alfie's expression abruptly altered. It became uncertain again and troubled. He brushed his nose with the back of one hand, dropped his eyes, and said: "In the loft."

Pat Malone drew fully upright, staring at his hostler. "You mean to stand there an' say those Rebs are up in my loft?"

Alfie nodded and sniffled.

Malone let off a loud groan as Hank stood up, picked up his soggy hat, struck it against a leg to get rid of all surplus water, then gravely worked at putting the shape back into its crown. He afterward set the hat atop his head with considerable care and looked at Pat Malone. "It could be worse," he said. "They could've been up in the lousy mountains where Leslie'll be lookin' for them." He paused, surveyed the soggy condition of his clothing a moment, then said: "I'd give a pretty penny to know how Frank Leslie found out there was any Reb gold in the first place."

"From Burris," said Alfie unexpectedly, and sniffled. "It had to be that way, Marshal. They talked a few minutes before Leslie killed the sergeant. I know that for a fact because last night, while the four of us were lyin' up there in the hay, Dave and Cap'n Saint George said they could see Leslie and Burris arguin' before Leslie shot him. The cap'n says he thinks maybe Burris let something slip about why we were back in the Conifer country. Then, when he wouldn't tell what it was he'd accidentally said, Leslie shot him."

"Weak," murmured Hank, heading over for the door. "That's kind of weak, Alfie, but I reckon we'll have to accept it until we get something better. Come on, you two, let's go up to the barn and have a talk with Captain Saint George."

Alfie moved swiftly to be the first one out of the jailhouse door. "You better let me go up there first," he warned. "They won't be expectin' anyone else, and they'll likely be kind of leery."

Hank swung the jailhouse door closed after them and considered the broken latch for a second before he turned and started ambling along with Pat Malone. Alfie was walking swiftly on ahead of them.

"Fine evening," Hank said dourly. "You got any idea where a

feller can trade in an aching skull for a new one that doesn't hurt, Pat?"

Malone didn't reply. He was watching Alfie's scuttling figure with a solemnly wondering gaze. When the hostler ducked down into Malone's barn, Pat said: "Yesterday I made the comment that this Saint George is smart and careful. Today I'll add to that, Hank. I'll say that, if Frank Leslie thinks he's going to walk up behind this feller and blow out his lights like he did with Burris, Frank's in for a big surprise."

Hank paused as they neared the barn's entrance way. He wiped excess water from his eyes. The brightness, any brightness at all, hurt them, and his head throbbed with a hard persistence. He was in no mood for generalities or light speculations. "Go around the back," he said to Pat. "I don't reckon they'll try it, but let's make sure. If anyone tries coming out that way, throw down on him . . . whoever he is."

Pat looked doubtful about the necessity for this precaution but he walked off without a word.

Hank stepped on inside the barn, looked right, looked left, and moved over closer to the loft ladder. Alfie's red-veined cheeks showed through the square up there. "Come on up," he said. "They're expecting you."

"I suppose they are," retorted the lawman dryly. "Alfie, you tell your friends to come down here."

"Marshal, they. . . ."

"Alfie, you do as I say!"

The hostler's head sucked back out of sight. A square-jawed, bearded countenance appeared in the opening and Hank traded long stares with Captain St. George himself. For a second these two stonily regarded one another, then without a word Captain St. George swung out and started climbing downward.

Hank looked down through the barn's gloomy interior, saw Malone out back, and beckoned. As Pat started up through his barn, other bearded men began climbing down from the hayloft. The second to last man had a little difficulty; this one's left leg was angled outward at an awkward angle that made his descent clumsy and slow. The last man down the ladder was Alfie.

Captain St. George turned when he stepped clear of the ladder and put a steely, dead-level gray gaze upon the lawman. He said nothing until his companions were also down in the runway, and until Pat Malone had come up to halt near Hank.

"All right, Marshal, Alfie's told us your problem," said St. George. "I reckon it couldn't be helped . . . Leslie breaking out of your jailhouse. But it complicates things for us."

Hank narrowed his gaze at St. George. "Not half as much as it complicates them for me," he returned dryly. "Captain, how much money is hidden here in town?"

Without any hesitation the ex-Confederate officer said— "Sixty thousand dollars in gold, Marshal."—and watched Hank's narrowed eyes gradually widen in purest astonishment. "Quite a lot, isn't it?" he said, in response to that look of amazement. "But then, during the war, the stakes were large."

Pat Malone sighed a big sigh. Without looking around Hank knew exactly how Pat felt. $60,000 was more than three men might expect to make in a lifetime.

"Another question, Captain. If it's not all there, what do you intend doing to old Jeff Stone?"

St. George paused a moment before replying to this question, then said quietly: "Let's cross that bridge when we come to it, Marshal. I haven't been able to see Stone yet, and until he tells me there's a defalcation, I prefer to continue believing him a man of honor."

Hank looked at the others. Pemberton he already knew. Alfie, too. The third ex-Confederate, though, the slight, wiry man with the hard, cold stare and the twisted left leg, he didn't know except by name. But in studying Gifford Bragg now, he could

241

see that this one, of the lot of them, might be the least amenable and the most deadly. Bragg had the build and the eyes of a man who'd be deadly if angered.

"Marshal," said Captain St. George, "suppose you and I walk over to Stone's store and talk to him."

"He's not at the store," put in Pat Malone.

"All right, then. Let's walk down to his house, Marshal," said the calm, quiet-acting ex-officer. "You want this thing ended as badly as we do. The only way to accomplish this is to see Mister Stone, and afterward. . . ." The captain raised and fatalistically lowered his shoulders. "Afterward, I think we can make arrangements to meet Frank Leslie, too."

There was something about this tall, quiet bearded man that inspired not just respect, but also trust. Hank nodded at him. "We'll do that," he assented. "But I want the word of your companions that they'll remain right here in this barn until you and I come back, and that means every one of them. No one's to slip out and go after Leslie. You agree to that, Captain?"

St. George inclined his head, turned, and gazed without a word at Pemberton, Alfie, and wiry, cold-looking Gifford Bragg. Each of those men nodded at St. George without saying anything.

St. George stepped out, heading for the yonder roadway. Hank didn't move out to follow him right away. He looked at Pat Malone who was his only ally now, and Malone would be out-gunned and outnumbered the moment Hank left his barn. But Pat seemed unconcerned. He said: "It's all right, Hank. I got a feelin' we're doin' the right thing."

St. George stopped out in the afternoon's reddening glow, waiting for Hank to come along. He said nothing until the marshal was up beside him, and they both stepped forth to walk along southward along the plank walk through increasing coolness.

"Marshal," he ultimately said in that quiet way he had of speaking, "we're not murderers. We want justice for the killing of Harold Burris, your brand of book justice or our kind of gun justice. But we didn't come here to start a war. Believe me, Marshal, when I tell you that every one of us has had all the fighting he'll need for a lifetime."

Hank paced along to the intersecting roadway, stepped down into the dust of Conifer's broad roadway, and hiked on across with St. George at his side. "I'll take care of Frank Leslie," he said thoughtfully. "What's bothering me is the trouble I think we're heading into now. Captain, I've got a hunch Jeff Stone doesn't have all your gold any more. I know for a fact he's spent some of it. I have no idea how much, and right now I'm praying it's only a small part that he's spent. But if I'm wrong, if Jeff thought no one was ever going to show up to claim that money, and went ahead and spent the biggest portion of it, I've got to warn you, if you try to exact vengeance, I'm here to oppose you any way that I can."

Captain St. George walked all the way to Jeff Stone's front gate before he turned, with one hand lying upon the gate, and said: "Marshal, there are two things I particularly admire in men . . . truthfulness and principle. You have both. I don't think we'll ever be enemies." St. George opened the gate and stood aside for Hank to enter first.

XVII

Jeff Stone met the two men at the doorway into his house. He gravely nodded without speaking, but looking as though this visit was no surprise to him, and stepped outside onto the porch, closed the door behind himself, and waited.

Captain St. George said quietly: "It's been a long time, Mister Stone. A good many years."

Jeff removed his spectacles, proceeded to polish them and

nod his head at the same time. He still said nothing, even when he replaced the glasses and gazed steadily at the ex-Confederate officer.

"I reckon you know why we're back in the country," said St. George in that same quiet tone.

"I know," said Stone woodenly. "Before we go into that, though, Captain Saint George, I'd like you to tell me which one of you killed my brother-in-law and why you did that."

Hank, wondering about Jeff's coldness toward St. George now, had his answer to that. He said: "Jeff, these men didn't kill Sergeant Burris. Frank Leslie did that."

Stone's eyes widened. "Frank . . . ?"

Hank nodded. "He met Burris out on his range. They talked a little, then Frank threw down on him. Frank told me it was an accident that he plugged Burris in the back. But that's not settled yet. At least it's not settled to my satisfaction. Anyway, forget Leslie for now. We're here on another matter."

Stone, though, shifted his gaze back to St. George and said: "Is this the truth, Captain?"

St. George gravely inclined his head. "Pemberton and I were returning from seeing Giff Bragg off on his way into town here, in disguise. Giff was to be on hand here when the rest of us rode in to see you, Mister Stone. We were back up a side hill and saw Leslie talking to Harold Burris. We saw Burris suddenly jump as though to spring around behind a tree. There were two shots. We saw Burris fall. It may have happened as Leslie says, but I think not quite like that. I think Harold said something about the gold. . . ." St. George ceased speaking for a moment, then said: "There's no point in talking about this until we can ask Leslie exactly what happened. Right now, let's discuss the gold. Where is it, Mister Stone?"

Without a moment's hesitation Jeff Stone said: "It's hidden in the wall of my bedroom in this house, Captain."

"All of it, Mister Stone?"

Hank held his breath as Jeff hung fire over his answer. "All but three thousand dollars of it, Captain," said Stone, without dropping his level eyes from St. George's face. "I used that three thousand for a purpose."

"What was that purpose, Mister Stone?" asked St. George, his face showing nothing at all, neither indignation nor suspicion.

"Captain, that money lay in its grave in my cellar at the store a long time. Last spring it occurred to me to dig down and see if it was all right. That was right after I got the letter from my wife's brother saying you planned coming here for it. The cellar was damp, Captain. That pine box we buried it in had completely rotted away and the bottom coins were badly eroded. I removed them. In fact, I removed all the money. I brought it to my house a little each day and sealed it up in the bedroom wall where it would be dry . . . and safe. Those three thousand dollars I put into circulation, a few at a time so as not to arouse any suspicion. I bought store supplies with all but a couple hundred dollars of it, and that money I deliberately lost at gambling to get them out of the area."

Hank fished out the coin he'd gotten from Rita Malone. "This one didn't get very far," he said, holding the coin so the other two could see it.

Stone gazed downward, then up into Hank's face. "So that's what it was," he murmured. "I knew the minute you walked up here yesterday that you knew something, Hank. Even before you started asking those questions. Well, I made a bad move, it seems."

Stone looked back over at St. George. He seemed to be awaiting some comment from the ex-officer, but St. George did not speak. He turned, walked over to a porch chair, and sat down. Then he said: "Forget the three thousand, Mister Stone. The boys and I had already decided to divide the money with you anyway. You're quite certain the rest of it is safe?"

Stone nodded, saying: "My wife isn't feeling well, Captain. After she heard of her brother's murder, she broke down. Otherwise, I'd take you inside right now and show you your gold."

Behind Jeff, the door opened and Harriett Stone stepped out. She looked pale and there were dark shadows under her eyes, but she had that stubborn set to her mouth and jaw that Hank had come to know very well over the past years. Harriett had a lot of iron in her make-up. She watched Captain St. George gallantly arise as she swept up beside her husband, and she said in a husky voice: "It's all there, Captain. I think, except for that money, my brother would be alive today. Please take it away as soon as you can. I don't like knowing it's here in the house. It's never done anyone any good, and it's done some good men a lot of harm."

St. George said softly: "Ma'am, I understand how you feel. And I'd like to tell you this. I never knew a finer man than your brother. As for what happened to him . . . leave that to the marshal and me. I promise you we'll see that Sergeant Burris didn't die in vain."

Jeff put out a hand to his wife. She took it and closed her fingers tightly around it at the same time continuing to gaze over at St. George. "Captain," she said, her voice softening, "Harold said in a letter that your cause still lives in the heart of every man who served it." She drew in an unsteady breath and let it out before going on. "Captain, I think it would be better if those of you who are left now took your money, built new lives for yourselves, and forgot the past."

St. George smiled softly. Hank watched that gentle smile transform the handsome officer's entire expression. "Miss Harriett," said St. George, "that's exactly what we plan to do. The past is past and life is for the living. But all the same, ma'am, men like Sergeant Burris deserve much better than life has given them, so, with your permission, the others and I would like to have a monument erected over the sergeant's grave."

"His grave," murmured Harriett. "Where is his grave, Captain?"

"In the little cemetery south of town, ma'am. One of our men . . . one of his old comrades . . . buried him there in the night. We've talked about this monument, ma'am. We'd like to have it carved out of living granite, Miss Harriett, in the shape and form of the kind of a Confederate soldier your brother was."

"No!" said Harriett Stone, her face turning white. "The war is over!"

"Harriett," said Jeff quietly. "Let them do it. The war is over, yes, but the memory of it shall live as long as the true men who fought it still live. Can't you see, these men want to do this, they need to do it? And Harold was one of them, never forget that."

"Ma'am," said Hank, breaking in here, "although I never knew your brother, believe me, I'm convinced he'd approve. I was never a Southern sympathizer . . . but I am now. Brave men are the same whether they wore gray or blue. Let your brother's old comrades do this, before they split up for the last time and go their separate ways. Just for this last time they will all be united, your brother with them."

Harriett looked longest at Hank when she ultimately said: "I'm sorry, Captain. I didn't fully understand. I'll be proud if you and your men would make that kind of a marker for my brother."

Harriett turned and rushed back into the house, leaving those three men looking gravely at one another. Hank broke that depthless hush a moment afterward by saying: "Jeff, we've got to go after Frank Leslie. I had him locked up for Burris's murder, and he busted out. I want you to stay here in the house. I don't know whether or not Frank will figure out where that gold might be, but until I get him again, I want you to stay close by your house. Will you do that?"

Stone said that he would. He also said to Captain St. George: "When it's all over, I'd like to see the others again. Of course I recognized the one who's been Malone's swamper at the livery barn when he rode back into the country, but I remember the others too, Captain. They were good men."

"Good men," echoed Captain St. George, and stepped on over to the porch edge to turn and extend his hand. Stone shook with him. St. George looked toward the house with a sad expression. "The weavings of the winds of war, gentlemen, reach a long way from where battles were fought." He glanced at Hank. "Well, if you're satisfied here, so am I, Marshal, and there remains one more thing to be done. Shall we go?"

Hank nodded at Jeff, joined the ex-officer, and the pair of them walked back down to the roadside gate, through it, and swung right to walk along stonily silent almost to the main roadway again. There St. George halted, drew forth from an inside coat pocket two cigars, presented one to Hank, put the other one between his strong teeth, and held a match. As Hank lighted up, St. George said: "Where will he be, Marshal?"

Hank exhaled, waited for the officer also to light up, then looked westward over the dusk-scented evening. "Probably he went straight back to his ranch, Captain. But that was several hours ago. By now he might be anywhere. He might even be heading back here."

"Why do you say that?"

Hank brought his gaze back to Conifer, ran it up and down the evening-shadowed roadway, and savored the good bite of strong tobacco. "Because, Captain, when Frank has thought it all out, he's going to come to the conclusion you or I would also come to if we were in his boots. The only people who actually know where that gold is hidden are here in Conifer."

"But he won't know I'm here, or that the men with me are here, Marshal."

"No," agreed Hank. "But he'll also know that he can't expect to find you fellers in the dark, and that'll leave him only a couple of alternatives. He'll think perhaps I know something, and he'll also wonder if perhaps, since Sergeant Burris was Jeff Stone's brother-in-law, which he didn't know before, Jeff might know something."

Captain St. George's eyes faintly shone with approval in the fading daylight. "I see you're also a shrewd man, Marshal. You'd have made a capital soldier."

Hank gazed at the ex-Confederate. "We'd have been an opposite sides," he said quietly.

St. George gave Hank one of those rare smiles of his. "Next to a good friend," he said, looking Hank straight in the eye, "an honorable enemy is most to be cherished."

Hank smiled back. He warmed more to this tall, bearded man, the longer he was with him. "Thank God that's over now, Captain. As for Frank Leslie, the reason I told Jeff to stay in his house is because I have a feeling he'll have visitors tonight. I've had that feeling ever since Frank busted out of my jailhouse. And now, if you agree, I reckon we ought to get back to the others."

"Of course," murmured the officer. As the two of them paced along side-by-side, St. George said musingly: "Marshal, what specifically do you have in mind?"

"Deputize your men along with my friend Malone, and slip back down to the Stone place and establish what you soldier fellers call a surround."

"Good," agreed St. George.

They were angling on across the shadowy roadway through ankle-deep dust when Rube Burrows came up to them, stopped when he recognized Hank's companion, and stared.

Hank said: "What's on your mind, Rube?" Then, seeing Burrows's round-eyed stare, he said: "Rube, shake hands with William Saint George. I think you two've met at the Trailhand."

Burrows shook with St. George and made a wry face. He was obviously recalling that other meeting when he said very dryly: "Yeah, we've met before." Then he looked back at Hank and said, in a different tone of voice: "Hank, I've been hearin' odd rumors. I heard that you locked Frank Leslie up after you took him outen my bar. Is that right?"

"It's right. What of it?"

"Well, I also heard that Starr and Henry Helm busted him out."

"Seems that the walls have eyes and ears," said Hank. "That's also true."

"Well, a few minutes ago, up at the saloon, Henry walked in through the back alley door and talked to some drifters that've been hangin' around town for the past week or so, then all three of 'em walked on out through the back door again." Rube, watching Hank's face and seeing the sudden grim interest reflected there, added: "That's why I went down to your office lookin' for you. Only you weren't there. To tell you that it looks like maybe Helm's up to something."

"Thanks," Hank said, a trifle bleakly. "Now go on back to the Trailhand, make sure Rita stays off the roadway, and just for once, Rube, don't stick your beak into something that might get it busted."

Burrows nodded, taking no offense at this, and, after nodding to Captain St. George, walked off. For a moment after the saloon man had departed, Hank and St. George looked at one another before continuing on toward the livery barn. Neither of them said anything until, just short of the barn entrance, St. George looked around again.

"You are a clever man, Marshal. Clever and solid. You've outguessed Leslie right down the line. My lads and I will be delighted to serve under a man of principle and resolve."

Hank, gazing over at the Trailhand where orange lamplight spilled outward over the doorway, said: "Captain, when this is all over, there's someone I'd like you to tell that to, for me. Someone who's been a long time coming around to believing I'm anything more'n just a lazy, easy-going feller."

XVIII

When Hank preceded Captain St. George into Pat Malone's lamplit little office, he came upon an unusual sight. Malone, with his six-gun in his lap, was scowlingly playing stud poker with Pemberton, Bragg, and Alfie, and, from Pat's bitter expression, he was losing.

As St. George came into the room, those seated men glanced quickly upward, all showing alert interest and expectancy. But it was Hank who addressed them, not St. George. He said—"Raise your right hands, all of you."—and, when only Pat Malone obeyed at once, Captain St. George raised his right hand and nodded at the others. Not until then, though, did Alfie, Pemberton, and Bragg lift their arms.

Hank succinctly swore them all in as deputy town marshals, then dropped his arm, and said gruffly: "Come on. The gold is safe and Frank Leslie is somewhere around here in town with his five riders plus a couple more saddle bums he's hired over at the Trailhand."

Pat was the first man to his feet. He looked eager as he stepped to a saddle boot leaning in a corner, drew forth the Winchester carbine, and stepped back toward the door. The others also stirred, but they kept watching St. George. Clearly

Alfie, Pemberton, and Bragg would take orders only from their wartime commander. St. George, with a twinkle in his gray gaze, said: "Boys, for tonight we'll be taking commands from Marshal Herman. He knows his way around, this is his town, and he knows our enemies a lot better than we do."

The ex-Confederate cavalrymen turned slowly to assess Hank. None of them said anything. All of them were armed with six-guns, and somewhere, concealed beneath his coat, Dave Pemberton had those two big knives. Hank led them all out to the darkening roadway, halted briefly there, then motioned them along and cut diagonally across the roadway.

He took his deputized men on through to the alley behind Burrows's saloon and southward to the intersecting roadway where he halted again. Up to now he'd said nothing. Now he did.

"Pat, take Alfie and cross the road. Go west until you're opposite the Stone place. Get under cover over there. If you see Frank or any of his crew ride up, be ready to let them have it. Captain, you an' Mister Pemberton slip along until you're in Stone's front yard. Hide in all that shrubbery down there. Mister Bragg, you and I'll stay right here in this alleyway. We'll have a clean sweep of the roadway east and west. Whichever way Leslie comes, we'll see him first and give him his one chance to quit." Hank looked at the others. "Agreed?" he asked, and, when the others nodded, he said: "Move out."

He and crippled Gifford Bragg stood back in formless alleyway gloom, watching the others silently fade out. It was nearly full dark now with the town's nighttime sounds beginning to replace the other, earlier day sounds. Gifford Bragg drew forth a twist of molasses-cured chewing tobacco, offered it to Hank, got a negative headshake, and worried off a corner of his plug, pouched it into his cheek, and said softly: "Marshal, I'd take it right kindly, when them fellers appear, if you'd sort of hold off on Leslie a second or two. You see, Hal Burris and me, we were pretty close all through the war."

Hank looked around at Bragg's steady, liquid-hard eyes. "Sure," he said. "I understand."

They kept their vigil a long time. Hank was beginning to feel restless. At his side Gifford Bragg rhythmically chewed his cud seemingly unperturbed, his eyes constantly moving, his head cocked for the sound of riders. He heard them, finally, after nearly an hour more of waiting, and he evidently was the first one to hear them, for when he spoke to his companion, Hank hadn't heard a thing except the usual night sounds.

"Horsemen comin', Marshal," he said laconically, and spat an amber stream out into the roadway. "Sounds like maybe eight or ten of 'em."

By Hank's careful calculation there would be eight men with Frank, including Leslie himself and the two drifters Rube had reported that Henry Helm had hired up at the saloon. He heard the solid jogging of those riders. He heard them halt over in front of his jailhouse, and after several minutes he heard them start moving again, this time coming on across the main roadway down this easterly side street where he had his trap set. He didn't see any of them, though, until they'd passed several hundred feet along toward the Stone house and come almost abreast of the alleyway where he and tobacco-chewing Giff Bragg stood, covered with darkness. Then he recognized Frank Leslie leading those men. He also recognized Starr and Henry Helm, but the other riders were back a little distance, bunched up making recognition in the night impossible.

As the last rider went on past, Bragg said softly: "Like slammin' the door behind 'em, Marshal. You'd have made a right fine strategist."

Hank let that go past without comment. He was watching those riders, and, when they were well beyond his place of

concealment, he said—"Come on."—and stepped out of the alleyway.

He and Gifford Bragg went along eastward until they had a
good view of the front of Jeff Stone's residence as well as all
those bunched-up horsemen who were wheeling in down there
to halt where Frank Leslie dismounted and stood a moment as
though sniffing the surrounding, quiet night.

Bragg, limping along, said softly: "He feels something's
wrong, Marshal. I've seen it happen a hundred times."

Hank slowed his steps. He had a good view of Leslie now
and therefore Leslie also had a good view of him and Gifford
Bragg. Leslie said something to Henry Helm. His foreman
started to dismount; he was leaning to the left preparatory to
swinging over his right leg, when one of those other men out
there in the roadway called sharply: "Careful, that looks like
Herman up there with that limpin' feller!"

Hank went for his gun. So did Gifford Bragg. Both of them
had cleared leather before Frank Leslie whipped around, facing
westward on up the roadway, straining to identify the two stroll-
ers coming down toward him. Helm eased back down across his
saddle and dropped his right hand. That's when Pat Malone,
from fifty feet behind those riders, sang out: "Don't do it,
Henry. You're covered from every side."

Malone's warning triggered what followed. Frank Leslie
sprang clear of his horse, dropped low, and streaked for his
weapon. Beside Hank, Gifford Bragg let off a spine-tingling
Rebel yell that rang down the night with all the savage abandon
that invariably accompanied that scream. Then Bragg also went
for his gun. What followed in this split-second private duel
brought home to Hank what the others had said about Bragg
being deadly with a gun. Leslie had already begun his draw
when Bragg let off that yell and also drew, and the two shots
were so close when they exploded in the night they might have

been only one gunshot.

A picket on the fence to the left of Hank, struck squarely by Leslie's bullet, broke with a loud sound. Hank flinched from the nearness of that shot but did not take his eyes off Frank Leslie when Bragg's muzzle blast redly lit the night. Frank was knocked backward; he staggered from impact, and, as his head jerked, his hat tumbled into the roadway.

Someone let off a shrill cry as Bragg thumbed off his second shot. That one, though, evidently missed, because Leslie caught his balance and started to straighten upward, bringing his gun hand to bear again. Then, although neither he nor Bragg fired again, Leslie suddenly gasped, dropped his six-gun, and collapsed.

Above him Henry Helm had his gun out and swinging to bear. Starr, too, and several of the other men upon their fidgeting mounts drew and fired. From behind those perfectly outlined men atop their saddles, Pat Malone and Alfie opened up. Over in front of them from near the porch of the Stone residence, two more guns cut in, adding to the solid, wild thunder that was now jarring every window in the neighborhood.

Hank saw Starr disappear down the side of his horse as the animal gave a tremendous leap sideways. He caught Henry Helm's muzzle flash aimed straight at him and ducked down even as he fired back. Henry, too, fell and struck the road hard.

Someone down there was crying out that he surrendered, that he'd had enough, but among those twisting, frantic men atop horses that were on the edge of panic, it was impossible to determine who was firing and who was not. Bragg let off that chilling Rebel yell again as he dropped to one knee and fired pointblank into the mass of mounted men. From over across the road Alfie's unmistakably hoarse voice quavered high with that same yell, and from in front of Jeff Stone's place two men, jumping up and rushing down upon those desperate horsemen, also screamed. It was perhaps as much the yells as the unexpected fierce and unrelenting gunfire that broke the back of resistance among Frank Leslie's men. They threw several more shots, then began yelling that they quit, that they would throw down their guns.

Hank, hearing these wild yells for surrender, started to call out for St. George's men to stop firing. He never completed that order; the ex-Confederates and Pat Malone, too, suddenly ceased firing with the same abrupt suddenness with which they had begun firing. Hank had a second to wonder at the precise manner of these seasoned fighting men, then Captain St. George's voice slashed down into the quick, frightening silence that came to the embattled roadway.

"Dismount, you men out there!" St. George called to Leslie's survivors. "Walk forward in front of your horses and throw down your guns in plain sight. Be quick about it. One wrong move and you'll be cut to pieces. Now move!"

Leslie's men moved. They came out into plain sight of their attackers, chucked down their weapons, and stood like stiff statues rolling their eyes around as Pat and Alfie, Hank and Giff Bragg, Captain St. George and Dave Pemberton converged upon them. Hank went directly over where Frank Leslie lay. At his side Giff Bragg limped along, halted, squinted downward, and said a harsh swear word. One of Dave Pemberton's big silver-bladed knives was sticking out of Leslie's back. Bragg turned furiously. "Damn you, Dave!" he roared out. "I had him an' he was mine."

Pemberton walked solemnly over, stooped, plucked out his knife, turned, and held it out, hilt-first, toward his comrade. "You hit him with the first shot, Giff, but you missed him with the second. He had you 'n' the marshal straight in front an' was bringin' up his gun. He'd have hit one of you sure . . . that's when I threw it. Here, Giff, take it. He'd have died from your slug anyway, in time. Take the knife. Keep it to remember this skunk . . . and also to remember me and Hal Burris."

After Bragg accepted the knife, Pemberton walked on over where St. George and the others were rounding up their prisoners. Hank, though, stood a long moment gazing downward. He was still doing that when Captain St. George came over to ask a question.

"You want us to herd them over to your jailhouse, Marshal?"

Hank looked up and around. "Yeah, Captain, I reckon so. Captain, Leslie's dead. We'll never know what passed between him and Sergeant Burris now."

"No," agreed St. George. "You know, I had a hunch it might end like this. Well, Marshal, the important thing is that Sergeant Burris is avenged."

"And those other two, Captain, Henry Helm and Starr, I've known them for almost ten years. Dead, too, and for what?"

St. George put out a hand, brushed Hank's sleeve with his fingers, and nodded. "I know how you feel. I've felt the same, many, many times."

Someone walked up to those two and halted. Hank looked around. It was Jeff Stone and he was carrying a double-barrel shotgun. Stone squinted at the dead men without a word for a long time, then straightened up, and turned to Captain St. George. "Is it all over now?" he asked, sounding very tired, very old and weary. "Is this the end of it, Captain?"

"This is the end of it, Mister Stone. Do you still want me to bring the men back to your house after we lock up these others?"

"Tonight?" asked Stone, looking uncertain about a reunion so soon after men had died.

Captain St. George said quietly: "Yes, tonight, Mister Stone, because you see as soon as we've divided the money, we're go-

257

ing to ride on."

"Well, but not for a day or two, Captain," said Hank, bringing his attention back to these two. "You don't mean you're figuring on riding out this very night?"

"I'm afraid that's exactly what I mean, Marshal. We have a long way yet to go. You see, it's our plan to ride on out to California together, before we split up. And after all that's happened here in Conifer, I have a feeling the others won't want to stay any longer than it takes to saddle up and ride out, either. I know that's how I feel."

Jeff Stone nodded and said: "All right, Captain. Give Harriett an' me an hour to prepare for it, then you bring back your band, we'll hand over the gold . . . and maybe we can all have a drink to the past . . . it's over now and done with, and with God's help it'll remain that way."

Stone turned and went walking back toward his house. Hank and St. George also turned, but they joined the others in driving the survivors of Frank Leslie's ill-fated attempt to force Jeff Stone's secret out of the old storekeeper over to Hank's jailhouse. The moment that band of men, some armed, some with their hands above their heads, appeared upon Conifer's main roadway, people began running swiftly down toward them from the northern reaches of town where that sudden, fierce, and quite brief fight had sounded to them like a genuine battle was in progress. Foremost among those excited, pale faces Hank saw Rube Burrows, and at Rube's elbow, Rita Malone. At that moment Captain St. George addressed Hank.

"Marshal, I've been thinking. When we all go back to Stone's for that farewell drink, I'd take it as a personal kindness if you'd come along, too."

Hank, still gazing over at Rita, murmured: "Captain, I'm not one of you. I wouldn't belong."

"Marshal," said St. George firmly, "you'd belong. As for not being one of us . . . only geography prevented that, I think, but whether that's so or not, believe me when I say you're one of us. All men of principle are one of us."

"Well, do you reckon if I brought someone along with me, it'd be all right with the others?"

St. George traced out the direction of Hank's gaze, saw Rita, gallantly bowed slightly as she returned his regard, and without taking his eyes off the lovely girl he said from the corner of his mouth: "Marshal, if you don't bring her, I'll be tempted to ask her myself. She's an uncommonly handsome girl."

They got to the jailhouse and entered, closed out all those curious yonder faces, and, as Hank locked up his captives, the others finally relaxed. Alfie was whispering to the captain when Hank came back from his cell-block. The captain said to his comrades: "Gentlemen, Alfie asks that Mister Malone accompany us back to the Stone's place, and I ask that the marshal go back with us, too. Do you boys agree?"

Gifford Bragg flung back his head and let off that frightening Rebel yell again, then they all did, and this was the strongest possible approval these heroes of a lost cause could offer any man, alive or dead.

ABOUT THE AUTHOR

Lauran Paine who, under his own name and various pseudo-
nyms has written over a thousand books, was born in Duluth,
Minnesota. His family moved to California when he was at a
young age and his apprenticeship as a Western writer came
about through the years he spent in the livestock trade, rodeos,
and even motion pictures where he served as an extra because
of his expert horsemanship in several films starring movie
cowboy Johnny Mack Brown. In the late 1930s, Paine trapped
wild horses in northern Arizona and even, for a time, worked as
a professional farrier. Paine came to know the Old West through
the eyes of many who had been born in the previous century,
and he learned that Western life had been very different from
the way it was portrayed on the screen. "I knew men who had
killed other men," he later recalled. "But they were the excep-
tions. Prior to and during the Depression, people were just too
busy eking out an existence to indulge in Saturday-night
brawls." He served in the U.S. Navy in the Second World War
and began writing for Western pulp magazines following his
discharge. It is interesting to note that all of his earliest novels
(written under his own name and the pseudonym Mark Carrel)
were published in the British market and he soon had as strong
a following in that country as in the United States. Paine's
Western fiction is characterized by strong plots, authenticity, an
apparently effortless ability to construct situation and character,
and a preference for building his stories upon a solid founda-

tion of historical fact. *Adobe Empire* (1956), one of his best novels, is a fictionalized account of the last twenty years in the life of trader William Bent and, in an off-trail way, has a melancholy, bittersweet texture that is not easily forgotten. In later novels like *Cache Cañon* (Five Star Westerns, 1998) and *Halfmoon Ranch* (Five Star Westerns, 2007), he showed that the special magic and power of his stories and characters had only matured along with his basic themes of changing times, changing attitudes, learning from experience, respecting Nature, and the yearning for a simpler, more moderate way of life. His next Five Star Western will be *The Last Gun*.